THE LOVE THAT
GOD FORGOT

THE LOVE THAT GOD FORGOT

Alexander Cordell

SEVERN
SH
HOUSE

This first world edition published in Great Britain 1995 by
SEVERN HOUSE PUBLISHERS LTD of
9–15 High Street, Sutton, Surrey SM1 1DF.
First published in the USA 1996 by
SEVERN HOUSE PUBLISHERS INC of
595 Madison Avenue, New York, NY 10022.

British Library Cataloguing in Publication Data
Cordell, Alexander
  Love That God Forgot
  I. Title
  823.914 [F]

  ISBN 0-7278-4848-8

For Paul and Susan

Typeset by Hewer Text Composition Services, Edinburgh.
Printed and bound in Great Britain by
Hartnolls Ltd, Bodmin, Cornwall.

Note for Reader

Drift Cottage existed on Flatholm within the perimeter of the walling constructed around the present foghorn station complex; the cottage's stone having been removed and used for the station's foundations when it was constructed in the year 1908, three years after the ending of the novel, THE LOVE THAT GOD FORGOT.

The fog siren sounded every thirty seconds and, it has been said, not only kept the islanders awake, but could be heard as far away as Swansea; by then all that remained of Drift Cottage, the home of Tom Mortymer and Jenny Wildflower, had been obliterated.

Within sight of the foghorn station there existed in 1897 a post office mast 110 feet high (a similar mast being built at Lavernock Point) for the use of the inventor Guglielmo Marconi, who, aided by technicians of the General Post Office, successfully and for the first time, transmitted a wireless message over the sea from Flatholm to Lavernock: the morse slip containing the words 'Are you ready' (signed by Signor Marconi and George Kemp of the Post Office) can now be seen in the National Museum of Wales.

A strange edifice celebrating this momentous happening has been erected on Flatholm: further detail regarding the Marconi experiments are available in the booklet 'Flatholm': sharing no part of the story of Mortymer and Wildflower, nothing of Marconi's experiments are included within the novel, but are of sufficient interest to be mentioned herein.

Alexander Cordell
Wales

Intreat me not to leave thee,
or to return from following
after thee...

Ruth 1; 16,17

Prologue

1900

If there exists a God of Journalists, which after bad experiences I doubt, He was surely on my side on the day Annie,
my mother, sent a telegram to the Fleet Street office of *The
London Mercury*, my newspaper. Her message said:

'Come home at once.'

Because one always obeyed instructions from Mother, I
was on Paddington Station within an hour, fighting my way
through khaki-clad hundreds, the less fortunates who were
on their way to fight the Boers in South Africa, and the lads
were singing:

"Goodbye Dolly, I must leave you, tho' it breaks my heart
to go. Something tells me I am needed at the front to fight the
foe. See the soldier boys are marching. And I can no longer
stay. Hark! I hear the bugle calling, Goodbye Dolly Gray."

Everywhere people were waving Union Jacks and the
place was a bustle of brass bands playing, wet embraces
and red-faced drill instructors bawling military commands.

Soon, I thought, I would be in this same place reporting on
the broken bodies coming home, the inevitable outcome of
our foreign adventures and unnecessary colonial conquests:
it was only a passing thought, for my mind was filled with
my mother's inexplicable request.

Hours later, after greeting her on Bridgend Station platform in South Wales, I knew the reason and was immediately
suspicious, for Dai Dando, an old retainer of the Mortymer
family, was with her.

1

Brushed up and toppered was Dai, his hat at a jaunty angle; as old as a dead crow was he and deformed by age; the antithesis of my mother who, inches the taller, appeared regal in her long white summer dress and broad-rimmed pink hat; aged fifty and emitting her usual air that she was not to be tampered with.

She said, "You are late, George," and presented me with a cheek.

"Blame the G.W.R."

"'Afternoon, young 'un," said Dai. "My ain't you grown!"

The people coming off the train pressed about us in smells of sun and hot cloth.

A word about these two while on the subject.

With Dai Dando knocking eighty and Annie a mature and unattractive matron, they lived together now as they had done for over half a century, first as servants in *Cefn-Ydfa* mansion, where once the Mortymer family held court; then, when Tom Mortymer and his Romany bride left the ancestral home after their disastrous marriage, they occupied Mansion Lodge, a little thatched two-up-two-down known ridiculously as *Corn Hwch*; translated from the Welsh this means 'the horn of the sow' . . . and a sow does not possess a horn.

In peace and celibacy they had lived together since the death of Old Bid, Dai's wife, once cook-housekeeper to the Mortymer household – he as coachman, Annie as a serving-maid: nobody disputed their right to do this, mainly, I suspect, because of Dai's great age and public knowledge that Annie's wild oats had been sown when she had me, quietly and illegitimately . . . when Tom's father, the master at the house, kindly took her in, he himself being a great one for wild oats in his time, said the locals.

Thus was I born in Great House, the mansion of *Cefn-Ydfa*.

Now, with Dai on the reins, I helped my mother, up into

2

the trap and the little piebald pony went clip-clopping along the Bridgend to Maesteg road.

"Where are we off to now, then?" I demanded.

"You'll soon see," said Dai.

"The old bird has found a skeleton," observed Annie.

"Pull the other one, Mam."

Dai said assertively, "I 'ave, right enough, young 'un! And I reckon it's worth a fiver, for I could 'ave called in the locals reasonable."

"But you didn't?"

"Keep things in the family, I always say."

"Where?" I asked.

"Where what?"

"The . . . the skeleton, Dai, where did you find it?"

"Down Ogpen Drift. My dog started sniffing around."

"Where's that?"

"Hold ye horses and I'll show ye. Mind, I reckon I ought to 'ave that fiver first."

"Any other time I got to chloroform him to get him out," said Annie, "now I can't keep him away from the place."

The pony trotted on; Wales shone in the evening sunlight; the pair of them were bowing left and right to neighbours, and as sure as hell, said Dai, if ye don't want to see any you'll meet a dozen.

"So the police don't know?" I asked.

"Not yet. Annie said to tell you first."

"It's in the public domain, mind," I observed.

"What's that, then? There's new words cropppin' up every minute."

"It means that the public has a right to know. If you've found a body you should report it to the police."

Annie made a strange lamenting sound, replying, "Up to you, George. We thought you'd be grateful, for it ain't every day of the week we get a murder in the Llynfi Valley."

"Have you any idea who did the murder?"

3

"Of course not," answered Dai. "Up to you, innit?"

He stopped the trap near Cwm Sychant, tethered the pony and put up a hand to Annie: lips pursed, she sat, immobile.

"She's right, mind," said Dai. "The roof's low, and it anna a sight for the fair sex. Sit tight, woman."

"Where now?" I asked, for the sun was going down.

"Follow me."

Actually, I recognised the old place; it came out of the shadows of my childhood: a few derelict miners' cottages watched us from battened windows, their open roof timbers staring up at the evening stars.

Time was, when I was a lad living in *Cefn-Ydfa*, I used to come up to Cwm Sychant and play dolly-stones with the urchins, and the old colliers of an earlier generation used to sit on their hunkers outside their doors, eating their lunch. A lot of them were the refuse of distant collieries where the roofs were low and the gas high: many were employed above ground at the big Oakwood Pit, and hung around the publics up in Nantyffyllon where the better paid ironworkers of Maesteg Ironworks were always good for a pint.

Now old Dai was scratching around in the coal-scarred hillocks, getting his bearings, so with a glance at Mother sitting in the trap, I joined him.

"Now you're going to tell me that you dreamed it?" I said.

"Round by 'ere somewhere, lad, for I aint' that far gone . . . there's a trap door in the drift roof, and a slope leading down." He knelt, struck a match and lit the wick of the lamp he was carrying.

"Jist that me eyes ain't that good, that's all . . . aha! Here it is." He rubbed away furnace slag from a flat in the ground. "Ay ay, here's their trap door down to the pitch; come on, George, give a hand," and he heaved at an inlaid ring-bolt.

4

Holding the oil lamp high, I peered down in the drift's darkness.

Below me, from a rope tied to the top rung of a down-ladder, a skeleton was hanging by the neck.

"That's 'im," said Dai.

I helped the old man down the ladder and we stood on the coal-step, looking at the skeleton of the hanging man in the lamp's wavering light; his socketted eyes stared back at us; his bones, hanging together in tattered rags, swung slowly in the disturbed air; about them was a smell of death.

A little draught moved; I held the lamp higher.

Behind us was a wall blocking further access into the drift; the rock roof was but a few feet above; the rickety wooden ladder upon which the body hung reached from floor to ceiling.

Dai whispered into my face, "I remember this old place; when the drift closed fifty year or more ago – they shut off this bit as a store-house for colliers' tools – fellas working the Oakwood over the river."

"How did you discover the body?"

"I were up 'ere on the scrounge, having busted me shovel: time was you could pick an odd one up off the heap in here, 'afore the vandals got at it, and when I was sniffin' around I saw that the manhole had been lifted."

"And you've told nobody about it?"

"Gawd, what do ye take me for? That old Graves is a peeler when it comes to the locals."

"Inspector Graves? Don't tell me he's still around."

"Large as life! 'You keep this to yourself, Dai Dando,' said Annie. 'My young George'll make a coupla bob out of it.'"

"Her young George reckons you ought to tell the police, Dai. It looks like a suicide, but you're – it could be murder . . . "

"What about your newspaper?"

"I'll send the article tonight."

5

"And what about me, son? They'll 'ave me bum in the county gaol directly it's on the streets."

"No they won't – all you do is tell the truth . . . hey, what's this?" I stooped and swept the floor with the lamp-light, for in moving had trodden upon something . . . and found at my feet – a pathetic little pile of rags that had dropped off the corpse: kneeling, I searched them, holding them up to the lamp, and they disintegrated into dust and the remnants of the dead man's coat. I found a stub of a candle, a broken quill and a tiny stone jar which could have contained ink.

"He were a writing chap, that's for sure," said Dai.

"Somewhere around here could be something he wrote . . ." and I crawled upon my knees, searching, but found nothing, saying: "The important thing here is to leave everything as we found it, and tell the truth of how you found it exactly as it happened. All right?" and I put everything back among the rags.

"Like Annie says, you're the gaffer," said Dai, and jerked his head at the corpse. "What about him?"

"Leave him to Inspector Graves."

"Mind, it don't seem decent, do it? I mean . . . "

I helped Dai up the ladder. "He'll have a decent grave, but all in good time. It's my guess that he's been hanging here for years; another few hours won't do him any harm."

Now, out of the chamber I replaced the trap door carefully and covered it with ashes and furnace slag, and Dai said, as we set off back to Annie, "Suicide or murder, eh? This is going to wake up Maesteg, whatever it is."

After calling at Maesteg police station and informing them officially of Dai's find, the three of us went home to *Corn Hwch* where I was to spend the night.

With the three of us seated around the fire, I said, "Mam, it's all so long ago now that it's like a dream – remind me about the Mortymers."

6

Said she, "You knows as much about them as I do, really speaking. Like I told you, I owes them a lot, especially Master Iestyn, for when I had me troubles, it was he who took me in. 'Never you mind, Annie,' he told me, 'it's only the good girls that get caught.' Then later he and Jenny Wildflower's mither got themselves drowned on their honeymoon, leaving Tom, his son, alone – remember?"

"Ay." Dai sucked his pipe. "Went swimmin', in the Bay o' Naples, didn't they?"

"Ach, ye daft thing, no! They took a ferry boat in Geneva and the thing went down. Then Tom fell for the Wildflower daughter; took her out of her Romany life and cut and carried her – lord o' the manor and the gypsy in the parlour, very romantic!"

Dai mumbled, "Weren't there a bit a scandal about that, Annie?"

"Not that I know of," came my mother's reply, and she elbowed him. "You wash out your mouth, Dai Dando: Tom Mortymer and his Romany was lovely people and I won't hear a word against 'em."

"I remember Tom Mortymer, of course," I said. "He used to give me flying angels and chase me round his study. And his Jenny Wildflower was the prettiest woman I'd ever seen."

Annie warmed to this. "She were as lovely as a daffodil Sunday, that Jenny, and like her mother Clare, she was a lady."

"But there was some scandal about their marriage; didn't it break up, or something?"

Dai studied his pipe with reflective interest; Annie lifted her teacup and drank, looking at nothing.

"Not that I know of," said she.

"Beautiful people, the pair of 'em, though," muttered Dai in contrition.

But I pursued it, saying, "They jumped the broom, Romany fashion, and cut their wrists to mingle their blood? That's what I heard . . ."

7

"Different people, different customs," said Annie abstractedly.

"Yes, of course, but why did Jenny suddenly fly off from *Cefn-Ydfa* and leave him flat?"

You could have cut chunks out of the following silence. I said, "Oh, come on, Mam, I'm family, remember?"

She sniffed and touched her eyes with a little lace handkerchief.

"Well, I don't know the ins and outs of it, but accordin' to Old Bid – remember Dai's missus – and she had ears to hear brown grass growin' – a letter arrived from someone saying they was brother and sister . . ."

"God, no!"

"No, Annie," interjected Dai, "you got it wrong. Half-brother and sister, I heard. My Biddy told it clear. Iestyn Mortymer, Tom's pa, had a leg-over with Clare, Jenny's mam, before George come on the scene."

"By that he means a love affair," said Annie with hostility. "But the old beggar's right – they shared the same father, but didn't know it. Sad, ain't it?"

"Bad cess or something they do call it," added Dai, going Irish.

"Incest," interjected Annie, "ye daft ole beggar. And that Jenny were a Romany, so off she goes, for her people don't fancy incest neither: off she goes to the bank, gets a lump o' money, hitches up the pony to her little red caravan and she's away to go."

I said, getting up, "But surely their parents warned them of the relationship?"

Annie nodded. "That's what I thought. From what Old Bid heard, and she had her ear to the panelling, not anything at all was said; yet anyone could see that Tom and young Jen was sparkin'. I said to Bid at the time, I said . . ."

Dai muttered, "Too full o' themselves, is my guess. Perhaps they intended to break that news when they come back from their honeymoon, but they drowned too soon."

The sense of it put an end to the speculation.

"What happened then? Surely Tom didn't sit around? Didn't he go after Jenny?"

Annie emptied her hands at me. "Half-brother and sister. There a law against it, ain't there?"

"There is up in Scotland," I said. "Death by hanging."

"*Diawl*," whispered Dai. "You can't have brothers and sisters a 'frolickin' in the same bed!"

"Don't you be indecent," admonished Mother. "It were a tragedy!"

"What happened in the end?" I asked.

"He hung around *Cefn-Ydfa* for weeks hoping Jen would come back, but she didn't. His Uncle Jethro, his father's brother, was over here from America, and they say Tom asked his advice." She paused, seeking words. "Mind, it were strange Mr Jethro should turn up then – just in time to take over the Mortymer tinplate works at Upper Forest . . ."

"And Tom then went after Jenny?"

Annie nodded; tears were in her eyes when she said, "Very sad, ye know. I mind when I was about twelve, 'afore I come into Service. There was a couple living next door but six down Colliers' Row, and they 'ad two children.

"Courted proper, they did, decent chapel people; and when they 'ad twin girls the whole valley turned out wi' a brass band to wet the babies' heads.

"And then, after the husband registered their birth, he came back home and put in for double trams, for things was tight and they needed the money. For a time nothing went wrong for 'em, for it was summer and the valley was like those babies, all dressed up in bonnets and lace bibs, and there was no father prouder in Maesteg than young Alfie Jordon – as English as they make 'em was he, wi' a fist on him for stunning mules, for he was a mountain fighter spare time . . ."

9

There was no sound in the cottage but the ticking of Annie's mantle clock and the coo-cooing of the *Cefn-Ydfa* doves.

She continued, "Then one day a policeman comes up Colliers' Row with a notebook and pencil and knocks on Alf Jordan's terraced door, and out comes Big Alf with lather on his face, poshin' himself up for Sunday Chapel, and his missus behind him with a baby in each arm all dummies and bubbles, an' that rotten ole policeman said, 'Are you Alfred Jordan?'

'Ye knows very well I am!'

'And are you the legal wife of this man, woman?' came the next question.

'Of course, sir,' said the wife.

'So your name is Jordon, too?'

'Ay so, Inspector. He's my husband.'

'Unfortunately, my girl, there's doubt about that. Accordin' to the Registrar of Births and Deaths you ain't this man's legal wife, but his sister. So I'll trouble you to hand those children over to neighbours and come with me.' He blew on his whistle and more boys in blue came runnin'."

Annie turned her tear-filled eyes to mine.

"There was trouble all right, for half the neighbours were on their doorsteps and the other half hittin' out coppers, and Big Alf fetched one the prettiest left hook I ever did see, and down he went with his eyes crossed.

"Then the Irish coming off shift got hold of it, and as fast as they brought in policemen from Bridgend the colliers got into them, while Big Alf, Mary and the twins went hell for leather for the railway station, with half the police force in South Wales behind them.

"But they cornered the family as the train was leaving, and beat Alf down with their truncheons and towed him off to the lock-up. Never dreamed of it, see? – either of 'em. They thought themselves properly married, but they parted 'em right enough – Mary back to her cottage and Big Alf

10

into the single men's hostel, till he were killed down Coal Pit two months later . . ."

She sighed. "Perhaps that was for the best, folks said – gettin' himself under a fall down Coal Pit. Some said he did it on purpose."

"It were a love that God forgot, really speakin', weren't it?" Dai observed.

"Could be," replied Annie, "though He don't miss a lot, mind."

At which she wept buckets, sobbing and wheezing, while Dai and I smoothed and patted her . . .

Next morning Wales was all over bright and gay, for summer, full and splendid, was into us, with coo-doves sobbing up in *Cefn-Ydfa* and swallows cavorting in the eaves.

I met Mother in the garden.

"Do you ever see Tom and Jenny Mortymer these days?" I asked her.

"Not in a month o'Sundays – they're coming and going over to Flatholm Island, they do tell me – they lived there once, ye know . . ." Here she went dreamy, making no eyes, and added, "Instead of writing about that old skeleton, son, I reckon you ought to write about them – the story of the love between Tom Mortymer and Jen Wildflower, his Romany sweetheart: they started off all right, but with one dreadful thing after another happening, got through it all because they was in love. Dai Dando weighed it up like he said – it was a love that God forgot."

"Tell me more."

"Don't ask me, it anna my business; besides, if I tell, you'd be as wise as me," and she added, "For it's their story, ain't it? Why don't you ask them to write it themselves?

And so, before returning to London, I took the idea over to Flatholm Island in the Bristol Channel, and put it to

11

them, but since re-opening their little island hospital for sick animals there, they were at first disinterested.

Jenny, Tom's wife, said eventually, "We wouldn't know where to begin, would we!"

"We haven't even got a title," replied Tom.

"Don't worry about that," I said, "I've got one ready made."

"What about it, Tom?" asked his wife.

"Us? Write a book?"

"Why not, we've enough time on our hands in the evenings. After all, the end of remembering is the beginning of forgetting . . ." Which I thought was a very strange thing to say . . .

That was the end of the discussion.

Therefore, I was amazed to hear within a fortnight, that Mother had received the first chapter with a request that she should put it into her safe in Upper Forest House, since they, the Mortymers, had no secure facilities in Drift Cottage where they were now living.

Years later, I read this book. It began restlessly and continued for over a hundred thousand words that rendered me sleepless night after night.

And its title?

THE LOVE THAT GOD FORGOT

Chapter 1

1880

Had it happened on any day but a Friday, I would have entered Drift Cottage first, and thus saved Jen the horror of what followed . . .

* * *

Within half an hour of reading, I knew, as an old hand in the business, that I was into a bestseller. But why the strict security?

By the time I had reached the end of the book, I knew why . . . and wondered if it ought ever be published. For this is what I read:

Book One

Chapter One

1880

The following is a record of the lives and times of Tom
Mortymer and Jenny Wildflower, dictated by the former and
set down by the latter, largely while living in Drift Cottage,
on the island of Flatholm.

Had it happened on any day but a Friday, I would have
entered Drift Cottage first, and saved Jen the horror of what
followed; but on Friday mornings I took our fish catch over
to Cardiff market on the mainland, leaving my girl to get
on with the bits and pieces that women usually save for the
weekend, and this left her alone on the Island. It was a fact I
later took note of, for somebody, clearly, had been watching
our movements.

"I didn't see it at first Tom," said Jen, shivering. "I came
into the kitchen backwards, barging the door with my bottom,
my hands full of washing, and there he was dead on the
floor."

Sam, our prize cockerel, lying in a pool of blood.

"And then I saw the note pinned up above the fireplace,"
and she gave it to me. Written in block letters in Sam's blood,
it read:

'Make the most of it you two, because you are next.'

We stood together in the little room, staring at the note,
the dead cockerel, the pool of blood.

"You were here all morning, love?" I asked her.

"Yes, Tom."

"Now come on, girl, *think*. Did you leave here for anything?"

She faltered. It would have been a shock for any woman, but dead chickens and pools of blood have a serious effect upon Romanies, and Jen Wildflower, having only recently left her tribe, was worse than most when it came to gypsy lore, I'd discovered. Now she said, sitting down, "Yes, I was away for about an hour."

"Where did you go?"

"Only as far as the Lighthouse, to ask about Mrs Morgan and her new baby."

"Did you see any strangers hanging about? Try to remember, Jen, it's important."

"No."

"There's footsteps in the sand outside the door," I said. "I noticed them coming up from the beach, but Sergeant Bostock could have caused those when he came last Sunday."

There was no sound now but the booming of the waves crashing on East Reach, Flatholm Island's perpetual music; faintly I heard, a distant wailing of gulls.

Jen said quietly, "It's a blood sacrifice, ye know." Her features, disconsolate, were piquantly beautiful in the coming dusk.

I shrugged, trying to play it down: give a Romany half a chance and they gobble such things into a turkey.

"Hadn't we better tell the police?" she asked.

"Of course not. Somebody killed a chicken, we'd be a laughing stock!" I turned away.

"But the note, Tom—"

"Forget it. Who ever it was they'd have given you a going over if they'd really meant trouble."

"At least mention it to Sergeant Bostock?"

I shook my head. "I'd have reported it to Sergeant Barrett

18

had he been around, but he's on leave and Bostock, who's standing in, is a bloody old woman."

"So you'll do nothing?"

"Oh, yes I will. Somebody is trying to shift us off this island and when we don't go he'll try something else; then I'll have him."

"Have you thought he might get us first?" she asked, and stooped and picked up poor old Sam. "He . . . he's still warm, Tom!"

Later, I swabbed up the blood and was taking Sam out when Jen called from the oil stove, "Where are ye going with that cockerel?"

"Taking him out to bury him."

"Oh, no you don't, Tom Mortymer. Nobody puts the breeze up me and gets away with it, give him here: he'll have an early Christmas."

"God no, we can't eat Sam!"

"You watch me," said Jenny.

Which was a Romany all over: one moment shivering with the superstitions of their tribal centuries, next exhibiting the practicality of their gypsy lives.

Chapter Two

We had arrived on Flatholm Island at the end of April after touring around in Jen's gypsy caravan, which we had now left in the care of Farmer Thomas, whose land extended to Sully: for half a crown a week rental we had left it, with our little piebald pony eating his head off, stabled for the next six months.

With our few possessions in an old suitcase, we had boarded the military ferry which ran once a week; the wind coming eastward that day was battering the Bristol Channel into a storm, and it was enough to freeze you solid.

"What you doing in these parts, then?" asked the boatman.

"Runnin' away from life!" bawled Jenny, cupping her hands to her mouth.

"Is that a fact? One thing's for sure, missus, there isn't much life on Flatholm, save rabbits and seabirds, an' when the breeze comes in from Bridgewater Bay it's enough to freeze ancestors." He braced his legs to the leaping thwarts as the sea came breaking over the gunwale to starboard. Grizzled and bearded, this one, a man of the sea, and he shouted next, "Accordin' to what they're saying in Sully, you're takin' over Drift Cottage – that right?"

"Four bob a week," I yelled back, as the spray suddenly drenched me, "enough to break us!"

The little craft, an old lifeboat, tacked expertly into the wind, then went about to the swing of the tiller and ran for quiet water in the lee of Flatholm. We glided calmly until the keel grounded on the shingle of West Beach; hauling our suitcase, I leaped ashore and Jen threw me our kitbag.

"Good luck!" I shouted.

The ferryman replied, "And good luck to you, ye mad lot, for you're goin' to need it!"

"Where's the cottage?"

"Take the path on the left to East Beach slipway. And if ye get lost on the way, Mister, ask God."

For the last year Jen and I had been roaming Britain in Jen's little red caravan, opting out of a life of industry and profit making.

Leaving my tinplate manufacturing works in the hands of Gaffer Adams, an expert handling my workforce of some ninety men and girls of the tin-trade, I had agreed to Jen's plea to adopt a wandering life for at least a year, before returning to the ownership and responsibilities of one of the most successful tinplate exporters in the Swansea area. "For one year, Tom," she had begged. "Give me my gypsy life for a single year and I will return with you to civilisation and become a dutiful wife."

And so we had wandered, sleeping in the caravan when the nights were frosty, and under the stars when the nights were warm and shiny. Bathing naked in the sea off St Bees Head in the Lake District, we were chased along the shore by a village policeman, and for doing the same thing in a river in New Lanark up in Scotland (Robert Owen's country) were fined ten shillings each by a stipendiary magistrate on the grounds of being 'dangerous to public morality'.

We were robbed by a pickpocket in Dover on our way to France via the ferry to Calais (and here we left Jen's caravan in capable hands) and were attacked again at knife-point in Montmartre, where I laid out our assailant; but not before he had lifted our last ten francs out of Jen's pocket: we

21

had begged a franc off a silk-hatted Paris gentleman and washed up for our supper in a pavement restaurant in the Rue de Ville.

The situation, as I protested to a disdainful Jen Wildflower, was now ridiculous; with enough money back home in a Morriston bank to buy the bloody restaurant, I was being treated by a fat French cook as a layabout and loafer, wandering beautiful France without tuppence in my pocket.

"It has got to stop," I said vehemently. "Do you hear me? I am going home!" and what began as a kiss of friendship in a tiny attic bedroom in the Latin quarter (and God knows how we were going to pay the rent) ended in heat and gasped breathing . . . yes, yes . . . in a little room with chintz curtains at a postage-stamp window which opened out on to the higgledy-piggledy sea of slate roofs . . . beyond which arose the beautiful towers of the glorious *Sacre Coer* cathedral.

This *pension* at a few francs a week was enough to ruin us. It was owned jointly by Mesdames Coustelle and Mavon, she who years afterwards at the height of *Vin blanc* jollity claimed relationship with the later world famous Georges Carpentier, the European Heavyweight Champion born to be known as 'The Flower of France'. Complicated, true, but having been a pupil of Dai Dando and learned the finer points of the Noble Art, friendship with such a person was later my only boast; all of which bored Jen to tears, who was intent only on us keeping body and soul together.

It was late spring and Paris was all over gay with flowers and pretty pavement cafés where, going from job to job to get the rent, we guzzled bad French wine – something all lovers do in Paris – and tore hungrily into hot crusted two-foot-long loaves straight out of the bakers' ovens, plastered with lashings of salted farm butter; then home again to watch

22

the stars come out over the city and make love until sleep encompassed us in the music of the Parisian streets – the cries of night lamp-lighters; the home-going revelry of dusk to dawn celebrations.

After a month in a *pension* and working overtime to amass sufficient money, I succeeded in paying the rent of Number 18 Stinkerque Attic for the next six months in advance; which allowed me later, when back in Wales, to continue this rental by banker's order; thus making the *pension* available on any flying visit to Paris.

I did not realise then, of course, how easily could be cancelled all its apparent advantages: on the face of it, an apartment in Paris sounded delightful . . . but my lover is absent now . . . Yet always will I remember that tiny room, the silk counterpane on the bed, the flowered curtains at the window, and the gasps of lovers under the Montmartre stars.

After leaving Paris we wandered France on foot; hitched lifts from farm carts, or sat in the cushioned seats of the opulent . . . where I listened to Jen's flow of garrulous schoolgirl French accompanied by expressive gesticulations, most of which had the locals in stitches: here again, I thought, the uneducated gypsy girl competing with the classically informed high school student; the enigma that was totally Jen Wildflower.

Our newly found happiness had to come to an end, as did the peacetime revelries of Paris: political thunder clouds were again gathering on the French horizon, due to harsh terms imposed by their conquerors after the Prussian war of 1870. But Paris in the spring of our visit was like a young maiden recovering from the effect of a tragic courtship, and as such will I remember her. We continued to send gaily-coloured postcards home to Wales.

23

Our newly found pleasures had come to us the hard way.

Earlier, during our courtship when Jen had lived with her mother in the caravan and I with my parents at *Cefn-Ydfa* (a mansion near Maesteg), our romance had been an on and off affair; this, caused by Jen's simultaneous attraction to David Grey, the adopted son of a local entrepreneur, had flourished literally under my nose; it came to a head just when I thought I had got her set up for the altar.

The outcome was her marriage to David, who took her to live with his family at what was known locally as the Russian Villa; their two-year life together was plagued with disaster, and came to a dramatic conclusion with Jen's miscarriage of a child, and the death of David Grey through consumption.

Therefore, although through the years my love for Jen had never faltered, I had caught her on the rebound as a second best. All my effort now, with no other woman in my life, was to bring happiness into the days of the one I loved.

Other elements, however, apparently determined to part us again, were slowly coming to their conclusion, and began from the moment Jen and I arrived in Flatholm.

Chapter Three

And so, at the end of a year of utter freedom, we had come to Drift Cottage on beautiful Flatholm and settled in to a life of 'do as you like' and to the devil with convention, and the outside world can take a jump, said Jenny, or words to that effect, and added, "Just you and me, Tom Mortymer, goin' naked from breakfast to loverin' time, just as we please, with no peeping eyes seeing what we get up to, an' no ten bob fines for doing an Adam and Eve act in public."

"Not quite," I replied. "We aren't the only people on the island, remember. If Bill sees you with your clothes off he'll get his rag out, and report you to Tidal Commissioners."

"Who?"

"Bill Dale, the lighthouse keeper. Besides, there's at least half a dozen sons and daughters of Mr Morgan and his wife, to say nothing of soldiers manning gun emplacements covering the Channel, and if they see you, I'll have to fight them off."

"Well, one thing's for certain – we've got our bedroom all to ourselves," said she.

A word about Drift Cottage.

At four bob a week it was expensive, because it was really nothing but a two-roomed stone tumbledown with a slate roof that leaked, an oil stove that didn't work and a bed that could have belonged to Christopher Columbus; but a double, at least, said Jen, patting it. At present the cottage was owned by Farmer Thomas of Sully, but initially, he told us, it was used by smugglers and other unsavoury characters activating in the Bristol Channel since 1700.

In the July after we had arrived, however, it looked pretty good, and still better after we had been over to Cardiff on the mainland and bought decent bedding, some rush-mat covering for the floors and print white curtains, stitched up by Jenny for the two small windows facing the sea; an oil painting of a ram dying in snow over the fireplace and a sampler saying 'God is Love' over the bed.

Looking back, it was the happiest time of my life, that summer, for the long Welsh coastline from Swansea to Newport was shining and expectant at the prospect of warmth, and the island ancient with memories of her Danish invaders, put up her spags and dozed, like us, in a big-bellied bumbledore July. And the death of Sam Cockerel, one might ask? Well, that was weeks away now and we had almost forgotten it in getting the place habitable. Indeed, it had left my mind completely, until Jen raised it on the morning I received the letter from Gaffer Adams, our representative of the tinplate works at Morriston.

"Somebody knows where we are," said Jen darkly. "I thought it was a national secret . . ."

"I had to tell Adams. He had to know our whereabouts in case something tricky turned up." I opened the letter delivered earlier by the ferryman, and read aloud:

"'27th July 1881
Dear Mr Mortymer,
I know that you instructed me not to contact you unless absolutely necessary, but something has occurred which makes it imperative that I do so immediately. Unless I hear to the contrary, I will visit you on Flatholm Island three days from now.
Yours obediently,
Gaffer Adams.

26

Upper Forest Works
Morriston'"

I lowered the letter. "He means business. Adams doesn't panic easily."

Jenny sighed. "For heaven's sake, Tom, can't they leave us alone? We've only just arrived."

"Something to do with the workforce, I expect; it can't be financial; he has the authority to do as he wishes."

"Perhaps that's the trouble." She was distant.

"What does that mean?"

"That you can be too trusting."

"Adams in money trouble? I'd stake my life on his integrity."

"I wasn't talking about Gaffer Adams."

"Who, then?"

"You're working with lawyers and solicitors too, remember. There's more of them in gaol these days than thieves and brain-thudders."

"Dear me! The legal profession wouldn't like to hear you say things like that!"

"When money comes through the door, loyalty flies out of the window."

Wandering around the little room, I replied, "If all he wants to talk about is routine management stuff, I'm not bothered . . ." and Jen shrugged, looking vacant.

How could we know that the information Adams was about to bring would scar us down the generations?

The morning was a diamond of brilliance, and the old molten bun sailing above a burnished sea set up the island in all her primitive glory. To remove my mind from the threat of Adams's arrival, I asked Jen to give me a hand with the completion of a big fish-trap I was building on East Beach; this, I congratulated myself, was guaranteed to keep us in fish (based on the tidal theory) for the rest of our stay on Flatholm, with some left over for selling in Cardiff market.

There existed on East Beach a ready-made slipway: originally constructed to serve Castle Rock gun-battery, it could be simply converted into a fish-trap by bolting across it longitudinal six-by-six inch timber baulks; these, spaced at reasonable intervals, would be flooded at high tide and fish trapped between them when the tide receded.

Since the position of our fish-trap was isolated and Castle Rock battery, which towered above us, occupied by the gunners only in emergencies, we had licence to behave as we pleased. Indeed, in those early days on Flatholm, we looked upon ourselves, Jen and I, as castaways; naked savages who owed allegiance to none.

We would return after work to the quiet sanctity of Drift Cottage; there to get outside huge bowls of Jen's Irish stew or the fruits of the sea; washing them down with draughts of wine, and wondering at the stupidity of land-based idiots who hadn't the intelligence to discover the simple delights of island freedom.

Living in deep communion with Nature was emphasised on the evening before Gaffer Adams came, when we arrived at the cottage hungry and tired after completing the fish-trap, to find two companions waiting on the doorstep to greet our homecoming. Bun and Shag, huddled either side of the door . . . eyeing one another suspiciously, but making no effort to escape as we approached.

"Keep still, Tom!" Jen commanded, and went quietly forward. Rabbit and bird stared up at her as if in mute surprise at her audacity, as she picked up Bun in one hand and Shag in the other, and took them into the cottage; one had a broken hind leg, the other a shattered wing; both half starved as a result.

With careless disregard Jen deposited them on the table

28

we later reserved for such casualties. "I'll see to you later," said she. "Right now I've got to get the dinner on the go."

Her affinity with all wild things was astonishing; their trust in her amazing: I have seen her walk among a flock of feeding gulls without them raising a feather, yet they had risen with squawks of alarm at the sight of me.

Thus began our Animal Casualty Centre on Flatholm; these two, plus Tom-cat who arrived later, were our first nonpaying patients.

The arrival of Gaffer Adams was more complicated.

For a start, he was a disappointed educationalist, and after us from the start, conveying to us, on the ferry coming over from Sully, his knowledge of Flatholm.

He was a small man, and had he been Irish might have been mistaken for a leprechaun, with his wizened little face and expressive hands.

We were silent, Jen and I, as he recounted volubly, while hanging on to the pitch and dive of the boat, "According to my encyclopedia, Flatholm is the jewel of the Bristol Channel: with Cardiff six miles or so to the north-west and Barry a little nearer, it is a beckoning finger to all determined to avoid the rush and commercialism of the cities . . ." He shouted into my ear, "Can you hear me above this palaver?" For the wind was getting up and there was a big sea rolling, spindrift flying and a flock of herring gulls shrieking demented above us. I shouted assent to get rid of him.

"It's about six hundred yards in diameter, almost circular, and in the sixth century was a haven for wandering monks, who used its tranquillity for scholarship and meditation." Jen nodded total agreement. Unabashed by our pent silence, Gaffer continued, "The disciples of St Cadoc visited here when it was known as Flatholm, but in fact it was called Bradanreolice by early Saxon invaders . . ."

"Is that a fact?"

" . . . which is a derivative of an Irish word meaning

29

'graveyard'." He continued, "Danish invaders took refuge here after their defeat at Watchet, many dying of hunger."

"Which reminds me to get the stew on the boil the moment we get in," shouted Jen, and gave me an old-fashioned look and a sigh.

So much for Gaffer, who was in good form: such an interest epitomised him, for he was meticulous in everything he undertook; which was why I had given him a free hand to run my tinplate works at Upper Forest in the manner he pleased.

The sea was quieter as the ferryman ran the boat, goose-winged and free, on to the shingle of West Beach. We clambered out, and our guest gave no indication that Jen and I had a shock coming that might end in us having to leave the island.

This came out after we had eaten herring soup and torn off mouthfuls of Jen's freshly baked crusty hot bread, followed by her inevitable rice pudding.

The lamp was burning low upon the white tablecloth; Bun and Shag, now splinted and bandaged, watched the three of us with enquiring eyes.

"First things first," said Gaffer, filling his pipe, "you're wanted by the police."

"Good God," I said. "What for?"

"Don't ask me, sir, that's your business. And the Scottish police, of all people."

Jen said earnestly, "You're joking!"

"True as I sit 'ere, missus." He made a face at the ceiling. "A few months back, maybe longer, you went up to Scotland, didn't you?"

"Yes, six months ago we went up to New Lanark to visit the Robert Owen Co-operative there . . ."

"Ay ay." Gaffer puffed out foul-smelling pipe smoke. "And soon after that I had a visitor – that Sergeant what's his name from Swansea – you know, the fat chap; you met him on the day the Mayor gave a send-off to our first export, remember?"

"Why is he involved?" I asked. "You said it was a Scottish inquiry."

"And so it was. The Scottish Office wrote to the Swansea police, asking them to check your whereabouts, and Sergeant Bush – aye, that's his name – called at Upper Forest to ask me."

"But you didn't tell him where we were"

Gaffer looked aggrieved. "Of course not. Last thing you said was to keep mum on ye whereabouts, so I did."

"When was that, you say?"

He puffed at his pipe. "About eight weeks or so."

"And you've heard nothing since?" asked Jenny. "Anyway, what are we supposed to have done wrong?"

"Nothin', so far as I know – they was only asking."

I interjected, "You mean the police in Scotland contacted the Swansea police and asked them to inquire about our whereabouts?"

"The two of ye, Mr Thomas Mortymer – and his missus." He took a noisy breath. "Can't be much to worry about. I've seen Sergeant Bush a couple of times since and he never mentioned anything."

"What can it possibly be?" asked Jenny, as if speaking to her soul. "We were only over the Scottish border for a couple of days . . ."

"Just long enough to look over the Co-operative, then come south again."

"Forget it, mister," said Gaffer. "Anyway, there's some'ut else, much more important."

Jen had got up to put the kettle on the stove, and stood there, I remember, looking over her shoulder at the pair of us. Shag made a sweet complaining sound, and she reached out and touched his bill.

31

"Things are beginning to go wrong, Tom . . ." said he.

"Come on, let's have it all, Gaffer," I said.

"It's the bank statements," said Gaffer.

"What's wrong with the bank statemeı ts?"

"Well, I ain't much on the financial side, as ye know, sir, but the new solicitors keepin' the Upper Forest accounts ain't too happy, by what I've heard. It's the O-H Siemens replacements, really speaking . . ."

"What about them?"

"You said you'd get 'em from Germany, remember? But you went off, and didn't, and two of the four wore out. They cost the earth, them furnaces."

"How much?" I asked.

"More'n two thousand pounds apiece – scandalous!"

"Can't you get an allowance on the old ones?"

"Two or three hundred quid at most."

"Well, you can't make tin without them, so what do we do?"

I saw Jen's glance as she made the coffee, and knew I was being short with the old man, but couldn't help it.

It wasn't the furnace replacement that was worrying me, not even the money, which was expensive at this stage of the firm's progress; no, it was this inexplicable business of the police inquiry that was dogging my thoughts at a time when I had come to Flatholm for the one elusive element necessary to our happiness – peace. A little poem out of the past was repeating itself in my head, 'Not for us is content and quiet and peace of mind, for why go seeking cities that you can never find . . . ?'

And I heard Gaffer's reply like a whisper in the world of sea and sand outside. "The trouble is, we've gone into overdraft . . ."

I got up. "What? That can't be true! Don't tell me that in six months away I'm in the red . . . !"

"Sir, you told me to keep up production, an' I have,

but two new furnaces at four thousand make a hole in the profits."

"But, when I left Upper Works there was a credit of over six thousand!"

"Oh, God, Tom," said Jen wearily, her back to us. "It's only money, isn't it."

Poor old Gaffer added, "I done the best I could, Mr Mortymer, but like I said, I'm no scholar when it comes to addin' up; I leave that to the accountants."

"Then why didn't you warn me about it before now?"

His eyes met mine. "You said you didn't want to know."

"To be accurate, love," added Jen, pouring the coffee, "you said you didn't want to be bothered." In passing with my cup she patted Gaffer affectionately on his bald patch, saying, "When it comes to profit and loss, Gaffer, they're all the same, take it from me. Don't worry about it, he's just an old pin'head, and he'll have forgotten about it in the morning." She held up a warning finger. "Meanwhile, there's a gale blowing up, so you'll not be getting back to the mainland tonight." She indicated the little suitcase he had brought. "Have you got the necessary in there?"

"I got a clean nightshirt and me shavin' tackle, in case—"

"Good enough, and if ye behave yourself you can sleep with me."

"Dear me," said Gaffer, "you are a one!"

After he'd gone outside to the toilet, I said, "What a ridiculous thing to say to an old man! Jen, really!"

"One thing's certain," said she, and kissed my cheek. "Since you've become a money-bags, you ain't worth sleepin' with."

Clearly, I was on my own when it came to the finances of the Upper Forest Works at Morriston. And if things went on the same way, I thought, I'd be back on the mainland to see both bank manager and police sooner than I'd intended.

33

The gale subsided before dawn and Gaffer Adams went home in the ferry boat.

Frankly, what with one thing and another, I was pleased to see the back of him.

I could never fathom from whom Jen had got her ability as a swimmer, for Romanies were mainly a landlocked people. Gaffer's visit to Flatholm that early summer was memorable, not for the news he brought, but for Jen's decision to go midnight bathing.

Personally I am not one for sea-dipping; in childhood my visits to the seaside had been restricted to paddling, and a bucket and a spade. Therefore, it had been a wondrous sight to watch Jen, as naked as with the midwife, go scuttling down East Beach and along the coaling wharf, to dive, shouting, into the waves; and then swim out until her shining body was a dot in the distance; there, treading water, she would raise a glistening arm, before diving under, while I waited with a pounding heart for her to reappear.

Indeed, on one occasion I had waited for half an hour, scanning the empty sea, before, with her graceful overarm strokes, she drove herself into my waiting arms. "For God's sake where have you been?" I shouted.

I feared that while the God of Romanies was glancing the other way, the sea Jen loved might one day take her from me.

Fate took her from me right enough, but it was nothing to do with the sea.

Chapter Four

In the middle of July, with Gaffer's worrying visit almost forgotten, Jen called happily from the shallows of East beach, "Down here, while you were still asleep, I found an acorn in the tide-swill!" She was naked again, and gathered handfuls of the sea and flung it above her so that it descended in a glittering light-spray.

"You watch it," I shouted as I hurried down to the fish traps, "they'll be reporting you to the parson," and joined her in the shallows.

"But an acorn, Tom! Don't ye realise what that means?"

The tide had left us a haul of herring, plaice and dabs and one huge tope was thrashing about threatening to swipe us.

"An acorn for luck, love!"

"Stop dancing about and give me a hand," I commanded, and she put her finger under her chin and smiled at the sun.

"Good luck, good luck! Forget about rotten old tinplate! Prosperity and happiness is stored in acorns, which is why pigs grunt with delight when they eat them."

For answer I lifted a box of herring and deposited it at her feet, saying, "Take that to the top of the jetty, and get some clothes on – they can pick you off for miles with a ship's telescope!" But she was in a tormenting mood and picking up a towel started to do a Turkish belly-dance act, covering up her vital areas with her handkerchief.

"That kind of thing got us into trouble up in Scotland, remember?"

"Come on! There's nobody to see me here!"

"That's what you think."

She was putting her skirt on now, topless. "Anyway, too much importance is put on this naked old business – we've all got much the same bits and pieces, haven't we?"

I said, "Unfortunately, not everybody thinks like we do – that's exactly what old Gaffer meant. This may be an island, but there's eyes and ears everywhere, Jen – and we don't want a repeat of what happened up in Scotland."

She replied thoughtfully, "Trouble with this old world is that it takes pure things and dirties them up. Anyway, we paid the fine up in Lanarkshire and got out of the place – what more do they want?"

"Put your blouse on, too, you're a big girl now," I said, and took her in my arms and kissed her. "And now forget about it – look, who's this coming?"

It was little She-cat, a kitten we had found hurt when about six weeks old; now she was coming down to the beach to inspect our fish-trap, which she did in wobbling intensity; Jen, shouting with laughter her woes forgotten, picked up the kitten, saying, "Where have you been, you dear little mite?" and kissed it.

"Consider yourself adopted," I said to the thing, and heaved more boxes up the sloping beach.

Jen shouted, "Didn't I tell you that acorns brought good luck? For ages I've been begging you to bring me a kitten from Cardiff!"

And more than good luck came with that kitten's arrival: this small scrap of life was responsible, proved by later events, for saving our lives in a manner scarcely to be believed.

But it was something else, not the arrival of 'She-cat' (as we immediately christened her) that took my attention on that sunlit morning: it happened when Jen had stooped to pick

36

up the kitten; her skirt had opened at the waist and for the first time, as she bent, I noticed the swell of her stomach.

Either she was putting on weight, or she was in child. Strange, I thought, that I had not noticed this before.

Delight seized me, and as Jen went about her work I stood indecisively, staring at her, wondering why she had not told me, for I had made no secret of my longing for a son. Then I realised that conception is a very private business to a Romany; one that has to be properly and officially announced – and not the subject of a casual discovery; nevertheless, I tried the usual opening gambit, asking as I seized another timber, "Are you all right?"

"Perfectly. Are you?"

After which she was as still and contained as a frosted lotus petal, so I merely said, "I love you, Jen Wildflower," which turned her into the Romany she was.

"And I love you, Tom Mortymer," said she, and held herself, adding, "so surely there ain't nothing wrong in makin' love under the stars, like we did in Scotland? But that bailiff chap turned it into some'ut dirty, wi' his old red face and leapin' about and shoutin'.."

I nodded, holding her, and she added, "An' that queer ole beak choking us off in the Court, when all he knows about loverin' is you put ye head on that pillow and I'll put my head by 'ere, and try to forget about it in the morning."

I listened.

"Proper lovering is doing it wi' nobody but the moon watching, for he's seen it all before, Tom – understand?"

"I understand."

"So you tell me now it weren't indecent? Even though we caught a ten bob fine for it and that woman swore after us in the street?"

"What are you trying to say?"

"Well . . ." and she hesitated, "like I said – suppose I came with a baby because of that New Lanark lovering? She moved

37

in my arms as if seeking escape. "Would . . . would you still love my baby?"

"Of course, of course!" I kissed her.

Dusk was gathering in the kitchen and with the kitten now sleeping in front of the stove and Bun and Shag eyeing us suspiciously, I saw Jen's eyes, wild and startled as she turned away her head. I sought her lips, and she shivered in my arms.

"Supposin' I birthed a girl, Tom?"

"A girl or a boy, it doesn't matter, so long as it came from you."

"You wouldn't think us cursed?"

"What are you trying to say?"

She turned away.

"Nothin'. It's my business, ain't it?"

I had no more words for her, but I'm certain sure, as she would say, that if you're seeking to know the outcome after making love to a Romany, you'd best keep away from the Wildflower tribe . . . conception being a very personal business.

Later, near to dawn, I awoke, to find Jen standing beside the bed and the moonlight on her face showed it was alive with unrestricted joy. She cried, "Tom Mortymer, there's new life kickin' inside me, and I feel it growin', *growin'*. Oh, my darling, ain't that wonderful!" and she opened her arms to me.

Romanies also make important pronouncements in unusual ways.

Chapter Five

Summer had come to the Bristol Channel in warmth and gorgeous colours and the wind blew gently across Jackdaw Point to West Beach, bringing fragrances of musk, and aromatic plants from the flowering gardens of Minehead and Cleveland.

With Jen living up to her name, the kitchen of Drift Cottage was a riot of colour; the flowers of ancient Bradanreolice, our island's Saxon name.

My Jen was an enigma: born into a gypsy tribe, her background until she reached the age of twelve was her mother's caravan and Romany fires: then, coming under my father's influence he gave her a High School education that put mine in the shade. Thus Jen became a phenomenon – on one hand the gypsy, on the other a classically educated student of art and literature – and from one role to another she switched with consummate ease, saying to me now, "Oh, come on, Tom! Read, *read*! Think of the treasures of literature – of Thebes, Athens and Sparta! All waiting to be laid at your feet!"

I answered, "You'll never make a silk purse out of sow's ear, girl: I'm a tinplate manufacturer – look at these hands." I spread them out for inspection. "It's no good trying to educate me up to your standard."

On her way to make the coffee she bent and kissed me, saying, "Darling, it's not a question of educating you, but to point out the magic that is waiting to be discovered: life

39

is enriched by writers and historians." She bent to the oil stove, turning up the wick. "Take Gibbons, for example, the chap you're reading now. It was while touring Europe over a hundred years ago that the idea came to him to undertake his gigantic history! Think of the dedication, the research he put into producing a work that's the envy of every historian! 'Decline and Fall of the Roman Empire'. He was born to inject world history into the hearts of us all: it's an offence against God, Tom, to deny Gibbons entry into your life." She put my mug on the table and blew on hers to cool it, making big eyes.

"Next you'll be canonising him," I said abruptly. "Don't go over the top, Jen – he has only written a book." I noted that when it came to Jen's split personality, the Highfield educationalist or the Romany, I preferred the latter.

"It is because I love you!" she said.

"And only because I love you that I take you seriously. Don't try to improve me, *cariad*! I'm a big thumping Welshman and thick between the ears."

"But you will read Gibbons, just to please me . . . ?"

I sipped at my cup. "Let's change the subject: when's the baby due?"

"At this stage it is nothing to do with you." She was cold, instantly back to being the gypsy.

"That's a good one. I'm the father and it's nothing to do with me? Last night . . ."

"That was last night; my baby has since moved but I'm not prepared to discuss it."

The glowing lamp was making grotesque shapes on the walls; shadowy hands reaching out for us; the place was suddenly cold, and I shivered. I said, "I only want to know when my son is going to be born!"

"A son, a *son*!" She swore softly under her breath. "You'll bring ill-fortune. What happens if it is a daughter?"

"I've told you before; whatever it is . . ."

40

Rising, she went to the window, staring out at the light-house and the golden stain of the sea.

"And I've told you before, Tom. Why don't you listen? Do ye want it born crippled? *Jawch*!" She bent towards me in unwarranted rage. "I ask ye to improve yourself and you put every obstacle in the way. Perhaps I'm only a gypsy but I've a mind that touches the stars, and I want the same for you! *Gawd*!" She thumped herself. "If you've got the brains to become an industrialist then you've enough to improve yourself!"

"All right, all right. So long as we have some peace!" I got up, too, and went to the door.

"And stop asking about my baby, for I can hear its heart, an' that's a bad sign. You wait your three months like me old mam said or you'll quicken the heartbeat, which might change him into a girl." She pointed a shaking finger at me. "It be ye own fault, mind; you don't respect Romany lore!"

I said furiously, "All I asked was when you were having the baby! How the hell we've got to classical literature and gypsy beliefs beats me."

"Oh, Tom, I'm sorry," she said, and wept. And when I took her in my arms and kissed her she began to laugh; softly at first, then in sobs, her fist against her mouth as if to stifle the indignity; and I remember thinking as I stood there holding her that it was just my luck to fall for a gypsy with such a temperament, when I could have enjoyed these early years of marriage with a soft-spoken woman of a tranquil disposition.

At this point Tom-cat came wandering in from outside and examined his empty milk saucer with plaintive cries; Jen picked him up and opened the front of her blouse and held him in her warmth. It was just as if nothing had happened to sully us. With the kitten purring against her, she dozed in her chair, and I watched her over my book and saw the tell-tale swell of my son; seeing in the eye of my mind a small one

41

of faltering footsteps; bright-headed, he was coming towards me with bubbling words of greeting, his arms held wide.

Yes, I saw him clearly, as one risen already from the womb of the woman in the chair, so soon to become my star-born. And I remember thinking, that this small scrap of humanity which she was fashioning beneath her breast would in a few months be a living, breathing entity I could hold in my arms. Even as I continued to watch her, Jen smiled in her sleep as if she had already been delivered.

Crossing the floor silently, I knelt and gently kissed her, and at that moment I saw a movement beyond the glass of the half-curtained window.

Straightening slowly, I casually walked behind Jen's chair, and saw, in a sudden flash of brilliance from the lighthouse, the crouched figure of a man, and he was staring into the room. Clearly I saw him, as if painted on the glass, in the instant before the lighthouse beam faded, leaving the world in darkness.

I went to the door, opened it quietly and peered out.

Nothing moved: it was as if the night had been shut by the slam of a coffin lid. Closing the door softly so as not to awaken Jen, I moved on slippered feet in the dark, eyes straining for a movement, my ears tuned for the slightest sound, and in a sudden buffeting of wind heard muffled oars, and ran swiftly down to the beach. A little boat was rowing out to sea, its oars making glints of phosphorescent light.

"What's happening?" asked Jen when I returned.

"Nothing," I replied, "go back to sleep."

Chapter Six

In retrospect, I understood Jen's reluctance to discuss her pregnancy; it being against her tribal law to declare her state until three clear months had passed since conception; but I knew that there was more to it than that in her case.

The coming of our Starborn, as we now called him, was Jen's second child; her first, the miscarried son of David Grey, my friend and rival – had been born dead about three years earlier. He, the son of the biggest industrialist in the Llynfi Valley, had beaten me to it in Jen's affections and married her under my nose; then died, leaving her free to be pursued by me.

A word or two about our past while I am at it:

The year of 1877 had not been kind to the Mortymer family, and the years preceding it not much better; the Wildflower family fared badly, too.

Our first casualty was my mother, a princess of the Afghan House of Barakzai who, by falling in love with my father during Britain's disastrous campaigns in Afghanistan, had produced me as a result. Then, after bringing me to Wales at the age of two years, decided to return to her own country later, leaving me to be raised by Iestyn, my father.

But fate had decided that he would not stay single and when Jen's mother, Clara Wildflower arrived with Jen to take up occupation on my father's land, the rest followed naturally . . . until tragedy struck and death intervened: both being drowned in a ferry accident during their honeymoon on the Continent.

This left me alone, then in my teens, as master of *Cefn-Ydfa*, our family mansion in Maesteg, and I naturally turned my interest to Jen. All looked set for a happy-ever-after until, as I said, my best friend David Grey arrived and I was virtually left at the altar.

Nor did David waste much time. Within a year Jen had been signed for, sealed and had delivered her first child in Rockfield, the big house where the Grey family lived.

That was the situation – all my ambitions in Jen's direction thwarted – until her husband's death from consumption.

From a happy and expectant life with David, Jen had nothing left save the loneliness of Rockfield House; her new relatives being not partial to Romanies . . .

For my part, with a beloved father dead and an uncaring mother returned to Afghanistan, I probably had even less . . . except an unrequited love for JenWildflower, whom I had wanted long before David Grey took her from under my nose.

But not for long, for we Mortymers don't take it lying down when the opposition arrives.

However, and this is important, whereas Jen had nothing left in the way of affectionate relatives, I did have friends in *Cefn-Ydfa*, where Old Bid, our housekeeper, and Dai Dando, her coachman husband, held court; to say nothing of Dozie Annie, our maid, and Angharad who was surely the most beautiful parlourmaid in all South Wales.

Beauty, as always, is in the eye of the beholder, and while I was as removed from the lovely Angharad as from Dai Dando (who has two cauliflowered ears) it would be unusual to omit a passing mention of this girl's grace and symmetry, for rooms lit up when she entered them. Nor, may I add, did she appear aware of this, but treated all with languid indifference; a curtsey here, a bow there . . . ignoring the covetous expressions of gentlemen guests and the ferocious glances of their female companions.

Upon me, of course, this beauty made not the slightest impression; I being in love with Jenny Wildflower . . .

But that was all past tense on the midsummer day I visited Swansea to see how my manufacturing profits were doing. Here lived friends from my earlier bachelor days, and one was Mr Opand my banker.

Bald, suspiciously benign, Mr Opand eyed me furtively over the top of his managerial desk in the opulent silence of Mills and Opand Ltd.

"You are aware, Mr Mortymer, that your deposit account is considerably overdrawn?" said he severely.

"Having received no recent financial statements, I am not," I replied.

Icily he answered, "Having no address to send you such statements, I fail to see how we could have appraised you of the situation."

"And the amount of my overdraft?"

"Let me see . . ." Opand adjusted his pince-nez spectacles. "According to our accountants, eight thousand two hundred and twenty-four pounds and nineteen pence." He lay back in his ornate chair and sighed with sadness at his lot. "Upon which the bank charges will be considerable, and for which I am hopeful you will be able to make restitution?"

"Enlarge on that," I said facetiously.

"To indemnify the bank to the extent that you are overdrawn, and ensure that your account is put back into credit, sir." His eyes goggled. "What is more, to ensure that it doesn't happen again."

"If it does," I countered, "I shall ensure that my overdraft goes elsewhere. Meanwhile, let's get down to detail. How has this debit occurred?"

45

"By cheque withdrawal, of course."

"By whom?"

It flustered him. "But surely, you should know that, sir!"

"I do not, which is why I'm asking you. In what name were the withdrawals made?"

He consulted papers. "By your Mr J Adams of Upper Forest Works, for one . . ."

"To meet the expenses of the Works?"

"Why, yes! You signed the formality giving Mr Adams that power, did you not?"

"I did. And what is the total of the cheques Mr Adams signed?"

I waited while he computed this.

"Five thousand one hundred pounds approximately."

"And the remaining money – who made that withdrawal?"

"Why you, sir, I am told."

"How?"

"Presumably by cheques. I do not have the evidence to hand, of course, but can easily obtain it."

"Don't bother," I answered, "you have no such evidence because I haven't drawn a penny out of my account with you since opening it."

It was an impasse; we stared at each other. His pince-nez spectacles came off; his jaw dropped.

I said, "Mr Opand, if you have allowed withdrawals from my account by someone other than Mr Adams and myself, you will find yourself in an unfortunate position."

"But we have your signed cheques, sir! Only last week I passed one for payment."

"Signed by Mr Adams on the Works' account, you mean?"

"No. Indeed not, sir. In your name – Thomas Mortymer."

The dull routine of bank sounds stirred upon the glass panelling of the room: distant conversation rose and fell against the clattering of outside wheels and hooves. It was midday; the tempo of Swansea's dockland was quickening.

I said quietly, "Something is very wrong here, Mr Opand. I want to see evidence of my withdrawals."

"Please wait, sir." Rising in nervous intensity he went into an outer office. "*Please*?"

I waited, inwardly fuming. His initial hostility was changing to one of patronising benevolence, and I thought of the hundreds of impoverished customers who had sat before him in nervous anticipation of his mood. Within a minute the door opened and he entered at a rush, beaming relief, saying, "Ah yes, sir; I thought my memory hadn't failed me." He spread before me many cheques, all authentic and properly signed by what was apparently my signature. "All passed for payment in cash over the past seven months," he added.

I examined them one by one, staring at my forged signature. It was perfect. Mr Opand resumed his seat before me. "You are satisfied that those are your signatures?"

"I am satisfied that they appear to be mine," I answered. "But I repeat, I have never drawn a cheque on this account."

"And have not received money from this bank in any other way?"

"Not a penny! The whole idea of my wife and myself taking to the road, as I earlier mentioned, was a challenge to that way of life – living off the land – self-sufficiency."

"Then these cheques are forgeries?"

"Of course."

The silence of the room clattered between us.

"And you have no idea as to who might have criminally forged your name?"

"None at all."

"Or of the identity of anyone who might have access to your personal affairs?" A thin smile touched his mouth.

47

"Of course. Mr Adams, my foreman who runs my Works, and my wife."

"So . . . ?" His eyes moved blankly over my face.

"So what, Mr Opand? If you are suggesting that Mr Adams is dishonest, you must repeat the allegation in front of him."

"Yes, yes, I apologise. But who . . . ?"

I got up. "You have passed the cheques, that's up to you to find out. In the interim I suggest the Bank pays back my missing money."

"And if the Bank refuses?"

"Then I will take you to law. The amount is trifling to bankers – about three thousand pounds? Please see that it is refunded by the end of the month."

Mr Opand drew himself up to his full height. "This is not the end of the story, Mr Mortymer."

"Oh yes, it is. You are responsible for passing the fraudulent cheques, not I."

With this I swept out of his office with all the dignity I could muster.

It was an ineffective exit; the last thing I wanted was to take on the bankers, but what pestered me more was the chain of events encompassing me without apparent reason: the killing of the cockerel, the threatening note; unknown footsteps in the sand, the stranger I had seen watching the cottage . . . his boat retreating from Flatholm. And now my money missing by forgery.

Of one thing I was certain: I had to keep this away from Jen; with her wildfire imagination she would gobble it into a turkey.

Chapter Seven

My first inclination, since I was in Swansea, was to visit my Upper Forest Works in Morriston and have a word to Gaffer Adams about the financial discrepancy, but decided against it: the honesty of Adams was not at stake; I would have pledged my life upon it. More, the overdrawn amount had been stolen by the forging of my signature, not his. The foreman's withdrawals had since been meticulously audited and every penny accounted for. Therefore, unless the man was exposed as a skilful forger of my name, he had no case to answer.

I did not, however, anticipate the clumsy lack of diplomacy on the part of the bank manager.

Without first consulting me, Mr Opand called in the police.

The effect upon Gaffer Adams was traumatic, and unaware of what was happening, I happily went on my way by hired coach to Cardiff, where, by previous arrangement, I was to meet Jen at the Royal Hotel in St Mary's Street; she having come over from Flatholm Island that morning.

She arrived at midday after having deposited our latest fish and rabbit catch with the Market merchants; then we planned to dine together, a treat we occasionally allowed ourselves.

The Royal Hotel was very up-market after the meals we usually grubbed together on Flatholm. Jen, aware of this, had done herself up in Romany finery.

If you think Angharad, the beauty who had become

the housekeeper at *Cefn-Ydfa* after Biddy's death, was incomparable . . . I thought, then look at this woman who is your wife.

Jen was even more beautiful with the sun upon her.

She wandered towards me among the Cardiff shoppers with her pink parasol tilted at a provocative angle . . . not enough to obscure her face, but sufficient to enlist the admiring stares of every male in sight; her eyes, the little devil, slanting at any lout who cared to flatter her with a glance.

I saw Jen before she saw me, and took note of her. She swayed towards me in a white dress with rose-pink trimmings at the waist and shoulders; designed, it would appear, to show off the fullness of its bodice; and a bustle that pronounced the effect. She knew what she was about this one, when it came to the sweet come-hithers.

I handed my lovely Jen up the steps of the Royal Hotel.

"Why the dog's dinner?" I asked her.

"Decided to give the lads a treat," came the reply.

"You've done that all right, you've stopped the ruddy traffic. That dress – how much did it cost?"

On the top of the hotel steps she paused, head tilted back, closing her eyes to the sun, and I saw the Romany in her behind the dressy apparel; the perfume of her touched my senses; I sniffed.

"What's that, then?"

"'A Night in Paris'. Two bob a bottle."

"What's the total damage?"

"Two pounds four-and-sixpence."

"How much did you get for the fish?"

"A guinea, including the rabbits."

"Then that's a few bob you owe me."

"Dear me," she said at the sun, "they weren't all born in Jerusalem. Who's paying for the lunch?"

"Joe Soap, as usual. Next month you'll have me scratching a pauper's backside in the Workhouse."

"What about a kiss while your waitin'?"

So, in the embellishments of the Royal Hotel foyer, halting the incoming guests in their tracks, I kissed her, and her broad-rimmed summer hat fell off and the black ringlets of her hair were in my fingers; and it was then, in the entrance of that unusual place, that I felt for the first time the roundness of her against me, and knew that soon she would confirm that she had conceived my son; but in her good time, being a Romany.

Suppressing my delight, I took her hand and formally escorted her to the dining room where a frock-coated waiter ushered us into its elegance.

"You have booked a table, sir?" he enquired.

"I wrote earlier. A table for two, in the name of Mortymer."

He consulted a book. "Ah yes," and positioned our chairs at an alcove table with a white, starched cloth and silver-ringed serviettes; a little rose-bowl, laden with flowers was between us and I winked at Jen over it.

"This is going to set you back, you old skinflint," said she.

"Oh no, it won't," I answered. "This comes out of housekeeping."

"Tell you what. You pay the bill and I'll think about loving you for a baby."

I closed my eyes.

I might have known, I thought: women are always at their most beautiful when making sons, and mentioned this.

"Don't count ye chickens," said she. "You might get twin daughters, just for the hell of it. Meanwhile what makes you think you're going to be a father?"

During the meal, Jen said, "The lad has just taken off his slippers and put his boots on."

"Don't be daft. You not fourteen weeks yet!"

51

"I tell you he's kicking me; probably he hates mulliga-tawny soup."

"It's wind, my love."

People were coming into the restaurant, the men with sustained interest in Jen, the women with the practised air of people who are not to be tampered with, and 'who is she, anyway?'

As for me, I spooned up that soup in the knowledge that I was suitor to a most beautiful companion.

Jen asked, "What happened at the bank?"

I shrugged. "Not a lot. The usual old soaking about income and outgoings. To tell the truth I don't know a lot about it."

I wasn't going to let her in on the forgeries.

"Is the old boy still making money for us?"

"Gaffer Adams? He's holding his own; exports have slumped since the American Civil War; nobody in South Wales is making a fortune."

"And the Co-operative?"

I put down my spoon. "That's the good part. Directly Gaffer makes a couple of thousands he builds another few workers' cottages – good stuff. The workforce is over two hundred, and if he gets an Afro-Asian order he's expecting his order books will be half full; we can't expect better than that with an absentee manager, the Bank says."

"Meaning you?"

The fish course arrived and Jen stared down at it. "What the devil's that?"

"Stuffed plaice."

"Did I ask for it?"

"It's the standard menu."

"Must have given itself up. You know, Tom, we could supply places like this with fish, have you thought of that?"

"Not really."

Then Jen said, "Don't look now, but there's a fella over there giving me the eye."

"You should be so lucky. Where?"

"The gentleman in the corner table dining alone." She sighed seductively to exasperate me. "The big handsome chap."

I glanced to my left. Certainly the man she referred to appeared interested in us. "Him?"

"That's right."

"God, he's old enough to be your dad!" I suddenly took a breath, for the stranger had turned; hitherto I had seen him in profile; now I saw him full face.

Unbelievably, he was the image of my dead father. Jen said, "Mind you, I like 'em a little bit older, ye know. Experienced. Especially when they come as good looking as that. Are you listening?"

I shook my head. The man was now looking steadily in my direction.

"It's you he's staring at, not me," she said.

Diners, coming and going, moved between us, obliterating the stranger; then my view of him cleared and for no definable reason there existed between us an affinity as strong as an electrical discharge. It was an impulse that was not of myself, but deeper, a phenomenon; and I think I knew that the man on the other side of the room was no longer of separate identity, but a part of me.

Amazingly, as if in acceptance of a relationship he recognised, the man rose from his table; with a long, hard look in my direction, he then crossed the room and left us staring after him.

"Good God!" whispered Jen.

I could not reply.

"You know each other, don't you!" she said.

It was as if my father, reborn, had shaken off his shroud and risen from the dead.

"I must be seeing things," I said.

Chapter Eight

I had just returned from a day and night in Cardiff where, for our largest outlay to date – over two hundred and forty pounds – I had bought a two-ton second-hand sloop; an eighteen footer of ship-lap hull-boarding which was built like a battleship. It had a tiller area, steps down a little companionway to a reasonable cabin, and a stout door leading to for'ard sleeping bunks for two adults and a child. ("And don't forget the child," said Jen . . .)

We named our boat *Aquila*, and flew a skull and crossbone pennant, and I've never been so proud in my life as I brought her into the coal-loading wharf up on East Beach, and set her down in the shallows on her double keel; which kept her upright when the tide was out.

The sloop would allow us to sail deeper into the Channel for bigger fish, and with this in mind, Jen and I spent the rest of the day on her deck; using it as a springboard to dive off into the translucent sea, with an eye out for prowling soldiers, most of whom were on shore leave.

Now, chattering with cold as we rubbed ourselves down at home, Jen said out of context, "I've been wondering this all night while you were away – who was that big handsome fella we saw in the Royal Hotel in Cardiff, Tom – the last time I was ashore?"

"Search me."

She answered, looking wistful, "D'ye know some'ut? He was just about the best-looking fella I've ever seen . . ."

I answered, and pushing back my wet hair from my face, "For a fella knocking thirty, I don't look so bad."

"You're better with your trousers on, mind."

Bun hopped over the floor with difficulty and sniffed at my hand; his leg was healing slowly, but not well enough for him yet to be released back into the wild, and Gull watched with an unblinking eye his attempts to ingratiate himself.

Around the open door crowded other patients we had recently collected. There was Shelduck, representative of the thousands of a species nesting on Flatholm, from whom we had extracted two air-gun pellets. Strikingly handsome, dark green in colour and with a bright red bill, his was a dignity unsurpassed, scarcely struggling in Jen's hands while I cut into his downy breast for the pellets. Soon, when his ducklings hatched (for doubtless he had a mate somewhere – certainly more than one female used to visit him while he convalesced) he would lead his brood over to the mud flats of Bridgewater since there is no food for nestlings on Flatholm.

Beside him, dozing in the doorway sunlight, sat Blackie, he of the deformed claw; still timid of me, Jen could do anything with him, even to carelessly picking him up to examine his crippled foot.

We had found him opposite Sully Island where we had set up our caravan. Clearly a cat had got him, probably while he was defending his young; when Jen approached to capture him he had initially fluttered away, dragging his wounded leg behind him and taken up a fighting stance at a hole in a thorn hedge.

Following him, Jen knelt to find that one of his brood had fallen out of its nest, and, having a tiny hand, had managed to replace it before his wife returned.

Elephants never forget; neither do blackbirds. Jen's reward was affection, for he would watch her every move. Though not giving a cuss for me, he would sit beside her in the sun,

55

allowing her to stroke his head; and when the time came for his young to leave the nest, he paraded them around the cottage door, ensuring, while doing so, that his mate was effectively chased away to a distance, so that only he could enjoy our approbation.

Then there was Rat, who was such a character that we allowed him the dignity of his true name – no 'Ratty' for this one.

As if allowing for the idiosyncrasies of humans (and clearly he was conversant with their cruelties to rodents) he never indulged in the slightest familiarity with either of us, but sat with unblinking disregard to our comings and goings; content, apparently, that we would never tread upon him.

He was impossible to entice within the cottage; irreverentially ignored the food we tossed towards him. The only real friend he appeared to accept was Bun, who allowed him, if the wind was cold, to lie within her furry warmth.

When the sun was upon him Rat was the most magnificent fellow; his well-groomed coat shone like burnished silk, and his tail, as he clearly knew, was a most desirable possession.

Rat's greatest pleasure was to lie within a half coconut we had suspended outside the cottage door. There, with his tail hanging down, he would doze within the tranquillity of our protection, if eyed occasionally by Tom-cat, who clearly cherished ambitions where rats were concerned.

Jen said, "They are the most persecuted of God's creatures. You know what Gaffer told me when he called here? Once, he said, when he was on a building site in the Midlands, he heard a lot of shouting and cheering one morning break; and going to find out what it was all about, saw a bonfire burning in the building's excavations where a rat was coming and going in and out of the bonfire, each time carrying one of her young to safety. Totally on fire, she came and went.

"Furious, he doused the flames, to find the smouldering

body of the rat in the ashes with her last baby in her mouth. Gaffer said that he called the men one by one into the foreman's office and sacked the lot of them."

"Good for Gaffer."

There was a silence, and I looked at our patients crowded around the open door; it being the morning surgery.

"I've heard this sort of thing before," I said. "The best mothers in this world are probably rats. And thank God for Gaffer; at least we've also got a few decent human beings."

In bed that night, I said at the window moon, "I've been thinking about old Gaffer lately. This business of the cheque forgeries is reflecting badly upon him."

"But you believe him innocent?" Jen asked.

"Certainly."

I had earlier decided not to say anything to Jenny about this, but now had to tell somebody because I was so worried about it.

She was handling it with better sense than I'd anticipated, saying, "Face it, Tom. Opand's a banker, so not likely to repay stolen money; after all, he's got shareholders to explain to."

"You mean, he'll have a go at poor old Gaffer?"

"Certain to. It's thousands of pounds. Take a cent off that lot and they bleed to death." Reaching over in the bed, she kissed my face. "You didn't do too well, ye know. You've forced the Bank into a corner by insisting on repayment. You should have stood the loss, you can afford it."

It was a mistake for which the innocent would pay; more than likely this would be Gaffer, I thought.

And so it proved.

Sleep wouldn't come to me that summer night and Jen wasn't doing much better, tossing and turning.

"Tom," she said from the dark, "coming back to that chap who was watching us in the Royal Hotel in Cardiff . . ."

"God, you've got him on the brain!"

"Why didn't he come over and talk to us, if he was that interested? Instead, he went off at a rush."

I sat up, having tea in mind. "He probably went to the lavatory, don't complicate everything."

"Do you think he might be a relative?"

"Aw, come on, Jen!"

"Anyone could have mistaken him for your dada."

"Not old enough – he was very much younger."

"Have you got any suspicious relatives I don't know about?"

I put my arm around her. "One thing's sure – they're all going to be Romanies."

"You could do worse," said she, and in the darkness of the window moon, I kissed her; and the kiss, initially of husbandly kindness, changed to quick breathing so that she reached up her arms and drew me down into the bed; with sudden gasping affection she covered my face with kisses.

"What about the baby?" I whispered.

"Gawd! We're not going to ask his permission every time; it's nothing to do with him!"

"I might hurt you, darling."

"Tom Mortymer, ye'll hurt me if ye don't! Come on, ye big handsome fella – give the girl a treat!"

It was not the last time I made love to Jen Wildflower, but it was a love-making that stayed for ever in my mind.

Chapter Nine

On our maiden voyage over to Weston-super-Mare in *Aquila*, a gale sprang up on the homeward run. It blew out our foresail and damaged the mast, which meant having the sloop towed back to Cardiff for re-rigging and repairs, and it was a month before we got her back.

Splendidly she arrived then, with a professional bringing her in on a fine tack like the old sea-salt he was. In a Force Seven gale he came, making me look like a novice by the way he handled her.

Our beautiful *Aquila*, now repainted white, came out of the pea-green sea, and shaking herself free of it like a terrier, lowered her main-sail and slid up to the East Beach coaling-wharf.

"She's here, she's here!" shouted Jen, and hand in hand we ran together down to the beach, followed by a string of hop-along patients, since this was supposed to be the morning surgery. Led by a staggering Shelduck they came, Bun doing his hop-step and jump, followed by Gull dragging his unhealed wing, Tom-cat arrived at a gallop and Rat brought up the rear with Donk, our new addition, he-hawing them along.

If ever there was a character, Donk was one. I had bought her off a passing tinker for a fiver to save her life, for the world had treated Donk with the hardship it usually reserved for donkeys. Aged, with her toe-nails so curled up that she could hardly walk, she had laid herself down between us while I cut and filed them, and Jen rubbed ointment into her back where the whips had made her raw. This was Jen's famous Romany mix, which she called 'The Balm of Gilead' – yellow dock mixed with goose-grease, and we used it for every variety of cut or sore.

Nearly blind, Donk was never out of our sight, and every time we went to market we brought her back some little gift; a piece of chocolate or a sweet to make up for the cruelty of earlier masters.

At sun-go-down and our new boat pulled clear of the tide, we were sitting in that peace which accompanies contentment, when Jenny said, "Bad fortune's coming, Tom."

"Now come on, don't start that!"

Lately she was given to these old wives' prophecies. Indeed, the closer we came to the primitive life, the greater Jen's need to be a Romany. All this, of course, she had got from the walnut-faced females of the tribe, most of whom had more suspicions than teeth.

"I tell you," Jen repeated, "it is coming. 'The croak of a raven and the scuttle of a mouse, heard together is a death in the house.'"

"Oh, aye?" Disinterested, I stretched out on the bed, waiting for supper.

Earlier, Jen had gone over to Sully with the ferryman and called to visit our caravan which we had lodged in Farmer's Field, for there were some queer old characters activating on the mainland about now. It was said that smuggling was over in the Bristol Channel, but some people had it that it was bigger than ever, with kegs of rum and whisky being loaded on the shore from little French freighters plying between Calais and Cardiff; and a few of these were tough old characters who would cut your throat for tuppence, said Sergeant Barrett, the Master Gunner in charge on Flatholm.

But that was yesterday, and this was today, and after locking up the caravan and seeing to our piebald pony, Jen spent a few minutes in catching a pair of hedgehogs, which she fondly called *hotchi-witchi* (the ancient Romany name for them) and these she had brought home for supper.

"Ye anna tasted anything till you've snouted *hotchi-witchi*," she announced.

"What are they like to eat?" I asked doubtfully, and she unrolled the dead victims out of a newspaper.

"After you've had one, you'll want more."

She pulled up her sleeves, adding, "Folks reckon it's a cruel business to kill a hedgehog, but Romanies know it's painless. Stupid bailiffs try to knock 'em off by dosing birds' eggs with poison – but that *hotchi-witchi*, he can eat a pound o' strychnine an' put two fingers up to the world, for he knows he's tastier than a bun and cleaner 'n a pig." While she was talking she was running a candle flame over the little bodies, burning of their spines.

"He was made for gypsies by God, we say, for *Hotchi* plumps himself fat by drinking from cows' udders at midnight." She waved the candle about. "You'll never get cows lyin' down if there's hedgehogs about, for a colony of them can suck a cow dry, an' cows knows it."

"How did you kill these?" I asked. "There isn't a mark on them."

"*Aha*! You *gorgio* chaps hit him dead with spades and flatten the dinner. Listen, all ye have to do is watch out for his tracks, for he always backs out from his nest in the hedges, and this loosens up the grass, for his spines then come back to front.

"He does this because he's scared of knocking his nose, for this is his tender part. The first thing you gotta do is get him undone, for he curls up into a ball when he sees you, and ye do this by rubbing a stick along his back, which he loves; then you tap him on the nose and the chap's a clay-cold; corpse. Easy, ain't it!" She broke into song then as she worked, singing like an angel, and I knew that were I

61

to live with this one for a lifetime, I would never unravel her complexity; that she would always remain a Romany in the midst of my accepted conventions; wild, free, and in touch with the creatures of the earth.

"If you think I'm eating that thing for supper, you've another think coming," I said.

"And that's where you're mistaken," said she, laughing. "For *hotchi-witchis* are eaten with the nose, not the mouth. After half a minute of him simmerin', ye won't be able to stop yourself."

After she had rolled the pair of them in balls of clay and set them over the embers of a bright fire the wind was perfumed with a smell that wafted over Flatholm and tickled the noses of the gunners in their barracks.

"Mind you, ye can do 'em by boiling, too," she explained, "and they're fit for a king laced with sorrel and agrimony, for the herbs bring out the taste."

"What about the insides?" I asked, examining my plate suspiciously. "You took out the entrails, didn't you?"

"*Jawch* no, Tom! Them's the best parts!"

I turned up my nose.

"Come on, get into it, ye don't know what's good for ye!"

It was dusk in the cottage now, and the glow of the oil lamp was turning her into a Romany in all her beauty; and I saw in her dark, aquiline features not what she was, but what she had been born to be: not the civilised wife of a commercial gent like me, but the woman of an untamed man who would dance her in a medley of spinning skirts around camp fires blossoming out of the past. And she would bear his children, not in a mansion like *Cefn-Ydfa*, to which I planned to take her when her time came, but lay her down in gypsy straw, which was the custom of Romanies world wide; thus would she keep faith with her birthright – birth in straw – enabling her blood to merge with the produce of the earth.

Was it wrong of me, I wondered, still watching her in that dim light, to canalise her spirit into acceptance of my conventional customs, when her roots were unconfined?

Thinking of this; tracing every line of her face and jet-black hair (which she always plaited before going to bed) I listened again.

"The same for fish, really speaking," said she softly. "Daft old lot, ought to know better. But they're the cleanest of the animal kingdom, our elders tell us, being washed into innocence; so it's a betrayal to catch 'em with deceitful baits, worms on hooks and flies in coloured jackets." She paused, smiling at the lamp.

"There they go, in full view of everybody, paddlin' away in the sun and not carin' about the time o' day; so ye creep up, see, slip in a hand, blow on the water to dazzle it till you reach him, then tickle him under the belly . . . softly, gently, mind, and he thinks it must be his birthday, that delighted he is by the warmth of your hand . . . too late he shouts, for his mam who has told 'im *and told 'im*, remember – for a thousand years after the world was young – to beware of the fingers of a human hand . . . and warm fingers an' all! Best be frozen under ice, says she, than end up on a plate in a savage's house, wi' ye fins in an animal's mouth." She sighed, her eyes shining.

"Mind, Tom, I always gives a prayer for a fish after I've tickled him out, for he's like a baby child, ain't he? That innocent . . . just wavin' there, and paddling among the weeds . . ."

I had no words for her.

Chapter Ten

Jen said, fearfully about a week later, "With old Farmer Thomas at Sully this morning, I heard a raven croak again – a third time croak, Tom."

"And now you're waiting for the scuttling mouse?" I laughed.

"Don't joke, my lovely!"

"Why not? We're getting gypsy warnings twice a month!"

Earlier, having been over to Cardiff market in our new boat, we had pulled it up on East Beach clear of the incoming tide, keeping it away from the Coaling Wharf; for the lighthouse-coaster had come in loaded with coal for the brazier and there was great activity on the beach: soldiers were working under the Keeper, unloading coal into handcarts and towing it to the lighthouse on the other side of the island.

Our lighthouse is worth a mention. Built by Bristol's Society of Merchant Venturers following a wrecking that cost the lives of sixty soldiers in 1736, its lamp consisted of a heavily reflected coal-fired brazier. Following another wreck, a new light was installed in 1819, and when Trinity House took ownership five years later it was the last of privately owned lighthouses.

"What's all this coming and going now, then?" asked Jen, for engineers, landing by boat from Bristol, were hauling ashore a giant mechanism on skids and wanted our Donk to give them a pull with it.

"They're fitting a clockwork engine so the light is operated mechanically," I replied.

"Why?" Jen shielded her eyes from the incinerating sunlight, for the sun was of molten glass that midday, reflecting off the shining backs of the half naked soldiers; the sea flat calm and hazed with shimmering mirages.

"To bring the lighthouse up to date."

"Expecting another wrecking, are they?"

Shelduck, She-cat, Bun, Gull and Rat were clustered about her feet; where ever she went the customers followed, each one seeking her favour. Blackie, on one leg, was sitting on her head.

"No, I don't think so," I answered. "Lighthouses need modernising, that's all."

Jen tossed Rat a piece of biscuit, then turned away with an expression of such sadness that I asked, "What are you bothered about?"

"Just seen a dormouse."

"What of it? Now don't start all that again!"

"It never fails, Tom. Oh God!" she added.

Jen was dressed that morning in a pink shift, a simple garment that reached to her calves, and her arms were bare to the shoulders; her skin, burned by summer to the hue of a walnut, turned her into the gypsy she was, and her long black hair, plaited and tied with red ribbons, reached to her waist. A vision manufactured by sun and wind especially for my delight, I thought, and noticed the envious glances of the labouring soldiers.

"It's going to happen, Tom," said she, turning away. "And laughing it off anna goin' to stop it." She looked about her. "Where's Tom-cat?"

"Probably after that dormouse you saw. Now come on, there's no superstitions on Flatholm!"

"Something's happened to him!"

"Don't be daft – look give me a hand with the boat."

She grasped its painter preparing to pull, but a young soldier saw her and came running, shouting, "Leave it, missus, I'll give a pound on that." I saw his eyes lower to the swell of her stomach.

I have heard said that young Chinese women can carry a child, without the bulge being obvious almost up to the moment of delivery; indeed, it was this same deception that made me sometimes forget Jen's state.

Do lovers ever learn, I wonder, the true value of loved ones, until Fate steps in and removes them?

Again and again this small event of the young soldier's thoughtfulness returned to me in the quiet hours of her absence.

My girl is lost to me as I write this; and although I search for her, I may never find her. But never again, if she comes back to me, will I take for granted her endearment; the perfume, the sounds of her.

Now I recall, the bulging muscles of the young soldier, and the wink he gave Jen when he thought I wasn't looking. The boat under our combined strength slid into higher water.

"Thanks," I said.

"That's all right, girl," said he, ignoring me.

I saw a glance of understanding pass between them, and now cursed myself for my inconsideration.

Jen looked like a little girl waving goodbye to the soldier with the animals clustered about her.

A letter was awaiting me when we returned to the cottage; it had been delivered by the ferryman, and was from Mills and Opand, my Swansea bankers; which was bound to be important because I had instructed them that Gaffer Adams, would continue to handle everything in my absence.

The letter read:

"34 Goat Street,
Swansea,
Glamorganshire

Dear Mr Mortymer,

It is with regret that I have to inform you of the passing of Mr Adams, your employee at Upper Works, Morriston, who has been found dead in his office. The police inform me that he died of gunshot wounds.

May I take this opportunity of telling you how bitterly I regret my suspicion that he was implicated in the fraud, for which he was being investigated.

The police tell me of their intention to interview you separately, for which reason I have given them your Flatholm address.

Yours sincerely,
A P Opand – Manager' 9th September 1883

The police did not waste time; scarcely had I time to digest the news than they were hammering on the cottage door. Jen, preparing rabbit stew, opened it.

All yesterday a gale had been blowing, but now it was sobbing in the eaves like a child crying in sleep.

"Mr and Mrs Mortymer?" The larger of the two, a man of great height and girth, entered with aplomb, his hand out. "I'm Detective-Inspector Graves," said he in a booming voice that sent Bun and the others scampering. "This is Sergeant Harris, my assistant." I took a limp hand. A contrast in size and type was Harris; an undersized man in looks and character.

They had got soaked coming over from Sully, so Jen took off their coats to dry them and I got hot dandy coffee into them. They didn't waste time in preliminaries.

"You've heard from Mr Opand of your Swansea bank?" asked Graves.

"This morning," I replied.

"You and Gaffer Adams were good friends, I understand," said the Inspector.

"Something more valuable than just owner and foreman," I replied. "In my absence he ran Upper Works."

"Complete trust, Mr Mortymer, technically and financially?" This from the other man, Harris.

"I had no reason to act otherwise."

"And your trust still extends to Adams, despite the bank's suspicion that he was responsible for deficiencies in your account?"

"Absolutely, and I resent the inference that he had anything to do with forged cheques."

"And his suicide?"

"I don't understand it, unless it was because of the false allegations made against him."

Graves said, filling his pipe, "Clearly, you haven't heard that he left a note . . ."

I stared at them.

"Making it clear that he was responsible for the forged withdrawals?"

Jen stood behind me, her hand upon my shoulder; the simple action of togetherness was comforting.

"Surely you read of that in *The Cambrian*?" asked Harris.

I shook my head. "This is Flatholm Island, we don't get the papers here, thank God, but I'd like to see that suicide note."

"Not yet: it's the property of the Coroner."

"When is the inquest?" asked Jenny.

"I don't know – you know what coroners, are." Saying this with finality Graves lit his pipe and puffed out smoke, adding, "But it wasn't only Adams's suicide that brought us here this morning, Mr Mortymer. How long have you and your wife lived here, sir?"

"On Flatholm? About six months."

"A little longer, actually," interjected Jen, catching my eye.

"And how long since you put Adams in charge of your Morriston Works?"

"About eighteen months. Why?"

"That stew smells good," observed Harris, and gave a schoolboy grin. Faintly, I remembered something my father used to say in the old days, 'When a boy's face shines, look behind his ears' and now smiled at my thoughts.

'Graves said, "And what did you do with your time during this intervening period?"

"We travelled the country – first Britain, then abroad – to Paris."

"A sort of Grand Tour!"

I laughed. "I wouldn't call it that; Grand Tours are for the rich. No, just that my wife wanted to return to her Romany roots; wandering is part of gypsy existence, though I can't think what this has to do with Gaffer's probable suicide."

Graves rose from his chair; walked around in silent contemplation and finished up at the window. "The pair of you went abroad, to Paris, you say . . . ?"

"Yes, I've mentioned that."

He turned to me, saying, "But before that your travels took you to Scotland, did they not?"

"If you know, why ask me?"

"To Lanarkshire, I understand; an unusual place to attract a Welshman!" He chuckled, sucking at his pipe. "Ah well, there's no accounting for taste, as my old mother used to say. But, do understand the investigative mind, Mr Mortymer, for we like the detail, don't we Harris! Why Lanarkshire?"

The rabbit stew suddenly came to the top of the saucepan; Jen rescued it and the little room was filled with a sweet, savoury odour; the incident did nothing to lessen the growing tension in the room.

I replied, taking my time, "Lanarkshire was once the

centrepiece of Robert Owen's social and Co-operative experiment, one that is growing in Britain today. We went to Scotland for information about it. My aim is to base Morriston Works on the same system."

"And you have achieved this?"

"Good heavens, no! It's an ongoing experiment and will take years to make it work successfully. Incidentally, Mr Adams was dedicated to the plan."

"And now he's dead." Inspector Graves smiled wryly.

There was a long pause. I expected this to be the end of the questioning, for clearly it wasn't leading anywhere, then suddenly Harris said, as if to himself, "Did you fall foul of the Scots while up north, sir?"

"What do you mean?" asked Jen.

I knew what they were getting at.

"Fall foul of the police," said Graves obliquely.

"In what way?"

"You don't remember?"

Angrily, I replied, "Of course she doesn't! Look, if you think you've got something on us, you'd best stop dancing around and come out with it!"

Unperturbed, Graves nodded, sitting down again. "While in North Lanark were you not indicted for a moral misdemeanour, and on that charge appeared before a local magistrate?"

I glanced at Jen; she sighed, turning her eyes up to the ceiling. "*Gawd*," she said, "I don't believe this!"

"Neither did I," put in Harris. "At first I rejected the Scots' legal report upon it; later, I realised that it was a most unsavoury incident."

"For which you were both found guilty and fined," added Graves.

I fought to keep calm; lose your temper with this lot, I thought, and there would never be an end to it; but what it was leading to, I couldn't even guess, and replied, "Guilty in the first degree – bathing naked in a pond on a Sunday. The beggar who reported us must have stood on a ladder with a telescope."

"But found guilty, nevertheless?"

"Yes, and fined five shillings each, plus a lecture about the values of public morality. We were naked in the same pond again soon after, but that time they didn't catch us."

"You put no emphasis upon morality, Mr Mortymer?"

"I've got no time for bloody hypocrisy, Mr Graves."

"You are married, I understand?"

"We are."

"Do you possess a marriage certificate?"

"We do not," answered Jen, coming to the fore. "But we have a signed paper from the hand of Romany Petla the Elder, who witnesses all local marriages in my tribe. It is properly signed and authenticated." She looked marvellous, now the educated Romany girl well up on her dignity.

"Which confirms that you jumped over a broom, presumably . . . !"

"And cut our wrists and mingled our blood," Jen replied, her eyes smouldering with anger.

"Which is one better, I suggest, than the sham some call marriage today. Ours is ended by death," I added.

"There's no need to become emotional," said Graves blandly. "It isn't our intention to cause you distress . . ."

I replied, "Really? Well I don't know what you're trying to accuse us of, but I tell you this – if you don't get yourselves the other side of that door in the next ten seconds I'll put boots into your backsides that'll land ye back in Sully."

"Assisted by me," said Jen, and went to the door and flung it open.

Bun, followed by Rat, raced for cover to Donk standing dolefully outside with Blackie between his ears. And I recall, even at that moment of contained fury, that Tom-cat was still not around . . .

The gale had passed; the sun in majestic splendour blazed down from the roof of the world.

The miscreants trooped out like criminals to execution, without a word, until Graves said, "The end of this meeting, perhaps, but not the interrogation, Mr Mortymer." He smiled, but not with his mouth. "For you will not get anywhere, except into Court, by threatening police officers. Further, you should prepare yourself – you and the woman you claim as your wife – for further investigation into an offence which has nothing to do with your foreman's death, but a crime which could land the pair of you in prison for a very long time. You know, of course, what I am referring to?"

"I haven't the faintest idea,"

"You will, in due course. Good-day to you."

We laughed briefly at the disconsolate pair going off an hour too early to catch the ferry back to Sully. Jen said, "A crime that could land the pair of us in prison, Tom? What on earth could he mean?"

"If we bathed naked again up in Scotland, I suppose!"

"But we were fined for that. You can't be punished for the same thing twice?"

"Aw, forget it! They're just trying to put the wind up us!"

I opened the cottage door again and the sun came in bowing first.

"I'm much more concerned with where Tom-cat has got to," I remarked.

"I'm not," came the reply. "I'm concerned with what those two meant – land us in prison . . . What for, for heaven's sake?"

I dismissed her remarks with a careless gesture, but was more concerned than she. Had I known what was to come to pass, I would have had good reason; the course of our lives was about to change in a way neither of us could have foreseen, bringing terror.

Chapter Eleven

With Gaffer's death, I suspected that soon I'd have to return to the mainland, to take over the Morriston Works.

"One last sail, then!" Jen shouted, and as we set about pushing *Aquila* out of the shallows, She-cat came bounding down the beach, mewing to be taken aboard, believing that she was part of its crew; so Jen waded back and got her, claiming that a cat aboard brought luck and that the Norsemen, those roamers of the northern oceans, wouldn't dream of slipping a hawser until the pet cat was aboard. Those Norsemen, said Jen years later, knew something about the feline race that we, the more elevated civilisation did not . . .

We pushed off from East Beach and tacked with the mainsail up into a south-westerly breeze, and the coasts of Cardiff and Bridgewater were misted and golden in the radiance of the day, as if God's painter had brought out his brushes and sprayed the world with burnished light.

Looking back, I will always remember that last sail with Jen, going after the big stuff, for deep sea cod were roving in shoals down in the caverns where the manta-ray fly.

Jen was at her best when at sea. Out of telescope range she would take of her clothes so the sun could get at her, and she was all over brown, a sea-sprite spewed up from the depths of the ocean.

Where is she now, I wonder; and where is my son she once carried in her womb?

*   *   *

"Prepare to go about!" I yelled above the wind, and swung the tiller and the little sloop breasted the waves, diving her prow deep into the big grey troughs and flinging the sea over her shanks, while Jen, fighting the foresail, braced her feet against the thwarts as green foam came pouring over the gunwale.

One of the enigmas of human existence is our inability to treasure every fleeting moment: we exchange them for the dross of a mundane life, letting precious times slip through our fingers; and the golden minutes that we take for granted go flying into the past; leaving a sad mourning for all our yesterdays.

So it was that day at sea with the silver fish harvest flashing in the cork-bobbing nets; at the other end of the floats Jen was hauling in the brimming shoal with excited cries . . . and the catch came pouring in to each new surge of the waves – flounder, herring, cod – and big fellas at that – flapping around our ankles!

"This is the life!" Jen shrieked above the wind, obeying the hunting urge when she could have been in my arms.

As if through some complexity of sea and sky, the wind died to a whisper, leaving us silently looking one to the other; the waves were unaccountably stilled.

Aware of this, Jen and I ceased our labours, and I heard within me a small incoherent voice calling her name.

I knew not from whence this call came, but my whole being was suddenly charged with the electricity of her presence; an awareness that snatched me up, so that I lowered the net-rope and stored it for'ard to where Jen was sitting.

As people engraved in stillness we sat, she in the prow, me now in the stern, and in that moment of mutual recognition of our need for one another, there was no longer sea, sky and sun; the battering tide diminished into gentle wave-lap; the tap-tap-tap against the hull were now the only sound of the day, and Jen, without moving her

74

position, smiled, brushed back her wet hair and opened her arms to me.

"Tom . . . ?" she said huskily.

The kiss is quiet in the beginning, a key unlocking an emotion that disturbs into gusty breath and strength. Trembling are the hands that twist and search; the words are gasped without design or meaning.

For long now I had not made love to my girl in fear of harming her; but now nothing counselled me against it, and I became one with her in thrusting strength.

All around us, beneath us and within reach of us was the fishy catch of the day. As primitive beings, exalted by the hunt, we made love in a delight we had never experienced before. And after the lightning of youth had flashed between us in sun-brilliance, we lay together, unmoving in the cradle of the ocean. Nor did we utter a single word.

I could have poured out my heart to her, but we did not speak. To have done so would have sullied a unity we had never before discovered; severing the chords of a new and exquisite understanding.

Now an awakening from the perfect trance . . .

"Good gracious me," said Jen, giggling. "How did that happen?"

She who was so soon to leave me . . .

"Again, please, Tom Mortymer?" her lips formed a kiss.

In gusty breathing, I made love to her again, yet in that tumult would have heard her step above marching armies.

Again and again I made love to her until the world was painted crimson with sunset; stars came out and the moon flooded the sea with brilliance.

Shadows had deepened into night when we got back to East Beach, and were surprised to find that none of our medical patients were awaiting us around the cottage door.

True, Gull's broken wing was nearly mended and his mate

had been pestering him to return to the colony; and Donk – well, with the Gunners in the barracks tempting her away with titbits, one never knew where she was activating from minute to minute; but all the other patients usually awaited our every homecoming and their supper.

But not that evening.

What clairvoyance possesses animals that they anticipate horror? I wonder.

"I tell ye what," announced Jen, "making love don't half make ye hungry! I'll get that Irish stew back on the boil!"

Kneeling, she lit the wick under the saucepan.

Looking back, my memory is hazy over what happened in the next half an hour, but I recall walking around the cottage to see where the patients had got to. Bun and Rat were always to be found . . .

Empty fields glared back at me and a strange foreboding began slowly to assail me. Then Jen shouted gaily from the cottage, "Supper up, Tom!" and I came through the cottage door in time to see her ladle out the contents of the saucepan.

"*Oh, my God!*" said she, and gasping, staggered backwards, her hands over her face.

Lying in the tureen was the steaming, skewered and tied-up body of Tom-cat.

Sick at heart, I left Jen sobbing in the kitchen and took the sad little corpse out for burial.

In the glow of the lamp I found the slaughtered bodies of Bun, Rat and Shelduck, he of the bright red beak who would no longer call for his mate from the waste of the sea; the bloody remains of six little chicks we had been rearing we found next, chopped to pieces; close by, Goat, the giver of our milk, lay dead with her throat cut; only Donk was

76

saved, he having wandered over to the lighthouse battery to be with the soldiers.

Jen said, weeping and screwing at her fingers, "I can't bear this, Tom. Please take me away from here – *please*?"

Next morning, after locking up the cottage and hiding the key in the eaves, I sailed *Aquila* over to Cardiff docks and sold her to a chandler for a song. It appeared that he had a buyer ready and waiting, and I should think so too – for a mere fifty quid.

Later I discovered the identity of this buyer . . . but at that moment didn't care; all I wanted was to get Jenny off Flatholm, and back to the mainland.

The following morning Jen and I, with a few packed possessions, caught the ferry to Sully. At Thomas's farm we collected our caravan and Lark, our piebald pony, and it's time he did something for a living anyway, said Jen.

Sunset found us rattling slowly along the road that led to Maesteg, and the mansion of *Cefn-Ydfa*, whose existence as my home, with the staff still waiting in attendance, I had almost forgotten.

"Lord of the manor again," said I with a levity I did not feel. "Now for the retired life of a tinplate industrialist, and get me feet up."

"That's what you think, me darlin'!" said Jen lightly, and wept for beautiful Flatholm.

Book Two

Chapter Twelve

The song of the robin, even when heralding the end of summer, said Jen, is one of the sweetest sounds of the countryside.

Sitting side by side in the caravan, we trundled along in sun-warmth down the road to Maesteg. Taking our time, we stopped early for night halts by watering places and started late on the road next morning, and there was a joy in us that we were back again amid the more prolific animal life of the mainland, for Flatholm had proved a sad old place when it came to our beloved wild things.

True, all but a few nightingales had already flown off to Africa, but those reluctant to go from the coppices seemed to burst their throats to sing for us, which Jen said was a lucky sign; to be approved of by night-birds, said she, was going half way to a fortune.

"Look!" cried she, and pointed joyfully at flocks of willie-wagtails and pipits flying southwards, wheeling and soaring like handfuls of cinders flung into the wind; wayside willow warblers, remembering it was late autumn, sang their melancholy ballads to us as if in consolation . . . for while it was true that our island home had brought lost friendships and death, it was a tug at the heart to see it fading into nothingness. A channel mist had come down, swallowing it up as if it had never existed.

"You are sad at leaving it?" I asked, and Jen kissed me.

"Nothing saddens me if we are together," said she.

The trout are very plump in the autumn, as if building themselves up for the frying-pans of men; and with about twenty species to choose from, says Jen, the rainbow fella is the one for me.

"Mind," she continued, in the clip-clopping of Lark, "ye canna pick and choose when the belly shouts, so mostly it's brown trout for Romanies. But since the gentry are daft enough to breed 'em in the western oceans, it's a rainbow I'm landin' once I gets me dabs on 'em."

"There's bailiff's water coming up," said I, "so it's a rainbow for supper if you're in the tickling fancy." I reined the piebald into a haven of alders beside a fine broad river.

"Tom Mortymer," said she, "you'll have me up in front o' the Beak again and coolin' me heels in the slammer – but give me five minutes and keep an eye out for the buggers." She leaped down from the foot-board, hoisted up her skirts and ran down to the river. With Lark grazing, I wandered after her, hands thrust into my pockets. There were no rivers on Flatholm, so I had never watched Jen go after trout with her fingers.

This is an art.

"Quiet, you," whispered she, "not a blink; don't even breathe!".

The secret, she told me later, is to make yourself one with the grass and wind, and behave as primaeval Man had done since the start of Time.

You creep, said she, to the place of the intended execution, making certain not to raise a finger above the surrounding country, because a trout has eyes which can look over his shoulder, and his old mam at his fishy birth gave him detailed warnings about the artfulness of human enemies.

"'The god of water-shadows,' she told him, 'is the large thing that walks on two legs, whom the water-rat calls Human; this monster has a big belly and a capacious mouth on him especially constructed for consuming trout like us; and those of us he cannot catch with rods, lines and deceitful barbed hooks dressed up as gad-flies, he drags out of the water with his hands, a pink weapon, possessing a thumb and four fingers.'"

I said, "Let's have more action and a little less old guff about it." Down on all fours now, Jen smiled at me, and crept towards the swirling edge of the river; slowly to turn, lie upon her back and slip a hand and arm into the water.

I watched.

And I wondered, as I crouched there of how many young hunters like Jen had lain in this every place and slipped in a hand for the bounty of the river! How many kisses, I thought, had been given and taken in this wild place where the river sang and the birds shouted their chorus over the still figure of a gypsy girl.

The thought was one banished instantly by the sight of a crescent of silver wriggling in the sunlit air, to land in flapping terror at my feet.

"Collar him, or he'll flap back in!" Jen now, on her knees in the rushes, shouting like a douche of cold water full in my face. "Come on, Tom – *wake up!*" Realisation struck me and I flung myself full length, grabbing the victim's tail in the moment before he slid back into the river.

Got him!

"Where have ye been?" she demanded, breathless. "Dreaming?"

"Trout for tea, I promised, but you didn't really believe it, did you!" Jen announced when on the final leg of our journey to Bridgend. "Do you hear me when I said that we are going to have a big golden pheasant for supper?"

Even Romanies must expect an end to one's credulity.

"Bet on it?"

"Give you ten to one." She took from her pocket a tiny bottle of what looked like cold tea, and while we were still on the caravan footboard, held it up to the sun.

"Now pull into the side of the road," Jen commanded, and I did so, reining Lark to a halt.

Jumping down, Jen walked the road verge until she found an area of short-cropped grass, over which she sprinkled the contents of the little bottle.

Returning, she said, "And now, my disbelieving friend, we will first drink tea." She went into the van behind me and put the kettle on to boil.

"This is a pheasant-raising area, do you realise?" I said. "The pair of us could end up transported for poisoning their beloved birds; they're reared by gentry for their love of being shot." I looked at her severely over the brim of my cup.

"Me, poison pheasants? I'm a Romany. Oh no, that's the last thing I have in mind – we're going to eat the things." Putting down her cup, she got off the footboard. Suspiciously I followed.

"D'ye hear that?" she asked, a finger up to her lips.

"Pheasants croaking," said I.

"More like pheasants singing?"

I followed her as she crept onward; sitting side by side on the road verge were a pair of cock pheasant three sheets in the wind; and like a couple of old drunks who had been out all night, they were croaking their heads off. Nor did they bat an eye as Jen walked up and belted the pair of them, and we returned to the van with a brace of pheasants for supper.

"Mind you," said Jen, as she basted them, "they ain't overloaded when it comes to brains. Raisins soaked in brandy they love – and get as drunk as coots on 'em – they just sit there waiting for one behind the ear."

Chapter Thirteen

We took the caravan to *Cefn-Ydfa* in Maesteg because it was the family home.

Built in 1728 by one, Anthony Maddocks, it had become famous for the legend that it was haunted by the ghost of Ann Thomas; she, forced by her mother to marry Maddocks, died of a broken heart in the arms of her love, Wil Hopcyn, they say.

The old place, rapidly falling into decay, was now scarcely habitable, and although I had one old retainer still living in the place, this trip to *Cefn-Ydfa* was more in the nature of a sojourn. With my new Works at Morriston expanding I had acquired a new home within sight of the industry.

"You say that Dai Dando is here?" asked Jen, as we took Lark and the van along the drive from *Corn Hwch*, the entrance lodge, and old Dai, my childhood friend, as if expecting us, was coming out of the mansion's entrance as we rounded the last bend before its forecourt; seeing us he waved delightedly.

"He's the only occupant now; his wife, Old Bid, and the two maids having gone on to my new house at Upper Forest."

"A new house?"

"One our solicitor has got lined up for us in Morriston."

"Dear me, you play your cards close to your chest! Supposin' I don't like it?"

"I'm renting it first and if you don't like it we won't buy it; don't meet your troubles half-way." I jumped

85

down from the footboard as Dai Dando came steam-ing up.

"Why, Maister?" cried he. "Welcome back, an' no mis-take! Eighteen months is it? It do seem like ten year to me!" His old pugilistic face broke into a wreath of smiles. "Only yesterday when Old Bid was going off, she says, 'You tell young maister that I ain't standin' for it, if he goes off without a word again . . .'"

Which needs a little explanation.

My father, while Chief Engineer to the King of Afghanistan, had an affair with his granddaughter, the Princess Durani, which resulted in my birth: for this the three of us were banished from her land, and came to Wales.

Later, however, short of an heir, the King demanded my return. My mother obediently returned to the Afghan court, but my father refused to leave Wales, or part with me. Wifeless, he married Clare Wildflower, Jen's mother; and they went on honeymoon to Europe to meet their deaths in a ferry accident; Jen and I, already childhood friends, were thus thrown even closer together, and after Jen's earlier marriage to my friend, David Grey, who died, she and I went to the elders of her Romany tribe, obtained a blessing on our marriage, and 'jumped the broom', mingling our blood in official gypsy fashion, as I explained.

Such was our haste to begin a wandering gypsy life that we left soon after the ceremony, so the servants in *Cefn-Ydfa* scarcely knew Jen as the new mistress.

"Ay ay, welcome, kindly welcome, Mistress," old Dai repeated in delight, and led Jen within.

Inside the mansion, the old man said, "Your solicitor chap called a week or so back and said you might be a'comin' home . . ."

I nodded. "Yes, I wrote to him and mentioned it."

"He asked if my Old Bid and one of the maids could go

86

over to the new house you're renting in Morriston, and get it cleaned up before you took it over."

"He seems pretty sure we're going to buy it," said Jen.

"On the basis of a month's rental first," I replied. "That's why I didn't mention it – I know the state of property these days – this old place is falling around our ears."

"That's what that gentleman Mr Jethro said when he come – 'Your master won't stick this old dump for long,' he said, 'take it from me.'"

"Mr Jethro?" asked Jen, giving me a meaningful glance. We were down in Old Bid's kitchen now, drinking tea, and a right state this was in as well.

"We don't know anyone called Mr Jethro," said I.

Dai grinned from ear to ear. "O aye? He knows you right enough, Maister." He gulped at his tea. "Knows the family, he do say. And posh an' all he were – a fine carriage and two white 'orses – a right dandy, beggin' his pardon. In fact, I anna seen so fine a gennulmun in all my life. Knows you, he does."

"Where has he supposed to have met us?"

"Where?" Dai looked nonplussed. "In Cardiff, recent. That's right – he see'd you in the city."

Jen put up a finger. "Would that be in the Royal Hotel?"

"What . . . aye, that's it! He said you was in there last time you was in Cardiff . . ."

"A big handsome fella," added Jen, nodding.

"And very interested in you, if I recall," I said wearily. "God, you've got them all over the place."

"Oh no, Maister!" admonished Dai. "No, I won't 'ave that. A decent, well set-up chap, this one, no womaniser, take it from me."

"Where is he now, then?"

"Gone north to the Top Towns."

"Which one?"

"Search me," said Dai. "Some'ut about goin' to the Top Towns to try to find his mam, he said."

"Blaenafon?"

"Ay ay, that's it!"

Jen looked at me; it was the way she looked. I said hastily, "Ah well, we'll forget about it for now. If he's a mind to, he'll be back . . ."

Dai Dando said reflectively, his head on one side, "Come to think of it, sir, he were the image o' ye dead feyther . . . like he'd come back from 'is drowning . . . to see for 'imself . . ."

"This is putting the shivers up me," interjected Jen.

Late, we wandered around *Cefn-Ydfa*.

From the window the old mansion lay stark black under the late September sky; eerily the coo-doves called to the stars; it was a night of floating cobwebs and unusual sounds; a shriek owl suddenly tore at the night-silence, then a nightingale sang.

"Look, love, *look*," Jen whispered, and clung to me, pointing, and I saw him clearly, black against the stars; liquid bubbles from his throat were sailing up against the moon.

Disturbed, I said, "But Jethro Mortymer! Here, in Wales! The man's mad, if it's him! Wanted for the murder of a soldier! Calling himself Mr Jethro! And here, of all places! He's just asking for it!"

"From what I've heard about your Uncle Jethro, it's just the sort of daredevil thing he'd do!" Jen chuckled, but I couldn't raise a smile.

What with one thing after another, I could do without my Uncle Jethro at the moment.

"But what *can* he be doing here?" asked Jen.

The night owl shrieked again from the woods.

I did not reply.

The more I thought of it, the more I realised that it

was bound to be Uncle Jethro, my father's brother. In my mind's eye I saw him again, tall, athletic, moving through the white-clothed tables of the Royal Hotel diners . . . the image of my dead father.

"Why return to the scene of his crime and risk arrest?"

"I'll tell ye," said she. "Ye have to kill a hundred Welshmen to get a pound of brains."

So I got no help from that quarter.

I was worried about the mysterious appearance of this man in my life.

That he had probably arrived under an assumed name with a forged passport would be understandable, since he was still being sought for murder; this, the only real information I had about him, had come from Dada.

It appeared that many years ago (with my father believed dead during the Chartist Rebellion of 1839) Jethro, his younger brother and what was left of the Mortymer family, had found sanctuary at Cae White Farm in Carmarthenshire. This was at the time of the Rebecca Riots when West Wales farmers were opposing the gentry's attempts to build toll-gates around their land.

Welsh farmers, fearing prison sentences under English law, disguised themselves when destroying the hated toll-gates, by dressing up as women.

Adopting the biblical verse of Genesis 24;60, which reads, 'And they blessed Rebekah, and said unto her, Thou art our sister, by thou the mother of thousands of millions, and let thy seed possess the gate of those which hate them . . .' they then ranged themselves in militant bands over the Welsh countryside, attacking the property of English and Welsh gentry.

During which, said my father (and he got it from the landlady of his local Black Boar tavern) my Uncle Jethro, a pugilistic old boy at the best of times, flattened an English dragoon who had followed him home from one of his Rebecca raids, leaving him to roll into a brook and drown: and thus was his murderer.

From that day (around the year 1843) after he had escaped to America, my Uncle Jethro was wanted in Wales for murder. Indeed I once saw a poster in an inn to this effect.

Jen said, after hearing all this, "When you lived in Cae White Farm in Carmarthenshire, did you ever meet a character called Betsy Ramrod, who ran the local inn?"

"Have a heart! I was scarcely weaned. My pa would have had the skin off me."

"Well, my mither knew her well, and she had a shine for the Mortymers even then, especially for your Uncle Jethro." She looked herself over in the bedroom mirror and preened like women do when they're broody. "And this I can understand, for he looked a real dandy to me."

"Behave yourself, he's old enough to be your grandpa!"

She patted her stomach and made big eyes at me, saying, "See ye in a few months, Uncle Jethro, after I've got this lot off my mind," She put her arms about me and kissed my face, adding, "Ye must admit, seeing him in the hotel that day, he's a real handsome Mortymer, if it's him."

"One Mortymer at a time, woman," I said, and what began as a peck of friendship ended in gasps and indrawn breaths, so that within the sudden tumult Jen reached out and turned the key in the door.

"You've got to make up your mind which Mortymer you want," I said, and lifted her in my arms and carried her to the bed.

"Give me half a chance and I'll show you," said Jen.

Down in the kitchen waiting for us, Old Dai wondered where we'd got to, he said.

Chapter Fourteen

With Jethro's appearance in Wales, events now came to a head with astonishing rapidity.

There were letters waiting on the hall sideboard for my attention; one with a Scottish postmark took my eye.

Opening it, I read:

> 'Office of the Procurator Fiscal,
> 24 St Andrew's Street,
> Glasgow, Scotland

September 24th 1883

Dear Mr Mortymer,

It is my duty to inform you that following your conviction (and that of the female accompanying you) and your subsequent fines for public misdemeanour at New Lanark Quarter Sessions, it has come to my notice that further allegations made against your characters are sufficiently important to warrant this official warning.

The Procurator Fiscal states that should the said Thomas Mortymer or the woman known as Jennifer Wildflower be, from this date, discovered within the official boundaries of Scotland the said persons shall, at the discretion of the law applied, be subject to immediate deportation and held in custody until charges under the Criminal Procedure (Scotland) Act are formulated against them. So take notice.

A B Mcbain, for

Procurator Fiscal'

I had just finished reading this astonishing letter, when Jen appeared in the kitchen, and I just had time to thrust it into my pocket.

"Oh, Tom, what a delightful day!" and I knew that the Romany girl had gone and that the beautifully spoken Jenny Wildflower had come in her place.

This needs amplification; at a later date I will explain this phenomenon; it being necessary, at that moment, to stay in control of myself; anything as emotive as such a letter might have a devastating effect upon our present tranquillity.

"Ah, we have some post!" said Jen, joining me and looking over my shoulder, and I opened the next letter with increasing dread; my mind still in a tumult from the first one.

This letter, also on headed notepaper, was a further shock.

'Coroner's Office,
9 High Street,
Swansea, Glamorgan

Dear Mr Mortymer,

Kindly acknowledge receipt of the attached letter written to you before his death, by Richard Henry Adams, whose suicide was conveyed to you on 9th September 1993, by Detective Inspector Graves.

Yours sincerely,

H M Knight

28th September 1883'

Attached to this letter was an untidy scrawl; written, it appeared, on a page torn out of a child's school exercise book, and this read:

'Upper Forest Works
Morriston, Swansea
7th September 1883

Dear Mr Mortymer,

Forgive me, sir, I got no option. I only took a sovereign or so at first, but I was still in debt, so I took more. After that it were easy, I forged your signature and kept on drawing the money. Mind, it were your fault sir, for you left me to do everything . . .

Please take care of my missus, she don't know anything about it.

Gaffer Adams'

I turned away; Jen took the letter out of my trembling hand.

"Nothin' wrong, I hope, Maister?" said Dai, coming in.

"We don't want to talk about it now, Mr Dando," said Jen, and together we went out on to the forecourt and stood there unspeaking, listening to the doves.

After a bit, Jen said, "At least he's at peace now, poor old chap. He really was a dear little man."

I heard myself say, "I don't understand it. It's his writing right enough, but it doesn't sound like Gaffer. True, he didn't go to the accepted schools, but he spoke beautifully – self-educated."

"We'll have to do something about his widow," said Jen.

Halfway down the drive to *Corn Hwch*, she asked, "Was that all the post you had this morning?"

"Yes."

We walked on amid bird-song. The day was glorious.

"Just wondered," she added, "because I thought I saw you reading another letter as I came into the kitchen."

"No, love – there was only the one."

There was a pause. "Sufficient for the day is the evil thereof, Tom?"

"If you like – something like that."

One didn't get away with a lot when Jen was around; she knew I was lying.

I had to lie. The Procurator's letter was terrifying, and I couldn't think of a reason for it. Reflecting back and putting even the worst possible implication upon it, our violation of public morals by bathing naked was something that had happened over a year ago, and for which we had been fined. It was scarcely a hanging offence . . . and now we were being threatened with deportation.

Something strange was going on, and I wondered if it was advisable to let it ride, or go up to Scotland to get to the bottom of it.

Jenny was implicated, too, of course, so she had a right to be consulted on what course I might take; the coming baby, too, had to be considered; he was more important than either of us.

In the event, I did nothing; the worst possible decision.

On the way back to the house, we called into the caravan to pick up a few things before packing for the journey to the new house at Morriston, and Jen said, "There's a few things need sorting out; I'm always promising, but never seem to get round to it . . ."

"Such as?"

"Oh, you know a few letters need burning – my mother was the most amazing hoarder; she never got rid of anything, and we never had room to move."

"Certainly, there's a lot of my father's papers that need sorting out," I said. "There's a wall safe in his study that's full of stuff; the last time I opened it was to get his will."

Locking up the van we started off again, hand in hand, and Jen idly remarked, "As I said before, you'll have to do something about Gaffer's wife. It's the least we can do for him."

94

"The beginning of next week – after we shut up here and get down to Morriston."

"You know her address?"

"No, but I can get it from the file."

It was like the last speech at the end of the beginning of Act One of a play, wherein the players set the stage for the denouement before the announcement of Act Two. Coming towards us from the mansion was Dai Dando, and with him was a woman I had not seen before. She was colourless, small, dressed dowdily and clearly distressed. Dai, accompanying her, said simply, "Gaffer Adams's missus, Maister. She heard you was home, so she arrived on the six-thirty . . ."

The circle of events seemed now complete; more – and this was incomprehensible to me – all our troubles seemed to date from the moment of my Uncle Jethro's arrival.

Chapter Fifteen

Mrs Adams, Gaffer's wife, had more about her than I'd thought. Sitting before Jen and me in my father's study in *Cefn-Ydfa*, she said, "You see, Mr Mortymer, my Jack and I were a queer pair, folks said, for he was educated; our place is stacked with his books . . ." She paused to dry her eyes. "And honest? Ye could look the world over and never find a more thrifty man, with his own or other people's money. And his accountin' books were that tidy." She sniffed and wiped. "He used to pride himself on his writing . . ."

"Yes, I know, Mrs Adams."

"So when that Mr Opand at the bank brought in the police about the forged cheques an' all that, he took it to heart. Couldn't sleep, and went off his food . . . The questions . . . morning, noon and night . . ."

She faltered. Jen had bowed her head to the prospect of a gush of tears and the woman fought for control, adding, "It just went on an' on . . . And if it weren't old Opand, it were that Inspector Graves – they was horrible to him, and as for his assistant, that man Harris . . .! *Well!*"

In her dilapidation she stared at us. "Ye see . . . he was out of 'is depth, if you get me? All his life he'd been honest, and now accused of forgin' cheques for thousands o' pounds."

"Surely, nobody actually accused him, Mrs Adams . . ." This from Jen; the female of the species being tougher when it came to practicalities.

"Oh yes they did, Missus! They 'ad him in tears more'n

96

once, for I was with him. 'It's for your own good if you tell the truth, Adams,' they said, and shoutin', too, not just polite . . . And as fast as he answered one question, they was after him with another.

"I tell ye, the neighbours heard 'em ten doors up, and folks comin' down and looking through our windows. It were the same at the police station – bawling and threatening, but he never really broke down.

"Mind, there weren't a lot of him, my Jack, but he were six foot up standin' on a chair . . ." Biting her lip she fought her anguish. "He was innocent, see, and that makes the difference, don't it? I'm a nobody, and I expect I'd 'ave agreed, just to get rid of 'em, but my hubby went to a good school, and that does somethin' for a man . . ." She faltered again, looking from one to the other of us.

"Have the police shown you the note he left?" I asked kindly.

"No, sir – just read it out to me."

"Did you understand what it said?"

She raised her face like a child baptised. "Not really. Only that he said he was sorry . . ."

I interjected. "But Gaffer didn't say he was sorry, did he? He wrote that he took the money because he was in debt."

This sat her up. "In debt? We ain't in debt! Me and my Jack don't owe a penny to anyone. Who said that?"

"The suicide note he left."

Astonished, she stared blankly. Jen said, "The police read your husband's suicide note to you, you say?"

"That's right."

"It would have been better to have read it yourself . . ."

She lowered her face. "Can't read, Mr Mortymer. Like I said, my chap was educated – he used to read a lot o' things about Greek and Roman people to me, and I used to listen . . ." She brushed at her tears. "Domestic servant, see? I was a skivvy at the age of ten . . . and he was the son o' the house. Folks said it wouldn't work, but we was happy . . ."

Jen said suddenly, "Would . . . would you like to see the note your husband left again, Mrs Adams . . . ?"

"Just told you – can't read, can I?"

"Just look at it, Mrs Adams," said Jen, and took it from me, and the woman began to shiver. "I know you can't understand it, but do please look at it."

She did so after fumbling with her spectacles, and slowly her face cleared of the grief, and she said softly, "Beautiful writin', ain't it? They always said he had a lovely hand."

"I know you can't understand the words, Mrs Adams, but is that your husband's writing?"

"Oh yes, it's lovely! We never had children, but I always said, 'Jack,' I said, 'if we have kids, you make sure they do that copper-plate writing, same as you. After all,' I says to him, 'if ye've had a decent education, it's right and proper that you shows it off, eh?'"

"Right and proper, Mrs Adams," said Jen.

After Mrs Adams had left, Jen asked, "Well, what do you think of all that?"

"Poor little woman."

I now had doubts about the letter's authenticity; the writing might look like 'copper-plate', especially to someone who couldn't read: but to somebody versed in Gaffer's personality and mode of expression, the words on the page denied the man.

Then who did write it?

Poor Gaffer, under duress?

Meanwhile, I was seized with a sense of approaching disaster; as if the chemistry of our existence had overnight developed by chain reaction into an engulfing detonation.

Chapter Sixteen

Maesteg, at this period of the Welsh Industrial Revolution, was a town of perfumes and smells: perfumes in the shape of flowering woods and mountains in spring and summer, smells approaching stinks, especially around the area of *Cefn-Ydfa*, when the wind was in the wrong quarter. The rancid assaults upon the nostrils came from mushrooming smoke rising from countless chimneys in the Llynfi Valley, chugging railway engines, the open doors of tinplate works; copper and chemical vents puffed out their poisonous deposits upon the roofs of the workers and laid waste the country.

Blackened spoil heaps replaced tummocky hillocks once green and gold under a burnishing sun; lovely hill slopes guarding one of the most beautiful valleys of Wales became blackened sentinels of a generation lost in Time. Our streets, wriggling like black vipers, were lined with the dross of a care-worn humanity cast out in the name of speculator profits: these, the coal-tattooed colliers and miners, worked out and pale, exhibited empty trouser legs and stumpy arms as the price paid for local and foreign exploitation.

Smoke and choke being brothers, this was the comradeship of the discarded; a tubercular refuse of spit and cough set amid the Palaces of Plenty; and we Mortymers, reluctant though I had been to recognise the fact, had played our part in the role of 'Devil take the Hindmost'; my attempt to change a system of riches for the owner and whippings for the slave had almost come to nothing.

A minute examination of the Upper Forest ledgers (with Jen and I burning the midnight oil) exposed the economic truth; that our enterprise, begun with bold hopes based on Owenite principles, had over the last few months been going down the drain.

"Face the facts," said Jen, getting up from the books, "you've been an absentee landlord."

Old *Cefn-Ydfa* usually so full of creaks and groans, was silent that winter night, with nothing but the screech of a Jinny Oolert owl to break the monotonous rumbling of distant industry. Also, for the first time I noticed that the Matron of Thirty was touching up my girl's features with autumn fingers. This could have been the onslaught of her pregnancy, I thought, watching her as she moved around my father's study; her natural slimness now exchanged for motherhood's ungraceful lines.

"Don't make the examination meticulous," said Jen, "the old girl won't stand up to it."

"I was thinking how beautiful you look."

Usually, this is the case; Mother Nature, compensating for weight, devises hints of natural make-up: the eyes become brighter in cheeks once shadowed by strain; teeth become whiter, breasts more prominent; and if a woman is not tortured by morning sickness (and Jen so far was not) her temperament was conducive to normality; for Jen could be a tricky old thing when on the Romany boil.

"What are you going to do about it, Tom?" she asked.

"What – the Works?" I shrugged. "When we get to Morriston in a few days I'll go further into it – for a start, the place can't continue without a foreman."

"Have you thought about getting out?"

"Selling up, you mean? Not really. I hate giving up the Owenite thing without a fight."

Taking her hand I walked to the study window and stood there with her, looking out on to the night, as I had seen my father do so many times. It seemed impossible that he and Clare Wildflower were lost to us, never to return.

Seeing their deaths in retrospect, they were the initial tragedy that preceded our bad fortune, and perhaps selling up and cutting my losses was the only real avenue left to me . . . before being dragged down into possible bankruptcy.

Now I followed Jen out into the forecourt.

"One thing's for sure," said she, "we won't think any more about it tonight." She put her face up to the wind.

"Smell that, love!" said she. "That's the kind of bread you eat with the nose, we Romanies say. Smell it?"

It was bread-baking time in the valley, and the wind was coming up from the rank-on-rank workers' cottages.

"Pay-day, of course!" announced Jen. "You can tell the calendar by them!"

This was a fact. Today was the first of the long-pay period when the Valley wives queued at the shops for flour and yeast.

Every cottage rank owned at least one baking oven at the bottom of its garden; the wives banding together in the communal effort of baking for the next fortnight. Bread money, carefully guarded to ensure its use for that purpose, was usually kept in places where males couldn't get at it without a struggle – in stocking-tops or down the front of bosoms.

That done, little groups of wives, each subscribing a penny towards the expense, would assemble for the ritual of pushing their prepared tins of dough into the communal ovens by a long-handled shovel; an occasion also for a gossip, and a babble of female voices would rise from the cottages.

Later, bakeries were opened by enterprising individuals, and later still the Co-operative movement took a hold. But in those early days of the Industrial Revolution, the fulcrum of social activity for wives was the baking of communal bread and collection of water from local wells and standpipes.

Jenny and I, hand in hand on the forecourt of *Cefn-Ydfa* for the last time, experienced the mouth-tingling smell of baking bread on the wind . . . for once obliterating the sulphurous stinks of the Llynfi Valley: a serenity of true domestic bliss.

In retrospect I am glad we made the most of it, for soon my girl was going to leave me.

Chapter Seventeen

Now the sequence of events contributing to my downfall unwound before me as innocently as the chanting of the alphabet by children . . . and continued with unerring accuracy.

Dai Dando said jovially, coming into the study, "Right, Maister, all we want now is the removal van comin' on time tomorrow, and we're ready for the off to Morriston." He put his fists upon his hips and looked well satisfied.

I asked, "Any regrets about leaving *Cefn-Ydfa*?"

"Well . . ." and he screwed up his battered face, "I'll likely miss me mates down at the Rose and Crown, o' course, but that's no loss to Old Bid, for she do reckon they're a bunch o' criminals."

"Still your mates, Dando!"

"Ay ay, but females dunna understand, do they? And she can be a right caution when she gets her dander up. She don't like the whampo, ye know."

"I don't blame her," I said, getting up from my table. "Ten pint sessions are too much for a chap knocking seventy – how you afford it, I don't know."

"It ain't the ale so much as the women, really speakin'."

"Yes, and you should watch that, too, Dando. Your trouble is that you stayed single too long."

Dai grunted. "Mind, a red-blooded fella like me do find it inconvenient to stick to one pair o' garters, beggin' ye pardon. And that's what Old Bid expects. Always 'ad me own way wi' the opposite sex, see, and when times come skinny, single roosters like me do find it difficult."

I said, pushing past him, "Single roosters like you, Dando, will find it harder still with your ambitions chopped off – there was a case in the paper last week – I wouldn't put anything past Old Bid if she caught you on the job."

"Dear me, you ain't half a one for puttin' the wind up a God-fearin' fella!"

My own troubles began when Jen came in from loading up the caravan that morning.

"I've been sorting out my mother's affairs," she announced. "Papers, papers, she's got them all over the place." She dumped a batch of them down onto the table before me.

I only half heard her for I was writing to my solicitors about terminating the rental of *Cefn-Ydfa*; the old place now being scarcely habitable. Jen continued, "She was a hoarder all right – lots of newspaper cuttings from all parts of the country. Look at this one," and she read, "'Cure for the cholera – a pint of wine, an ounce of camphor, another of mustard, some black pepper and bruised garlic . . .'"

"That's enough to knock anyone off," I replied abstractedly.

"Don't be daft, you rubbed it in. And Joseph Tregelles Price, the Neath ironmaster, gave a Christmas dinner, in 1794, to every prisoner in Monmouth Gaol."

I nodded, writing. "It's more than they'd get round this part of the world."

"And an old chap of sixty got three months on the treadmill and fifty lashes for leaving his place of employment."

"God bless our employers."

"Have you heard of Sydenham's Antibillious pills?" she asked.

"Not lately."

"Or Elixir Paregoric?" and she whirled about the study with her long plaits flying, and sang, "If the wind had only blown the other way, I might 'ave been a single girl today, instead of stuffing paregoric into kids that 'ave the colic, if the wind had only blown the other way," and bending, kissed me.

"Hop it, Jen, I've got work to do."

"A fella called Sabbath Williams died by 'A visitation of God' – it was on his Death Certificate."

"Which could happen to another I could mention."

She had effectively stopped me working, yet in this mood of jocularity, although it appeared strangely forced, her presence had a scintillating effect upon me, for it was Jen at her best. Thus, when her mood quietened suddenly, I took no heed of it; for this is the way she was: one moment within an exhilaration of joy, next sunk into a slough of apathy . . . so I just went on writing.

Later glancing up, I saw her in deep thought, staring down at a paper trembling in her hands.

"Anything wrong?"

Jen closed her eyes. "No, darling, no . . . !"

It was the last time she used such a term of endearment.

It was only after she had left did I realise that her eyes were red as if she had recently been weeping.

It was some time before I had finished my work in the study, and with a hard day tomorrow and the prospect of moving the furniture to Morriston, I went to bed early. Jen had preceded me and appeared to be asleep. Not wanting to awake her I slipped quietly into the bed beside her.

I awakened late, surprised to find that Jen was already up and about, apparently, but there was no sign of her usual activity or her tuneless singing in the bathroom; nor was she to be found in the dining room where Dai Dando, standing in for Old Bid, brought in the breakfast.

"Have you seen my wife, Dai?"

"Down the Big Wheatfield early on, sir – crow-starving, I expect, for they was cawing some'ut terrible."

"She was getting the van ready for the road, I suppose."

Later, however, when Jen still hadn't come for breakfast – and this was after ten o'clock – I sent Dai down to the Big Wheatfield where the caravan was kept, usually with Lark grazing nearby; then I wandered down the drive to *Corn Hwtch*; but the occupants there had not seen her, they said, and the road to Bridgend was empty.

An hour later, when Jen still hadn't returned, I quickened my search for her and was actually running by the time I got back to *Cefn-Ydfa*; there to meet an agitated Dai Dando.

"The caravan's gone, Maister!"

It took my breath. "It can't be!"

"I tell ye, it's gone, sir. Pony an' all."

I actually shook him for sense.

"The missus, sir – she must 'ave took it . . ." and out came a gush of words. "I followed its wheel tracks in the grass, it rained last night, see? And it took me goin' north through the valley . . ."

"But she must have gone past *Corn Hwtch* Lodge, and they haven't seen her."

"What time were that, sir?"

"I don't know, you fool!"

"What time did she leave 'er bed, Maister?"

"I don't know that, either. But why?"

"Reckon you can answer that better'n me."

I said, breathless, "Are ye sure she's taken the caravan?"

"Who else?"

"Then why didn't the keepers hear her pass *Corn Hwtch*?"

"They ain't overloaded, mind; twice to the synagogue come Sunday – ain't normal, says Old Bid."

"For God's sake, Dai. Think, man, *think*."

"Could be she's north above Cwmy-felin by now, or

106

even beyond Caerau – he can travel, mind, that little Lark."

"But why should she leave now? We're just off to Morriston!"

"Don't ask me, sir. Women are queer; I never know what Bid's up to from minute to minute."

But I didn't really hear him, for I was looking at my watch. "How long has been gone?"

"Long enough so you couldn't follow 'er easy, sir – or she'd 'ave gone past *Corn Hwtch*. Cut across the fields, didn't she?"

"Let's get back to the house; she might be back there by now."

But she wasn't.

We found no sign of her, the search fruitless from the outset; the pony and caravan had gone, and Jen with them. Desperately, I ran up the stairs to the bedroom; the room, suddenly empty of her, stared back at me with hostility.

But on the floor, hidden on Jen's side of the bed, was an envelope; I ripped it open and read:

'Dearest Tom, I'm sorry, but there is no other way. God bless you and bring you happiness. Jen'

Attached to this message was a letter, and I recognised the writing at once: it was from my father to Clare Wildflower, his wife.

I read in growing astonishment:

Cefn-Ydfa Mansion
Maesteg

My dearest Clare,

I write this to you with reluctance, feeling closer to you now than at any time since we met.

It must have become clear to you, as to me in recent months, that an affection is growing between your Jenny and my Tom.

107

As yet they are still children, but an affection born in puberty can become a bond which could grow through adolescence into love.

Since I am father to them both, we are faced with an intolerable situation, and one which is better faced now than later, when their love might prove too strong for us to sever.

The blood relationship, you understand, is too close to be tolerated. God knows what malformation might be visited upon the children of such a union.

This, my dear Clare, is the outcome of the sins of the fathers, and I will never hold you responsible for a situation I forced upon you. Let us continue to be lovers, but temper our actions with foresight; and here I suggest that while I keep Tom here in order to train him for the life of business awaiting him, our Jenny should go away to boarding school, for which I will pay expenses. Meanwhile, I beg you to do all you can to discourage their present close friendship.

Iestyn Mortymer
6th June 1868'

I do not know for how long I sat there in the study with the letter shaking in my hands.

Jenny Wildflower was my half-sister; we shared the same father; the realisation dawned upon me in waves of sickening intensity.

The removers arrived and because I could not think coherently, I left it all to Dai Dando, wandering around the emptying rooms in a soporific dream.

In that trauma I indicted my father and Jen's mother, Clare, for their stupidity in not confiding earlier to us the truth of our relationship. Instead, impelled by their own love affair they had gone blindly on, it appeared, from one emotional peak to another, concerned only with themselves and without a single thought for the outcome. My father I considered to be mainly at fault, for I remembered Clare's reluctance to encourage my affection for Jenny; but Dada had done little to allay my interest in her, though it was happening right under his nose. And how had he handled it? By the infantile act of sending Jen away to boarding school; by which he had brought us closer; absence making our hearts grow fonder.

Empty, I fought back tears, the pathetic emergence of the weakling.

Dai was coming and going with questions during that first terrible day of Jen's absence, and I answered them automatically; it was only when he was about to leave for Morriston that I realised I would be left alone in *Cefn-Ydfa* with but a few sticks left of furniture.

"Until the Mistress comes back . . ." said Dai.

"Perhaps she isn't coming back," I replied bitterly.

"Aw, come on, sir? You know women, they fly off the handle, but it don't mean nothin' . . . take my Old Bid, for instance . . ."

I said, "I . . . I want to stay on here for a bit to give my wife a chance to think about it. You get the furniture over to the new house, and I'll be with you the moment she returns . . ."

He cackled, "Bid's thought o' that, an' all, for we've been sending notes back and forth by Angie . . ."

"Angharad, the new maid?"

"Ay ay, Bid's arranged for her to stay here with you until the Mistress comes back to ye, son . . ." His old eyes clouded. "With your pa gone, you're sort of our son now, really speakin . . ."

I nodded, wishing him to the devil.

"And Angie were keen, mind. Fair play. 'You leave the Master to me, Old Bid,' said she, 'for sure as fate he won't eat properly otherwise – he ain't no good at cookin'.'"

109

Chapter Eighteen

Now I lived in a universe of nights and days. Hours dragged into uneventful weeks, sitting alone in my father's study awaiting Jen's return. The horror of the situation confronting us swept over me.

Half-brother; half-sister! And Jen had a baby coming . . . Nightmare dreams contained my days and sweating, tossing nights; I could neither comprehend the outcome, nor a reason why we were being subjected to such suffering; surely no punishment could be so bitter . . . for the offence of falling in love. We were being subjected to a curse from which there was no escape.

After this realisation came legitimate anger and a distress greater than anything I had known; and through it all Jen's face stared at me through the desolation.

What should I do?

Was it right to pursue her? If so, to what end? To build false hopes upon a past that now was a mountain of decay?

The more I sought escape, the more I realised that none existed. Jen was as lost to me as if she had put on a shroud and stepped into her grave.

The bottle called me. I'd sit there day after day, staring at the amber slant of the whisky and the beckoning solace of the port, a lurid enemy, and in my swimming senses heard Jen say: "Start that, boyo, and the pair of us are lost . . ." or, in her more refined mood, "Do not be seduced by whisky Tom; a man with your soul can do better than that. Anyway, what about me? There are no short cuts to my peace of mind, for I am carrying your child."

Then once in the night hours, I heard her say, "So you think you're in trouble, but what about this Jen Wildflower? The tribe won't be keen to have me when they know I've had a child by my half-brother.

"How much better it would be if I were back in *Cefn-Ydfa* with your arms about me, but see my situation. I cannot leave because nobody wants me, and I can't stay with you because it's against the law. Are you listening?

"Since leaving you I've been making discreet enquiries. Are you aware that the letter you received from Scotland was because of our incestuous relationship, yet you hid that terrible letter from me? But I found, and read it . . ."

I groaned in sleep, seeing her apparition standing by my bed; it withered and shrank in alcoholic waves as I reached for her.

On the third week of Jen's departure, the wraith of Jen appeared again.

I was in the sweating drowse of another drunken nightmare when my eyes opened in bright moonlight and I saw her standing beside the bed with terrifying clarity.

She said, smiling, "Have you stopped to wonder who could hate us so much that they betrayed us to the local authority? Someone who knew we had taken the van over the Scottish border?

"Consider it, Tom, *who*? I can't think of anybody who would do such a terrible thing to us.

"Somebody has been following our every movement. The same person, no doubt, who killed our animals on Flatholm.

"Do you remember the note we found beside the dead body of Rooster, the first to die? And did Gaffer Adams really steal your money? A *lot* of unexplained things have been happening. Do you realise that Scotland could even have us hanged for breaking her law against incest? And yet, my love, despite all these allegations I do not feel the least immoral. True, we share the same father, but does that really make us criminals?

"I love you still. Whatever they do to me, how ever the world judges me, nothing will change that love. Although we are parted, nothing will dilute the respect I have for you, even though the world no longer allows me to call you my husband . . ."

I sat up in the bed calling her name . . . in time to see the door slowly closing; it was as if she had never existed; only her perfume told of her passing . . . and I drank from a second bottle of brandy . . .

During the day, wandering around the grounds and talking to myself, I would sometimes go down to *Corn Hwtch*; the keepers there, old Jewish people, would hide behind their curtains, thinking I was demented.

People were beginning to gossip; the tradespeople, usually seen by Dai Dando, would arrive fearful of the master of *Cefn-Ydfa*; he who communicated with ghosts.

"Mind you, missus," I heard one old girl say to another, "these gentry toffs ain't all they're supposed to be, ye know. She were a real smart piece, that Wildflower, but there's always a fancy man around the corner . . ."

"I heard talk as how he roams around intoxicated – gone off his rocker they do say.

" . . . Mind, some do 'ave it that they're really brother an' sister . . ."

"No!"

"O aye! Insisterly, or some'ut or other, they do call it."

London cockneys these two, come south with the industry.

"Gawd, mate, you ain't edicated, are ye? *Incest*, ye mean, girl!"

112

Gabble gable, gobble gobble.

"Don't care what they calls it, but's a damn disgrace, I say. Shoot the bloody pair of 'em, I would. Jist fancy – brother and sister doin' it!"

Soiled women, these; dirty in the mind and mouth.

"One thing's for sure, Girt, if she's that free with it she anna got my complaint."

"What's that?"

"Doctor says I've got a dilapidator in me passage."

"No, love, no – a dilapidated passage; I got one, too."

"Have ye? Dear me, I feels better already."

I lost myself in the market-day crowds, and grieved for Jen. To this day I never knew how our tragedy had been learned by such people.

Drinking hard, I continued to wait for Jen in *Cefn-Ydfa*, refusing Old Bid's blandishments to move over to Morriston, where, she said, she had got the new house in a state fit to receive its new master; sending Angharad, the new parlourmaid recently taken on to tide me over until things were more settled.

This Angharad, as beautiful as her name, had replaced our poor little Molecule, the maid who briefly served us before finding a grave in Llangynwyd church cemetery.

Angharad was proving the antithesis of Molly Cule (her real name) in every shape and form. For where Molecule was the lisping workhouse-bred child, Angie (as Old Bid called her) was the epitome of womanly grace and deportment, and any man with an eye for beauty would have to be blind to be unaware of her; possessed as she was with an animal magnetism that put potential suitors off their food.

Tall, Welsh-dark, aesthetically refined, she had captivated the Morriston house from the moment she had entered it apparently. Her hair, like Jen's, was long; she wore it in a single plait that began at the crown of her head and finished

113

in the vicinity of her bottom; and her smile, wide and gentle, belied the passion being generated within: there being more to the lovely Angie than was superficially apparent.

"Good-morning, sir!"

She had arrived on the ten-thirty from Swansea and with a suitcase, clearly intending to stay.

"'morning."

I was unshaven and gruff, and after another drunken, sleepless night, was not in the mood to pay her homage.

"You have no news of the Mistress, sir?"

"Nothing."

"Biddy says she thinks she must be ill – going off like that without a word." She was beautifully spoken.

I yawned with purpose, it being too early in the morning for conversational platitudes. Nor did I want to conduct an inquest upon Jen's behaviour with a servant I scarcely knew, and inwardly I cursed Old Bid for not having the sense to send me Dozie Annie, the other maid, to perform such a duty. My nearest neighbours, the Maddox, were probably the source of present gossip and it didn't need fuelling with a gypsy in the parlour, a role Angharad looked like filling to perfection.

Indeed, I began to wonder if there lay a hidden philosophy behind her presence, for Old Bid had never been enamoured of my relationship with Jen . . . there being no snobs like the working class, and match-making, according to Dai, was Old Bid's stock-in-trade.

"How long is it now, sir?" Angharad stood before me, her hands clasped, her smile kind, as if in acknowledgement of my sad situation and determined to do well by me.

"Three weeks – I don't know, probably longer."

I was wishing her to the devil via Morriston.

"Where could the Mistress have possibly got to?"

"God, I don't know! D'you think I'd be loafing around here if I had the faintest idea?"

Angharad bowed her head; astonishingly, tears were in her

eyes and I was instantly contrite, saying, "I . . . I'm sorry, but I'm at my wit's end, not knowing whether to go searching or sit here awaiting her return."

She did not react to this; she was staring past me towards the window.

"The caravan horse is back, sir. Isn't that Lark, your wife's piebald pony?"

I actually pushed her aside in my haste to get outside, for Lark, free of his caravan was standing aimlessly on the forecourt.

Weary and travel-stained was he; I led him round to the stables and was feeding and watering him when Angharad joined me.

"You've got a visitor as well sir," said she, and pretty she looked, I recall, in her long black servant's dress and lace poke-bonnet.

"Oh, God," I said, "not now!"

"A real gentleman, too, sir, come up from the station."

I was now brushing Lark down. "If he's selling anything, send him about his business."

"I hope I haven't come at an inopportune time, Tom Mortymer," said a voice, and its owner entered the stable, offering his hand. He was large, handsome, and the image of my dead father.

"Your Uncle Jethro," he said, "you've heard of me?" He added, "Last time I saw you – and the first time, come to that – was when you and a lady were dining at the Royal, in Cardiff; I knew of you, but clearly you didn't know of me."

Words had left me; I just stared, gripping his hand.

He continued, "Actually, I called here some time ago and talked to your coachman, Mr Dando."

"Yes," I replied, "he mentioned it."

I am over six feet tall, but he topped me by inches; beautifully attired in his morning suit, he removed his hat and his blue eyes danced in his brown face, assessing me.

115

I gathered my failing wits, and said, "You must forgive me, Jethro. Everything seems to be happening at once, and . . ."

"That is why I am here," said he, simply, and came closer, putting his arm around my shoulders. "The last of the Mortymers, are we not? – you and me. Thin on the ground now, Tom, we'll have to make up for lost time."

Angharad, I noticed over his shoulder, was carefully watching us.

From the outset I never trusted this woman. Constantly she gave an impression that she was assimilating more of my affairs than was good for me.

With Jethro's arm around my shoulder I walked back to the house discussing mundanities, because, following at a respectful distance, Angharad was within earshot.

Chapter Nineteen

Later, with Jethro and I hard at it drinking whisky, Angharad, in the study doorway, said, "I've brought you coffee and sandwiches, Gentlemen; is there anything else you want before I go to bed?"

We thanked her and she drifted away.

"For God's sake!" said Jethro after she had gone. "Where did you find her?"

I poured us more whisky. "Soon I'm moving down to Morriston; most of the servants are there already; Angharad is staying over to see I eat properly, she says."

He grunted some reply, and I took the opportunity to study him better in the light of the lamp, saying ineffectively, "Beautiful women aren't at a premium in *Cefn-Ydfa* – you should see my wife."

"Where is she?"

"Can we discuss that later?"

It appeared to suffice him. Vaguely, I thought, watching him, that it could have been my father sitting there. Younger than he, of course, but with the same massive frame and dignity. I judged his age at fifty.

"You knew that my father died, of course."

"Not till recently, when I looked for him in Blaenafon. I visited there to see my mother, your Grandma Mortymer, but she had died about a month before I arrived, so I didn't see either of them." He stared down at his cigarette. "Dear God, it's been about forty years!"

"If you recognised me in the hotel, aren't you a bit late in making this contact?"

He shrugged. "Two reasons: firstly because I'm a wanted man in Wales; secondly, the kind of business I'm in isn't conducive to an unexplored family relationship."

"Well, I like to know the company I'm keeping. You killed a soldier, didn't you? I'm in enough trouble as it is without sheltering a wanted man. The police here aren't idiots."

Jethro rose; going to the window of the study he looked out, his back towards me. "It's a long yarn. Can't it wait until later?"

This man, I thought, was an enigma. While his intonation and Iberian good looks were clearly Welsh, his manner was brashly American. Reasonable, I supposed, having living most of his life in that country.

"I want to know about you now," I answered.

"Well . . ." and this was a drawl, "you asked for it." Returning to his chair he picked up his whisky. "For the past twenty years or so I've been employed by the Pinkerton Detective Agency in New York. You've heard of them?"

I shook my head.

"Then your education's been neglected. Allan Pinkerton is the man who organised and founded the American Federal Secret Service! *Come on!*"

"Never heard of him."

"You soon will, for now he's moving in over here and has sent me to set up Pinkerton branches in Wales and Scotland – England won't give us a licence. Actually, I was staying at the Royal in Cardiff, working on the Welsh aspect when you bowled in there. I assumed the beauty I saw you with was your wife?"

He was ready to change the subject.

"If you knew who I was, why didn't you introduce yourself?"

"I've already explained – one has to work slowly and

118

carefully in my game. My agent, pointing you out, said you were living on an island somewhere, and this threw me. Later I traced you here, to Maesteg". He took out his watch. "I've got to get going, they'll be locking me out." He suddenly appeared as one needing to escape.

"Where're you staying?" I asked.

"The Old Tavern, Maesteg."

"Where's your luggage?"

"I dropped it off from the station coming through."

I said, "I can't offer you a bed here, the place is ramshackle – no fit bedroom: the maid has one, I've got the other."

"Don't worry, don't worry." He stretched himself, shaking his black-curled head. "You know, Tom, it's a hell of a thing to come back to a place and find the family gone. D'you realise that we're about the only surviving Mortymers?"

He was beginning to repeat himself, adding, "Iestyn, my brother – I heard of his death soon after it happened – meant a lot to me . . . Your grandparents are dead and gone, my two sisters, Edwina and Morfydd – God, she was a nut in her time believe me – and Mari, my brother's wife – she meant a lot more . . . Gone, all gone. Mind you, even without this Pinkerton work, I reckon I'd have come home one day looking for the family. It's a Welsh tradition . . . Which brings me to your wife again, what about her?"

"It's too involved for this time of night."

But he persisted, saying, "Since she isn't here and another woman is, I guess she's left you!"

"I wish it were as simple as that. The woman here is a maid. I don't know her any better than you do. She's here until I move to Morriston."

"Why did your wife go off?"

"Persistent, aren't you!"

"I might be able to help," he said.

I sighed.

"Another chap?" He fluttered an eye.

119

"Jenny? Don't be ridiculous!"

"Then why?"

I glared at him for reply, watching as he poured more whiskies, and suddenly hated him and everything he stood for. His presence now appeared as an invasion of my privacy. How the hell could one man tell another that he'd been living with his half-sister and brought her to child? His insistence in prying was akin to cutting the stitches of a partly-healed wound, for, strangely, although Jen was lost to me, I was suffused with a sense of relief that the crime against her was not now being perpetuated.

Yet the torture was heightened by Jen's predicament. Winter would soon be upon us; how could she survive without shelter or friends? She had left me without redress or knowledge of her whereabouts, and anger gainst her, with the help of the alcohol, was also beginning to dilute my foreboding.

Jethro's voice raked me from the reverie. "Perhaps she can manage on her own, Tom, but what about the child?"

The lamp was guttering noisily, short of oil, and shadows darkened about the man sitting opposite me in variegated tones of gold, shadowing his features.

"The child?" I repeated stupidly, for the whisky was now really getting me. "How did you know Jenny's in child?"

"I'm one of the Pinkertons . . ." Suddenly he looked ill at ease.

I got up. "No. Not good enough. How did you know?"

"A branch in Scotland – remember?"

"What of it?"

"The first thing the Scottish Office wanted from me was proof of identity and credentials . . ."

"So what?"

"It gave me access to personal files; when one enrols staff you're entitled to know their background – everyone employed by Pinkerton must be whiter than white. While selecting my people I had an opportunity to look up the Mortymers . . ."

"And learned our history!"

"Well . . ." he drawled this and my anger increased, "I wouldn't say that your record is lily-white north o' the border. Bathing naked is against public morality!"

I closed my eyes. We were common knowledge because of a minor offence; and this had opened the door to the facts of our relationship. Now anyone with a wish to set up a commercial venture had access to our secret.

"Would you like to tell me about it?" Jethro smiled innocently.

"It's my business, and Jen's. Leave it."

"And pretty serious stuff it is, too, by the sound of it!"

I drank my whisky at a gulp. "Look, stop your bloody American third-degree and get back to where you came from!"

"I'm only trying to help."

Rising, he momentarily faced me, and we looked steadily into each other's eyes: he said, scarcely audibly, "Tom, I don't know what it's all about in detail, but it sounds to me like some unholy mistake . . ." and such was his expression of sudden kindness that I was tempted to let the whole thing flood out, if only to share it with another human being.

"How far is she gone?" he asked.

"With the baby? About seven months."

"That couldn't be worse. She's got to be found at once."

I raised my voice, swinging away from him, "Exactly. So I shouldn't be sitting here exchanging mundane platitudes with you, should I? The moment you've left here, I'll go after her . . . She took the caravan when she went, but the horse has returned – you saw it when you arrived . . ."

"That's the best lead we've got. When did she go?"

"Oh, weeks!"

"If she's dumped the caravan and turned the horse loose,

you only have to give him his head and he'll take you back to her."

"You think so?"

"I know horses; anyway, it's worth a try. For heaven's sake don't hang around hoping she'll come back – get after her, man!"

Suddenly, unaccountably, he was very much in charge . . .

Scarcely of my own volition I went to the study wall-safe, took out my father's letter to Clare and tossed it on to the table beside him.

"What's this?" He picked it up.

"Read it. It tells the whole sorry tale."

He read, his expression unchanging; then: "God Almighty," he breathed. "And your parents didn't warn you?"

"Not a word; and they must have seen what was happening, but hoped Jen and David Grey would make a go of it before I got to her."

"The man she married first?"

I nodded. "He was tubercular, and soon died."

"That happened after Iestyn and Clare were drowned?" (He knew of this, too.)

"Soon after. But I've got to be fair. They did their best to keep us apart: Dada sent Jen off to school in Devon; Clare wrote to the headmistress there and stopped my letters."

"Then after their deaths you and Jen got together?"

"Of course. Nothing to stop us; she was a widow."

"And eventually you married?"

"Not the way you mean. Jen's a Romany; she took me to the tribe and we jumped over a broom. Then we set up the caravan and went off to Scotland."

"Why Scotland?"

"Well, I'd bought the Upper Forest Works in Morriston – and my idea was to open up Robert Owen's ideals in Wales – a Workers' Co-operative; and the best way to achieve that was to copy what Owen had done up in Lanarkshire."

"And while up there you fell foul of the Scots!"

"For which we were fined ten bob, Jen and I. But there was more to it than that. Being fined brought us to their attention; look at this." I gave him the letter I had received from the Scottish Office.

"I know," said Jethro, "I've already seen it. And it appears to me that a third party has been feeding the Procurator with further information."

"About the relationship, you mean?" I was amazed.

"Of course. You've been banned from Scotland for something worse than such a minor offence, and somebody had a hand in it."

"I can't think who!"

"Didn't you have some trouble with one of your servants? Dai Dando mentioned something about a butler, but didn't go into detail."

"What – Bill Bumstead? That was donkey's years ago."

"What happened?"

"He stole jewellery from my mother and went to prison, it was really a storm in a tea-cup."

"It might not have been to him. How long did he do?"

"In prison? I forget, I was only a lad at the time."

"Your old Dai remembers thumping him, nevertheless! He told me!"

I laughed. "Yes, Dada was away, and Bumstead went out on the end of Dai's boot. God I'd almost forgotten about that!"

"Where is he now, this Bumstead fella?"

"Still with the Grey family, as far as I know."

"Does your wife have any contact with them now – the Greys?"

"No. After David died she was only too glad to get away from them, Jen said."

He shrugged, empty. "Ah well, there's probably nothing in it, but I'll check out this butler character." He got to his feet with an air of finality, adding, "Vendettas never happen without good reason, and this could be one such, though I doubt it. But there's a reason for every dirty trick, and a counter when a supposed injustice is involved. Leave it to the Pinkertons!"

I answered, "I don't want revenge, tell them. I just want Jen back."

Momentarily we stood together at the front door, listening to the distant thunder of the Valley works. A cock was crowing, I remember, appearing as a symbol out of the night, and we smiled at each other as it crowed again.

Lying in bed in the same attic room of my childhood, I fell into a drowse of approaching sleep; to awaken almost instantly, it seemed, to a faint light blooming on the landing; and saw on a nearby table the personal card Jethro had left. I read the card again:

'Pinkerton Detective Agency
   New York, U.S.A.
   European branches – Glasgow, Cardiff'

It appeared legitimate.

Accepting this, I began to wonder if, since Jethro said he was once a metal-worker, he'd be prepared to drop into Upper Forest Works from time to time and keep an eye on things for me while I went in search of Jen. I hadn't yet replaced Adams, and administratively the place could be going to pot. I decided to ask Jethro to fill in for me briefly.

Although I had denied knowledge of the Pinkertons, I'd learned enough of their strong-arm methods from my father, who had condemned them in the same tones he used for the infamous Molly Maguires, a movement gaining ascendency in the American labour market. Anyone whose contacts

124

included such organisations, I concluded, would have to be suspect; violence being the keynote of their ethics.

It was a dilemma.

A board creaked outside on the landing. It alerted me into readiness; simultaneously, the air was suddenly perfumed; and I was not surprised to see the bedroom door come open.

I was sitting up in bed when Angharad entered.

Here was another, I thought: in terms of trust I might prove unfortunate in my choice of companions these days; certainly I didn't trust this one farther than I could have thrown her, and did not know why.

"You are awake, sir?" she asked.

"I am now."

"Like you, I cannot sleep, and saw the light under your door."

"The moon, Angharad."

"May I come in?"

"You're in already. What do you want?"

Like most mavericks, I am usually available for night visitations from attractive women, and Angharad's beauty would have tempted a saint.

This visit, however, was inopportune, however exotic the situation; and while I have ever been prepared to sacrifice myself upon the altar of womanhood, now was not such an occasion.

"What do you want?" I repeated, and was astonished by my discipline.

"I was wondering, if you might like a cup of tea? Or is there anything else I can do for you?"

She was wearing a simple cotton nightdress, and as she bent above me the divide of her breast was comforting.

I lay there with waves of Angharad's black hair falling in perfume upon me; and saw her eyes shining like opals in her high-boned cheeks.

125

But somewhere out there Jen was alone in the night; and the memory of her was violently opposed to my present erection of mind and body.

"Who told you to come to my room, Angharad?"

"You were alone. Your wife has left you, and . . ."

"Wrong, girl, she has not. Go back to your own bed."

"But the way you look at me . . . ?"

"Wrong again, Angharad." I literally pushed her out of the room.

Jen would have given her something else to go on with. As for me, I sat on the bed after she had gone and wondered if I ought to have my head read.

Missed it by inches.

Women would have claimed that this was because I was in love with Jen, and this is where women go wrong.

Being in love is nothing to do with it. It was a situation which men understand and women do not. The male, it is universally accepted, possesses no conscience; but there are certain limitations.

Conversely (and women, I had noticed are not appraised of this fact) few men like the gift of sex to be presented on a plate and their co-operation taken for granted.

Astonished at my strength of purpose, if not morality, I put my head on to the pillow, and for the first time in weeks slept like a baby, dreaming of Jen.

Chapter Twenty

Now, at last I was going in pursuit.

It was over two months since Jen had left me; I was going to search for her.

That I should have respected her wishes, never occurred to me; nor that perhaps I ought to leave the situation as Fate had planned it.

But what if I found her? Would she reject me for a again?

Nothing could fill the void of emptiness that I was now suffering. Had I been asked – What right have you to try to revive in her a love that had become morally dead . . .? I would have had no answer. More, the fact that we were blood-related, and that a renewal of our love could end in disaster did not occur to me.

I knew only that my life was empty of the sounds of her; that a chasm of nothingness had been created.

Saddling Lark, I brought him round to the entrance of *Cefn-Ydfa* and tethered him.

Angharad was awaiting me in the study as I entered it.

"So, you are going to try to find the Mistress, sir?"

I nodded. "That's the general idea," and opened the bureau where – and it seemed a lifetime ago now – my father wrote his endless letters: it now being necessary for me to write a couple of my own; one to Jethro at the Old Tavern Inn, in town, telling him of my intention to leave that morning and belatedly asking him to call in at Upper

Forest Works from time to time; and another to Mr Opand at my bank, saying it was necessary to fill Gaffer Adams's position.

To have gone to Morriston, surveyed the situation and made the appointment myself would have been sensible, but sense did not enter this particular curriculum. Too much time had been wasted already.

So I wrote the letters, drank the coffee Angharad had prepared for me, and put into a haversack the sandwiches she had wrapped for my journey.

Angharad was charmingly aloof that morning; alluring, she stood nearby as I fired the sealing-wax, saying quietly "You look tired, sir. Did you not sleep well?"

I blew out the candle; the tang of smoke stung my nostrils.

"Actually, I was doing passably well until I awoke to find I had a visitor. Thereafter, sleep was impossible."

She ignored the cynicism. "You are wasting your time going in search of her, you know."

"No, Angharad, you are wasting your time." I went to the door.

"She has been gone for two months. Is that the action of a woman who loves her husband?"

"Believe me, she had good reason!"

"So I understand from gossip, but it would not have deterred me. If I loved a man, I would stay with him, whatever the world said."

"No doubt. But the situation demands sensitivity, and my wife possesses more than her share; perhaps you lack it," and then I wondered what I was doing exchanging such platitudes.

"But she is not your wife, is she, Mr Mortymer?"

I raised my eyes to her face.

"Nor ever will be," she added.

I swung open the door, saying, "Don't let it worry you.

Return to Morriston, arrange with Dai Dando to collect the rest of the furniture here, and continue the role for which I pay you – that of a servant."

To my surprise she was not the least abashed, but smiled at me, one eyebrow slightly raised, as if dealing with a fractious child.

"There, in Upper House at Morriston, I will await your return, sir."

She was standing in the doorway of *Cefn-Ydfa* as I rode off. Turning for one last look at the old pile, I saw her with one arm raised.

That, I comforted myself, was the last I would see of Angharad.

I could not have been more mistaken.

I took the road to the Rhondda Valley, because that was the direction Jen and I had taken when we had earlier left Maesteg on our disastrous journey to Scotland.

I was filled with a heady sense of well-being, for at last I was active. The crisp late October morning seemed in tune with my mood.

I rode until the sun was directly overhead; and Lark, appearing glad to be free of the van, led me confidently to wherever he was going.

To the summit of Cefn Mawr we went, and it surprised me that Jen had presumably chosen such a mountainous route with the caravan in tow; for the roads soon resolved into sheep tracks, and in places almost disappeared; but Lark appeared nonchalant in what I assumed was a pursuit.

We debouched north of Aberdare in the country of Hirwaun.

Darkness found us east of ancient Sarn Helen (and the tracks of the Roman legions) and heading for the Brecon Beacons; here was Lark's pronouncement of his accuracy, for I heard on the mountain wind a gypsy violin playing.

Following the sounds, I came to the high edge of a Romany encampment and a jutting crag that shielded me from eyes. Crouching, I looked down on to the camp-fire activity.

Romanies! Their coloured dresses were bright in the light of the bonfire. Men and women dancing within three red caravans parked in a triangle; and an old man sitting on a box was playing his fiddle to the moon.

Trust Jen, I thought. It was sixth sense to a Romany – they were always able to track the tribe. Doubtless she had preceded me here.

With Lark contentedly grazing, I went down the sheep tracks and into the clearing.

One was safe with Romanies, especially if you acted naturally with a hail-fellow-well-met attitude; formality of any kind being to them anathema; and I thought, standing unseen, that I was privileged to see my girl's people as they had been for thousands of years; realising, too, in the vacuum of Jen's departure, how little I knew of the tribal instincts that possessed her personality, and better understood the roots from which she had sprung.

They derived, Jen had told me, from Northwestern India, and began their tribal journeyings over Asia, northern Africa, Europe and America. These very gypsies I was watching now had peopled the Byzantine Empire in the ninth century, spread over the Balkans before the fourteenth century, and thereafter populated Germany, Italy and France.

Jen had spoken of all this reluctantly; and since the Romany language is influenced by the host country, she had to introduce strange words – the jargons of horse-traders, peddlers and thieves . . .

Vaguely I wondered as I slipped and slid down the hill towards the encampment, now pulling Lark on the rein behind me, if Romanies in their own environment were as civilised and honest as Jen had claimed.

One thing was sure; I would soon find out.

The moon was a silver crescent lying on her back with her harlot's skirt above her knees, watching, as I strolled into the Romany encampment with a confidence I did not feel.

Chapter Twenty-One

The dancing stopped immediately I entered the clearing; the surrounding trees seemed to imitate the statuesque immobility of the dancers. Silence followed like the slam of a coffin lid.

I have heard of kings and queens among gypsies, but it is mainly a fiction, Jen had said; the individual tribes being led by selected Elders.

Such a man approached me now as I stood near the bonfire. Apparently he was a friend of the fiddler, for he patted his head in passing, and came in a crotchety gait, having foregone his youth.

"Aye, stranger!" he cackled. "Are ye come in peace?"

"Ne'er to break a head, Old Man," I answered, and bowed to him.

"Then ye'll be welcome to a bite and sup, but dunna touch up our women or the young fellas'll be after ye."

"Mister," I said, copying his Irish intonation, "I've enough of them wacklers to serve me back home. And I'm arrived following the path of one of 'em. Can ye hear me?"

"Ach, for sure," said he, "for though me eyes are turnin' up to the stars these days, I've ears to hear fleas scratchin' in a wig-sack." He prodded his stick in the earth and regarded me with pouched eyes. "A woman, d'ye mean?"

I nodded, coming closer and with an eye out for the young ones, for Romanies, I'd heard, bred arrogance in their hairy males, with a wish to flatten the nearest stranger in order to impress their sweetheart darlings; and sure enough, one of these, a bull of a man, dropped the hand of his partner, came closer, eyed me, and said, "Ay ay, drink and eat if ye will, but first tell where ye picked up that piebald, for I saw one frantic like him by these vans a month an' a bit ago."

The old man came closer to look me over; his opaque eyeballs rolled in their cataracts and the firelight flushed his walnut skin. "Ay ay, Lija," said he suspiciously, "you'd be right. I may forget a man, but never a pony; how come ye by it?"

I looked around the assembled dancers; the men in their waistcoats of variegated colours and brown leggings; the women, from slim Dianas to busty matrons in voluminous skirts; all still motionless, and their circle about me had narrowed.

"Has ye tongue gone loose?" asked the young man, now beside me.

"The pony's me personal property," I said. "Last time you saw the animal it was pulling a Romany van with a woman on the reins, and goin' north, lest I'm mistaken. But she must have loosed it from her van and sent it home with a slap on the rump; I'm after returnin' the woman to me bed, so I rode it north again."

"A Romany female, did ye say?" asked the Elder, peering, and the people pressed closer about me in the hope of catching a word, for there's no noses longer than a Romany's, said Jen, when bent on another's business.

I nodded.

"Has she a name?"

"Jen Wildflower."

Silence. An October night-bird ceased his twittering; there was no sound but the crackle of the bonfire; then a woman shrieked, coming to the fore, "The Wildflowers of Cymma Creek, and them heaved over to Maesteg, an' no husband – him dead?"

133

"The same," I answered. "I'm husband number two."

Laugher at this; then consternation and excitement; like an Irish Parliament it was now with everybody talking and nobody listening, and the Elder flung his thin, blue-veined hands upward and cried falsetto, "Bless me soul to hell, fella, for I was about to fetch ye one on the jaw for a horse-thief that you're not! Listen and understand." He prodded Lark in the ribs. "I recognised the pony for the one that was pulling her van, but it went lame on the woman, and she bought another and cast this one to graze wi' the tribe till she returns. But it broke its tether and came back home, eh?"

"That's the size of it!" said I.

"Irish, are ye?"

"Welsh."

"Ach well, sure to God we can't have everything, and anyway, Welshmen are only Irishmen who've never learned how to swim." He slapped me on the back and roared with laughter. "Is it now the husband o' that pretty woman that you are?"

"I am, and jumped the broom proper."

"And now she's stitched up ye shirt-tail and left you?"

"So she has!"

"Did ye treat her poorly, then?" asked another, "for she looked a right misery to me, wi' talk of burning her van and wanderin' the roads till her spags were blood and dust." He shoved his young face up against mine till I went Irish, too, with a wish to land him one, and he continued, "Sure, she was a sweet Welsh thing wi' the breath of old Connemara Irish on her cheek, and I'd have given her one meself if she'd worn it. What ails your manhood that you let her get away?"

"My business," I said, and up came another huge gunk of a chap with a face on him like a navvy's arse.

He said, wagging me a finger, "Mind, I'll be the first at ye, if you've harmed her, mun, for you'll have forfeited membership o' the human race. Was I the only man to see

134

the creature's tears, and her wi' a belly on her for a Galway matron?"

The Elder held up a fist for silence, saying, "You've a woman of your own, Cabri, so no sobbin' over the one ye haven't collected, or I'll land you one in the gob. There'll be no violence at all at all against the stranger; folks who come to our fire are guests. Do you realise that the girl was after turning herself into two?"

"In child," I said.

"Seven months, she said." And he paused, eyeing me. "Are you asking where she's gone?"

I nodded.

"Then do ye see that piebald?" and he jerked his head at Lark.

"I do."

"It's brought you this far and done ye fair, mister, for there's a Romany shoe on it, since I checked. Which means that there's an animal's nose on it better'n any man here; so stay the night and eat your fill, then go; ye can follow the van's wheel ruts till ye get to the meadow lands, then give the thing its head.

"Meanwhile, sleep your fill and keep off our women or I'll give ye to the young 'uns in the morning," and saying this, he led me to a caravan outside the ring of the fire, and the bed he indicated had a soft down mattress and hand-made lace on the pillow, which is what Romanies always keep in case of a guest.

I awoke to a morning of sun-glare, with birds going demented about me and the beech woods down in the valley all over golden, and creeping mists making ghosties among the branches like witches.

I was instantly aware, too, of a presence in the tent; so awakened with a fist under the blanket ready for the nearest Romany chin.

But smooth and fair was this chin, and the face above it wreathed with auburn curls, and her name, said she, was Effie Culpepper, and her first sounds told me she was a Cardie Welshie.

"Ay ay, boyo!" and she put a finger to her lips and flapped me into silence.

"What d'ye want with me?" I asked her.

"A bit o'quiet, mun, or the brutal sods of Irish will hit us flat before cock-crow. Welsh, ain't ye?"

"Like a leek."

"Then why do you put on the Irish gab?"

"To save my skin, missus, for there is rowdies around by 'ere, and they anna too fond o' Welshmen."

The girl came closer and squatted on the ground beside me, and her face in that pale morning light was that of a nun. I'd seen the likes of her a dozen times and more down among the Cardigan Romanies, also her voice held the same lilting music.

"It seems you're after a maiden who come in a red van and a puddin' under her apron?"

I nodded. "Aye, for she's me girl."

"About a month or two back?"

"Aye!"

She made a face at a sun-shaft coming in from the flap. "Were she a South Wales Wildflower, and the pony pullin' her the one you're ridin' now?"

"The same."

"Then you'll not get the truth of her from this wild bunch, for they're as thick as fleas for Galway Irish and they'll break the bonces o' decent Welshmen, and not linger 'em among their tribe.

"Which is why they sent the Wildflower woman on her way wi'out so much as a fill o' the belly, the poor wee soul.

"For this lot's on the move, see, and the child your woman carries looks like a seven month blood to me, so I stayed

136

and felt her bag, bein' a Welsh sister, ye understand, tho'
I sound like an Irish; and I reckoned the child needed a
turnin', so I did."

"Are you telling me she's ill?"

"She anna yet, but soon will be, lest ye can hire a better
turning woman. Knowing this, the Irish elders sent her
on, see?"

"Where to?"

"Och, come on, don't look so ghostly! They may not be
Welsh, but still human. 'Take this girl down to the Ossie
Midwife,' said the boss-man, 'but she's gotta have clean
fingers, remember.'" The girl smiled at me. "Irish and tough,
see, but good people when you get to know them. And Ossie
Midwife's the best turnin' woman in Brecon county."

"And did you?" I sat up beside her.

"Did I what?"

"Did you take her to the midwife?"

"Ay ay – to Struet Cottage in Brecon town."

"When was that?"

"I jist bloody told ye, Mister. About eight weeks back."

"Might she have had the baby by now?"

"Depends, but more'n likely."

"What's your name?"

"I just told ye that, too – Effie Culpepper."

"Effie," I said. "Can you take me to her? For she's my
woman and the baby's mine and I want to take it to a
minister and have it baptised. You say you turned the baby
for her?"

"I did, but likely it's turned back again by now: some
Romanies stand high in the womb."

"You'll take me to her?"

"It depends."

"On what?"

"On who ye are, mister. What's your name?"

"Tom Mortymer."

137

She drew herself up, thin in her sack dress and pulled in the top as if I was halfway down it. Such was the effect upon her that I could have bitten off my tongue, for she rose, staring down and saying softly, "If you're a Mortymer I've said too much already, mister, for you're the last bugger in the world she wants to see!"

And she pulled back the tent flap and was through it, running like a hare towards the broken dawn. And then she went Irish on me, shouting back, "Bad cess, *bad cess to ye*! She told me all about you, you big, fornicatin' bastard! Your own sister, is it? *Your own sister?*" and fetching up stones at her feet, showered me with them till I snatched at Lark's rein and went hell for leather with him in tow until I was clear of the encampment.

Jesus! It took me five hours and a quart of black coffee to get me sober.

Chapter Twenty-Two

Two days later found me on the outskirts of Brecon town and Lark taking his time among the rocky outcrops of the lovely wild places. Though my pace was leisurely, there was building in me a surging excitement at the prospect of finding my girl; though how she may receive me was doubtful by the sound of it.

And I was as drunk as a coot.

Here, sitting by the road verge that led to the town, was a tramp. A merry smile had he and a pair of tin ears that would have been the envy of Dai Dando and sitting upon them was a face as battered as its owner, and he shouted soprano, "T'is fighting around the September fairs I am, me darlin'! From one to the other I goes at a guinea a time for the love of it, understand?"

"No," I answered, dismounting unsteadily from Lark, who went off to tear at the grass. "I've had enough bloody fighting to last me a lifetime."

"Is it a titty-dancer ye are then, me son?" and the tramp rose and took a fighting stance, "for I'm trimming the chops of any fella who fancies his chance with Dai Swipo!"

"Not a titty-man, either, mister," said I. "With you knocking sixty and me half your age, I'll land you one that'll send you back to County Cork. I'm not after bother."

"Ach, for sure, me love, you're a chap after me own heart, so ye are! But the years are knockin' on, like you say, and I hoped you was an easy touch, see? Where're ye bound?"

"Senny town."

"And you're after a woman, they say!"

"You're a mind-reader, Irishman."

"And you hope to find her in Brecon town?" he asked.

"God willing."

"God don't come into it, me lad – not where women are concerned, for they're the spawn o' the Devil. T'is women, ye see, who have landed me in the mess I am now. A pair of tits and it's bonkers for Dai Swipo, though I'm a leg man mainly speaking, mainly above the knee. Napoleon were the same, they tell me, but his woman put the knockers on him. . .

"You ever kept pigeons?"

"No."

"Then you've never lived, son! A loft full of racing pigeons and a woman upstairs in the feathers is all a man needs in life, except for a bowl o' Irish stew, take it from Swipo." He laid back on the road verge with his broken boots cocked up, the stub of a clay pipe sticking out of his bearded mouth and his face a bunch of laughs. "Ay ay, me darlin', ye realise, do ye not, that pigeons and butterflies have a big thing in common?"

"Never given it a thought."

"O aye!" He struck a match and puffed out smoke from purpling lips, then made a queer whistling sound; and to my amazement a white butterfly as big as a baby's hand, flopped out of the sun and settled upon his waistcoat. Even Lark, grazing nearby, raised a head to peer at him; animals having great interest in the paranormal, as is not widely known.

"Now take this species," said the tramp. "He's a *Nudaureta* from South Africa, and over here by magic – to make my point about pigeons and butterflies. And if I raise a hand and snap me fingers like this, his big sister arrives . . ." and another butterfly flapped out of the sun and perched upon his hand.

"The *Gynauisa maia*, don't ye see 'im, but he ain't really

there, mister, as you'll be the first to understand, since it's a long, long way from Africa!" Grinning with a rhubarb mouth he took a breath, adding, "Now you're a gent and I'm a tramp, see, so intellectually there's bound to be differences between us.

"But 'ave you ever stopped to think that women are like butterflies? Even ugly ones 'ave got a soul that the male o' the species don't understand? Have you ever stopped to consider, for a start, that we got fancy buggers like Leonardo da Vinci and suchlike waggin' fingers about their bloody genius, yet not one of 'em can fashion a baby's fingernail? – yet the meanest whore can turn out a sprog at the wink of a sailor's eye! And beautiful, mind, just like a butterfly!" He brushed two more off his waistcoat, shouting, "Go on, bugger orf, the pair of ye," and he spat. "For I'm telling you this, lad, when it comes to the human race ye can forget about men; like the old Molly Maguires say: 'Woman, the Mother of God, shall never be violated, as Irishmen we stay pure to the edicts of God Almighty'. Which is why I travel the valleys knocking hell outta men, while bowing at the feet of every woman who crosses me path!"

His hypocrisy was evident.

"Yes," I said, "after you've been to bed with them." I added, "You stink, man, I can smell you from here."

"Not true. I put women on a pedestal."

"Only so you can see their bloody legs."

At which he knocked off his bowler hat and bawled with laughter, crying falsetto, "Women and birds! There's little to choose between them, pigeons especially – if you're a fancier for one you've got a fancy for the other!

"Shall I tell ye some'ut that made me a path to a fortune?

"I was racing pigeons all over the country, see, but losing twenty per cent to hawks, until I noticed somethin' in Nature that came different; and it were to do wi' butterflies.

141

"Dozing in me garden one day I saw that while birds swooped on insects with plain wings and gobbled 'em up, a butterfly with eyes on its wings didn't attract their attention.

"So I thought, 'Dai Swipo, me lovely, if ye paint eyes on the wings of your pigeons it'll cut down your losses.' So I collected up me birds and painted two black eyes on every wing – four eyes to a pigeon, and I never lost a racer to a curved beak thereafter; ain't that bloody marvellous?"

"Ay ay," said I, "and you're a marvellous bloody liar." Which set him off again, rocking with laughter.

In fact, it was the truth, for years later, speaking to Dai Dando, I said, "You keep losing your racing pigeons to hawks and kestrels, you say? That's easy – try painting false eyes on their wings and see what happens – it's an old liar's tale, but it's supposed to keep predators away . . ." and damn me, he raced those pigeons for years after and never lost a bird. Which goes to show that you can't take every tall yarn with a grain of salt.

"You still don't believe it?" I asked Dai later.

"Of course not, Maister – it's a coincidence, that ole tramp was pullin' your leg."

"Not so," I answered. "Look it up in an insect book and you'll find that two South African species of butterflies have eyes on their wings. The *Gynanisa maia* and *Naururetta Zaddachii* never attract predators."

I never expected to see that old fighter-tramp again, but you never can tell with a male witch, for that's what he was for certain. You don't have to travel to Transylvania to come across the paranormal; you can discover it through travelling innocently in search of your wife outside the town of Sennybridge.

This I knew for sure when the old sod shouted after me,

"That woman you're chasin', Welshman – would she be named after a flower and full to the breech wi' childer?"

Although it took my breath, I did not reply to this, but reined Lark into a faster trot, and the old reprobate bawled then, "No hurry, me darlin', no hurry at all, at all; the girl's empty in the belly already, the sweet thing, and the poor mite is half-born. And a son an' all, would ye believe it – your heart's desire, eh? Which shows ye what happens when ye go to bed wi' your sister!" He laid back again shouting and kicking his legs in the air. "Meanwhile go to Number Seven, The Struet. Old Nick, me Master, tells me so, and ask for Primrose, though you'll be lucky to get her through the door, for the woman's beef to the heels . . ."

I saw him through tears, knowing this to be a Purgatory of my own making, and that I was in the company of sorcerers: learning from an apostle of the Devil that my son was lost to me.

As I galloped away I looked back, but the road was empty. Nothing was there but the green sward where the Thing had lain, and the empty road that led over the hills to Brecon.

But then I heard a voice that seemed to come from the earth beneath me, and the voice cried shrilly, "Give 'er one for me, Tom Mortymer – give 'er one for me! Meanwhile, what you need is a drink, my son, for you're a ten pint fella if ever I saw one – call in at the next public, me darlin', and we'll wet the baby's head!"

What with one thing and another, and my half-sister turning my mind, I was as stoned as a crow before I got to Brecon, and had to sleep it off.

Chapter Twenty-Three

Night shadows were falling by the time I reined in Lark outside Number Seven, The Struet, in Brecon town and they can write all they like about the Fourth Crusade which brought the foreign lands to ruin.

The Crusaders who looted Constantinople's gold in 1204, and carried off its works of art to St Marks in Venice, had got nothing on the plundering Normans who gave poor old Brecon a going over before the coming of the English horde: yet still she stood, this noble old town, with two fingers up to the foreign aristocracy who had built an English barracks upon her holy soil. And as I tethered Lark to a pony-post in The Struet, I gave a thought to the clash of alien swords and the River Tarell which once ran red with our Celtic blood.

I had raised a hand for a knock on the door of Ossie Primrose, the midwife, when the thing came open and a corpse came out feet first; carried by top-hatted funeral bearers and followed by wailing relatives, it came, its retinue sniffling and wiping, the only dry one being the corpse, which was of a young girl with a winter rose in her hand.

Respectfully I stood back, hat in hand as the cortége passed me, and last of all came Ossie Midwife, whose Christian name was Primrose, and never in my life have I seen one less like a spring flower. Drunk as me was she as well, patting her bosom with purps and pardons; her sack dress was stained all down the front with dinner, and the smell of her gin set me back a yard.

"Thank you kindly, my duck," said she with an unsteady curtsey. "Kindly bring ye lady in and I'll see to her directly." She nodded at the corpse. "I 'ave to take 'em in rotation, you understand? First in, first out is the rule o' the establishment." She slammed the door behind the mourners.

"Am I addressing Primrose, the Brecon midwife?" I inquired within.

"At ye service, sir, so cross me palm wi' silver for a start, for all fees are paid in advance, you understand? Ladies in the family way being buggers for sharp departures – a 'usband in a Hanson cab and the sods are off."

I said, "There's no lady accompanying me. I am here to inquire about one."

"Well, I never did – there's a turn up! Have a little tot o' gin wi' Primrose, son, for you're a likely young fella if ever I saw one." She winked a baggy eye. "What's more, if you're the man I take ye for, you can call me Prim." She slapped me on the back, slopped gin into two glasses and offered me one. "Life's all ups and downs, me lovely, ain't it? And when I clap eyes on a fruity chap I do make the most of it. Single, are ye?"

"Ossie Primrose," I said to cool her. "You're the loveliest woman I've set eyes on this side of Christendom, and we'll come to an agreement between now and the morning. But first answer this question. Did a lady named Wildflower call here recently and ask you to assist in the birth of her child?"

Primrose bulged her baggy eyes with recollection and emptied her gin at a swallow. "Well now, your worship, I gotta think, for I'm so much in demand that they come and go like shellin' peas. Wildflower did ye say?"

"Yes, yes!"

"A little elf o'a thing who looked like a tinker-girl?"

"That's her – a Romany!"

"Did she walk a piebald pony?"

"Exactly! The horse outside!" I was stupidly eager, being unversed in the ways of Primrose. "Did you birth her baby?"

She scratched her blowsy face, and I saw behind the plastered paint and powder, the woman she might have been before her death by men; and she moved away from me and crossed the floor of the jumbled room with its double bed and tables laden with medicine bottles, then turned with a broken smile, and said, "Maybe so and maybe not, me son, but either way it's goin' to cost ye. Five guineas." I paid it into her grimy hand.

"Would she have called in her labourin' the name of Tom?" she asked.

I nodded.

"And babbled about an island out in the sea, wi' seagulls and rabbits and suchlike scampering?"

I saw her through a glaze of unshed tears, and nodded assent.

"Then it'll cost ye again, me lovely, for she cost me. I turned the babby twice and sent for the surgeon – he's the butcher on the Friday Shambles, ye know, but this were a Sunday and he charged me overtime. He be a sod, that Rhys Evans, but he did her no good; brought it out in bits an' pieces."

She raised her face with an angelic smile, adding, "Pity, too, for it were a boy . . ."

I drank gin with Primrose because in some measure she had served Jenny, but could not see her for tears.

Out on the doorstep, she said, "I 'ad her for five days – that Rhys do come hard on miscarriages. But she walked out on her own, mind you, not like the poor soul ye saw going to Church; and paid me fair, like you done. Money weren't a bother to her; straight outta 'ere she goes, and books herself in at the Wellington . . ."

I was not surprised. At another time, in another life it

seemed, we had stayed at the Wellington Hotel on our journey to New Lanarkshire.

Primrose added, "A Romany, perhaps, but a'spendin' gentry money?" She peered at me in the light of the street lamps. "What's she to you, anyway?"

"She is my wife."

"O aye? That's queer! I asked her about that, for she was wearing a bridal-ring. But she came all over huffy wi' me, and said she weren't married to anyone."

The October night was cold with him and rain was sweeping the streets of Brecon, with a few vagrants huddled in dark corners of the town. Pallid children pestered me for alms outside the Wellington, which was just across the way from the midwife's place.

This was a coaching-house serving routes to West Wales to as far down as Pembroke, north to Holyhead on the Roman Road, east to London and via Bristol to Penzance. I hurried Lark through sheeting rain and ran through the coachway arch in hope of finding Jen's caravan on the stable cobbles, but found my hopes to be forlorn; according to Primrose, Jen had been gone for over a week. Yet, even as I fruitlessly searched the Wellington stables, there was within me an excitement at her growing nearness: every footstep seemed to ensure our eventual meeting.

That my pursuit would end thus was as certain to me as the sun would rise next morning: but how would I be received?

From what I had heard to date she might very likely send me about my business. This thought chilled me as I reached the Wellington reception desk, where sat a sleepy clerk. I asked, "Have you had a lady named Wildflower staying in your rooms recently?"

He studied his register with planned indifference.

"Wake up, damn you!" It jumped him into life, his finger tracing down the pages.

"Miss Wildflower, sir? Stayed two nights."

"When?"

"Twenty-third and twenty-fourth of this month."

"She arrived in a caravan, did she not?" Somewhere in the building a chiming clock struck eleven.

"Don't know, sir."

I glared at him. I was weary, disappointed and sick with the knowledge of the death of my son.

"What room have you got for me?"

"Number Ten, sir; first floor, sir."

His strangely liquid eyes, his spotty complexion reeked of his adolescence; unaccountably, I hated him.

"Come on, man! Come on!"

"Number Two, sir. She . . . weren't well, so the manager put her on the first floor."

"I want that room. Please arrange it."

"There's a gentleman due in it, sir. He's booking in from the London coach at dawn."

"Put him in Room Ten – the one you were going to give to me."

"I . . . I dursn't, sir."

I put five sovereigns on his desk and picked up my bag. "Take this up to Room Two; also a bottle of whisky."

"Yes, sir."

Normal human beings who claim to elemental decency can, when disturbed, be absolute bastards, and I was one.

A little later, before midnight, I was dozing between sleep and wakefulness, having adopted my usual position of sleeping between Jenny and the door. Now needing her nearness, I slid over to what would have been her side of the bed, and lay there within imagination's joy.

A footstep on the road outside brought me to awareness; getting out of the bed, I went to the latticed window, looking down.

148

A man was standing on the cobbles below, staring up at me.

In a flash of the moon I saw his face momentarily, but quite clearly, and the face I saw was mine; the cheeks running with tears.

I stared down at the man below; he stared up at me; and to my further amazement, put his hands over his face and began to sob.

With shoulders shaking, he sobbed, raising his wet face to mine.

There came to me then a poem out of my childhood:

'Still is the night, by darkness overtaken, this hour my darling's presence did grace: tho' she the town has long forsaken, here stands the house in the self-same place. And here stands a man, who upwards is staring, his hands hard-wringing, in, out, bursts of woe. I shudder; his form with mine comparing, the moon to me doth my own features show! You pale companion, you counterfeit fellow, why act this hideous pantomime? Why ape the pangs that here I suffered, so many a night in former time?'

When, a few moments later, I lowered my hands from my face, the vision had gone.

I have read of *doppelgangers* but have seen but one; a grief so indelible that it can be conjured out of the soul.

"*Gawd!* What a bloody awful state you've got yourself into, ye drunken fool!" said Paddy Infernal, and his face then on my pillow was an inch from mine.

Chapter Twenty-Four

I decided to make Brecon my first staging point. Jenny's enforced convalescence at Primrose's and the Wellington Hotel having shortened the delay.

Being also concerned with Jethro's handling of the Upper Forest management, and how he was settling into the new house at Morriston, I decided to inquire into this as well, for Old Bid could be a tricky old girl when it came to strangers. There was also the presence of Angharad, with whom my uncle's undoubted virility might prove a complication . . .

Therefore after breakfast next morning, I sat in the Wellington and wrote:

'To: The Manager, Upper Forest Works
Morriston, Near Swansea, Glamorgan.
Please report management and domestic situation to me at Wellington Hotel, Brecon. Will be here until October 28th. Tom Mortymer.'

Taking this message to the Lion Street post office, I sent it by telegraph to Jethro.

Giving him my whereabouts was necessary because I had promised to tell him my movements if he, in turn, would report his taking over at Upper Forest: it being essential to keep a hand upon my financial affairs in future.

Not that I distrusted Jethro; but nurtured suspicions of anyone after the Gaffer Adams débacle.

150

Pursuit of Jenny had brought me fear of the present and uncertainty about the future. Minute and inconsequential day-to-day happenings were beginning to assume the proportions of great obstacles. Where earlier I had been able to laugh away minor mishaps, each now built within me an unusual sense of adversity. It was paranoia fed by self-inflicted loathing; a sudden realisation of my sin against social ethics. I had lain with my half-sister, a relationship condemned by God.

In recognition of this, Jen had left me with terrifying finality and begged me not to follow her; yet here I was in pursuit of her with nothing but a pledge to continue the affair should I succeed in persuading her to return to me.

To what end should I continue such a fruitless journey? I asked myself.

Yet hope, who makes a restless bedfellow but a happy breakfast, always managed to rise anew at memories of Jen. No sanction, public or private, diluted the longing to have her in my arms.

Next morning I received from Jethro a reply to my telegraph. Noticeably he didn't append his name; though it was marked 'Poste-Restante' it required me to pick it up at the Lion Street post office; the message read:

'To: Mr Tom Mortymer,
    Have settled into Upper Works management; home orders static. Exports high. Angharad taken over running of Morriston House; all going smoothly. You claimed no enemies; Dai Dando appraised me of an important one whom I am investigating. Will report.
    Manager, Upper Works
    Morriston, Glamorgan

So all was going on well without me. The important point – that of having an enemy, did not occur to me,

151

until I remembered the night years ago when old Dai had booted Bumstead, the butler, out of the *Cefn-Ydfa* for his presence in my mother's bedroom. This incident had done more than anything to ensure her return to Afghanistan and move my father into the arms of Clare, Jenny's mother.

Indeed, since the two of them then lost their lives in an accident abroad, my mother's betrayal of her marriage was probably the fulcrum of our subsequent troubles, and Bumstead's sentence to penal servitude for theft.

Bumstead, returning to Wales after his sentence, had then been employed by David Grey (Jen's father-in-law) and as far as I knew was still with him, and it seemed improbable to me that the butler, now so comfortably settled, would nurture a supposed injustice for over fifteen years and prove responsible for our succession of disasters. One could take crime detection a little too seriously, I thought, including Jethro's Pinkerton Detective Agency.

So Dai Dando's equal suspicions of poor old Bill Bumstead, once our own butler, appeared ludicrous.

More worrying to me was Angharad's sudden elevation to the running of Morriston House, until now palpably Old Bid's preserve.

What happened next, however, relegated such worries into minor importance.

The reception clerk at the Wellington Hotel, clearly after a tip, was in no way a simpleton. Next morning his dowdy mood of indifference had changed to one of ingratiating smiles.

"Good-mornin', sir!"

I gave him a nod.

"Did ye sleep well, sir?"

"Badly."

His small, cockney face perked up. "Got a lot on ye mind, 'ave ye, sir, like most business gentlemen?"

I eyed him. Clearly he had something under his high-buttoned morning coat that was about to come out. He then proceeded to scratch away at a large brass-bound ledger while I awaited his pleasure. Glancing up, he gave me a gummy smile. "Yes, sir?"

"What have you to tell me?"

He peered around the hall, saying secretly, "While you was out, a lady called, sir."

"Really!"

"And asked for you, sir."

"Whom?" I asked huskily.

"Well . . ."

I got him by the front of his coat and shook him to rattle his bones. "Her name – quickly!"

"What's it worth?"

"My God," I whispered, and walked him round his desk to face me. "Her name! Instantly!"

He paled before my wrath. "Well, it were old Primrose. You was lookin' for a lady, she said, and she has only just remembered . . ."

"Remembered what?"

"She's got information, sir." He sagged in my grip.

"What information?"

"Gi' us a sovereign, sir, and I'll take it round to her . . ."

Pushing him away, I strode out into winter sunlight.

Back at Seven Cottage, The Struet, I hammered the door. A window creaked open above me and the grimy face of Primrose appeared.

"Well, Mr Mortymer! You're welcome to come up, mind . . . !"

"I understand you have something to tell me."

"'ave I?" She was nonplussed. "Who says so?"

"That obnoxious clerk at the Wellington!"

153

"How much?" I called up to her.

"How much for what, kind sir?" She smiled with a rhubarb mouth.

"If you have information about Miss Wildflower, I want it now."

"'ow about five sovereigns, your honour?"

Out of the window a little leather bag descended on the end of a string. "Live and let live, sir, innit?"

I seized the bag. "If the information's worth it. If not I'm coming up there!"

"No violence, darlin', or I'll call the Peelers!"

I counted five sovereigns into the bag. It sailed up and the face peered down again, saying, "Goin' off to Frenchie parts, she said in her ravings. Had enough o' Wales to last 'er a lifetime, she said, an' what's more, she were goin' to burn that bloody old caravan – she could use the language, mind – you ever heard a Romany in labour?"

"Anything else?" I shouted up, now being barged about by pavement crowds.

"Nothin' more, mister, now piss orf! No, wait, sir *wait*!" and Primrose bawled down to me, "She burned her van on the Redcoat road, and was then booking on the next stagecoach to Dover."

At the risk of catching something, I could have climbed up and kissed her.

"Why didn't you tell me Miss Wildflower was going to Merthyr for the coach to Dover?" I demanded of the Wellington clerk.

"Ye didn't ask, did ye?"

I shouted. "You must have boarded her luggage. Did she have labels on her cases?"

He scratched his ear.

"What was her destination, man?"

"Paris, it said on the baggage."

Her wanderings over, Jen was returning to the Rue de Stinkerque and our attic where lace curtains, fringing the windows, looked out on to the higgledy-piggledy roofs of Montmartre.

Chapter Twenty-Five

I rode Lark out of the Wellington Hotel stables in sunlight, for the November morning was brisk and fine. We wriggled our way through market crowds and over the Usk Bridge to the junction of the Merthyr-Llandovery road.

Here a prize-fight had just begun, which, against the law, was being held beyond town boundaries, and a crowd was assembling composed of community toughs with bent noses and cauliflower ears, with gentry toffs following in gigs and landaus.

Perfumed and top-hatted at that time of the morning, these gents had gathered for the final bout, a *piéce de resistance* after a night of debauchery in local taverns. Upon their arms walked the prized harlots of the neighbourhood from bouncy tap-maids to flouncily-dressed ladies; most with their noses high enough to drown in a rainstorm, but available at a guinea a time; the clientele of what was called the Noble Art.

This was Breconshire in the 1880s, a sad tapestry of rich and poor, where the slam of a door could mean starvation while high-flight financiers of the old slave plantations lolligated in luxury.

The contestants' blood was beginning to flow as I trotted Lark around the perimeter of the baying crowd, for lust was in the spectators now; their wine-flushed faces sweating with blood-fest as one gigantic man beat another into a battered hulk.

The crowd was lowing like cattle at an empty manger as

I reined Lark along the ancient Redcoat road leading to Merthyr Tydfil, the Town of the Saint.

A word about this town; bigger and wealthier than Andrew Carnegie's Pittsburgh at the time, it was to be the greatest steel-making centre known to Man.

Ruled over by the Crawshay Dynasty, a succession of family ironmasters right through the Industrial Revolution, it sent its products to the ports of the world: engine parts to Egypt, steam locomotives to the Sudan and India, railway lines to the Argentine and giant engineering enterprises to the Continent. Its workforce numbering tens of thousands, it embraced every trade imaginable; and from the moment the Dynasty had cast its shoe over Wales, there began a migration of peasants and workers from the towns of Britain under the banner of the cry, "*Merthyr, Merthyr!*"

The immigrants poured into the new metropolis whose streets, the starving claimed, were paved with gold.

Seeing the glint of quick profits, the ironmasters cornered them, flinging up row after row of terraced cottages with neither water nor sanitation for workers prepared to work for a bag of potatoes.

Ireland's Great Hungers of the 1840s being followed by plagues of potato blight, caused bottomless coffins to bury a generation; and Merthyr, from the Crawshays at Cyfarthfa to the Guests of Dowlais waxed fat within a famished community. Industrial disputes arose, fanning the flames of earlier disputes, such as the *Bread or Blood* riots of an earlier decade, which culminated in the hanging of the innocent Dic Penderyn.

The man who today lies in Vaynor churchyard, Robert Thomson Crawshay, with 'God Forgive Me' on his grave is testimony to the avarice of industrialists who sucked the lifeblood out of an army of peasants.

The dirt track road upon which I rode now, was a secondary access up the Brecon Beacons leading to the iron town.

Originally, the only road ascending from Brecon, it was now used exclusively by Brecon Garrison for putting down local disturbances linked with iron and coal production in times of trouble.

Often it was jammed with military reinforcements rushed to Merthyr by a nervous English government that feared Merthyr might prove the tinder spark of the labouring classes.

This eventually occurred in the outbreak of the Chartist Rebellion.

Now all was quiet under an early winter sun, and I began to wonder why Jen should have chosen such a location for the destruction of her caravan, the legendary final act in the demise of a Romany in expectation of a better life.

Swallows were assembling for migratory flight, swooping about me in clusters, and collecting in chattering groups in wayside gorse where the late autumn crocus (never to be confused with meadow saffron) were doing their best to survive the onset of the cold; and to my joy I noticed perching on a bough a red-necked phalarope, one of my favourite waders, resting on his way to his breeding ground in Scotland!

All Nature seemed to be alive on that solitary ride in search of the remains of Jen's caravan, and I thought it sad that during one of the earth's loveliest seasons, we should be apart while the rest of winter's world was preparing for a new and generous spring.

In a lonely lay-by, one constructed to prevent vehicle congestion in the mountain ascent, I discovered what was left of Jen's caravan; a dark pile of wood ashes from which sprang hooped iron and the remnants of burned wheels.

Dismounting, I walked around it, recognising items that leaped out of my boyhood: a melted brooch I had once seen Clare Wildflower wearing; broken pottery, knives, forks.

Kneeling I picked out of the ashes a baby's spoon, vaguely wondering if it had been used by Jen in childhood . . .

To my astonishment, deeper parts of the ashes were still warm; proof that the fire had been active recently.

Suddenly knowing a biting loneliness, I looked down into the valley. Beech trees laid a carpet of copper hue for as far as I could see, a glorious autumnal foliage, that ended in a sea of conifers with their regimental fire-gaps.

I remembered ancient Tretower, where the villagers that had laid out such forests, interspersing oaks with such meticulous care with seedlings that they later grew rank on rank on the hillsides, into a design depicting the French and British infantry, the cavalry lines of the Battle of Waterloo.

Nostalgically, I recalled the old cider house on the Abergavenny road where one could become tipsy on a jug of home-made scrumpy, and as drunk as a lord on two . . . With this sudden evocation, a catharsis close to tears, a new emotion contained me, one of unmeasured joy, and I could have shouted aloud at its recognition – that in the dead ashes of Jen's caravan lay the renewed spirit of a return to love; and a knowledge that out of the phenomenon of the flames would arise a new understanding between us.

Soon, I thought, she would be in my arms again. No doubts assailed this sudden chemistry of change; it was unsullied by threats of blood relationship and public scandal, and it needed a toast to celebrate its existence.

Therefore, I took my new gin-flask from my hip pocket and tipped it high, gasping to the sting of it, slobbering within its hot bite to my throat. I drank, allowing the scalding gin to run down my face and soak my shirt; and when the flask was finished, fighting for breath and feeling reborn in heady swims of the gin, I turned and faced the valley. With a fist raised high, shouting with exultation, I leaped into Lark's saddle and spurred him hard along the road that led to Merthyr.

Chapter Twenty-Six

At the bottom of the valley, not far from the junction of the Brecon to Merthyr road, was sitting Dai Swipo, the tramp I believed to be a witch; and had I been told he had dropped out of the sky on a spider's thread, I would have believed it.

"Good-day to ye again, me foine young fella!" said he, and pushed his bowler to a tilted angle. "Is it still chasn' after that sister o' yours ye are? And her half-birthin' ye childer?"

"She is not my sister!" I replied.

"Is that a fact?" he winked. "Tell that to the Peelers, me son, for if ye land north o' the Scottish border ye'll dangle on the end of a rope for it; they've never repealed the death sentence for incest, ye know!" He lay back in the grass, shouted laughter and spluttered.

"Ach now, me darlin', forgive an old coot for takin' the piss outta the rising generation, for it's a sad, sad state you're in, and me heart bleeds for ye, so it does! Did she lose her son, like I said?"

I nodded, hating him, yet forced to stay by some hypnotic influence, and he added, eyeing me from his grizzled face, "So she's away to foreign parts now, is she?"

"How did you know?" I eyed him.

"Aye, well now, t'is a terrible question, that, for it involves the human state wi' all kinds of weirdies and ghosties, to say nothin' o' the *tylwyth teg*, the Welsh hobgoblin lot. Can we just say, ye lordship, that when fella humans like you come to the end o' their tether and there's nowt left but cuttin' a throat, they finish in the hands o' the wizards and sorcerers, and there's no end to the demonology we get up to, be God!"

The wind ruffled a feather on his hat and there came to me a stink of his decay, where earlier had been the scents of November.

Vaguely I wondered if he was a living corpse.

"A witch, are you?" I was still in the saddle, looking down at him, and sensed Lark's unease, for he was showing the whites of his eyes as I reined him in.

The tramp said, "Well now, me lovely, a witch would be too hard a term for one blessed by the Devil wi' the unholy powers of divinity. And while it's true that if ye wave a crucifix I'll likely disappear in a puff o' smoke, it's best to keep on the right side o' Paddy Infernal, as I'm known back home; and the way to do that is to cross me palm with gold or silver, though it tortures ye!"

"You're like the rest of the voodoos," I said, "Fee-faw-fum palaver, and I don't believe any of it." I made to spur Lark away.

"Now, is that a fact?" The tramp got up and came to the saddle and held on to it, breathing raw gin all over me. "Sure to God, I'd rather 'ave a disbeliever sayin' so than a snivellin' weaklin' doin' it behind me back, so I'll give ye a chance to redeem your luck, son. For ye can have an incantation that'll drop that horse dead in its tracks, or a pastoral preferment that will lift your soul from its load o' troubles – but at a price!"

I smiled down at him. "I thought so."

"Ay ay, ye can have me prelate's blessing free, and sell your soul to me Master, who is a friend o' the banshees; or you can cross me palm with sovereigns and make your way to the bosom of she whom you call wife, wi' no interference from the Devil, though I canna say the same for God." Here he crossed himself, his bald eyes darting around.

161

"And if I don't?"

"If he don't, me son, then Satan help ye for the only hope ye've got to date is to sell your soul to me . . ." and I saw through his shattered face the distant spires of Brecon, and knew that the face before me was not a face at all, but the mask of one who was not really there. This, the second vision to come my way, the first being the *doppelganger*.

He continued, "Take note. That pimply clerk in the Wellington lied to ye, son. If your sweetheart raved about takin' a trip on the Paris stagecoach, that was in her delirium, for neither came to pass so far. Are ye listening, or have your ears gone loose?"

I nodded.

"For the truth of it is that having burned her van in Romany style, she fainted on the roadside until a gent and his harpie came by and loaded her and her luggage on to his carriage . . ." With which he made a queer little whistling sound at the sky, adding, "and the three of 'em took off for the town of Merthyr."

I eyed him. "Is this the truth?"

"God in heaven, would I lie to you? May fleas infest me balls should I ever break faith wi' such a marvellous fella, for it's backed by the personal integrity of Dai Swipo, otherwise known in the nether regions as a Paddy Infernal, like I said." He slapped his thigh and bellowed laughter, adding, "Try the Star Inn where Nelson roughed up the feathers with Lady Hamilton."

I shouted, "If you're lying to me I'll return and have the tabs off you!"

"Then take it, or leave it, ye son of a bitch. Dear me! Of all the disbelievin' sods in the County o' Breconshire, me Master loads me wi'you! Bad cess to ye, Mortymer! It's enough to make a fella take a vow of chastity." He made a strange lamenting sound. "Go, *go*! It's the truth I'm tellin' ye, for honesty is the best policy so long as it pays. *Away!*" and he fetched Lark a clump on his rear to make his hair curl, and we were away at a gallop up the road to Merthyr, but when I glanced back, the road was empty.

God help me: he even knew my name.

Were all who unknowingly committed incest condemned to become the property of Paddy Infernal? I wondered.

"Have another swig o' that flask, ye sweet thing," whispered a voice in my ear, "for sure to God, now you've sold your soul to Beelzebub's Brew, you're goin' to bloody need it."

Chapter Twenty-Seven

The trouble with the paranormal is that when you've made a witch of your conscience and manufactured a devil, you have to watch your step.

So far, without the help of Divine Intervention, I had managed to follow Jen's flight by assistance from a Romany tribe; also Effie Culpepper had helped me, as had Primrose and the Wellington hated clerk, if under duress.

But now, having bought information off a pupil of His Satanic Majesty, I had scraped the bottom of the barrel, and would doubtless pay a price. Still, I comforted myself, having sold my soul, I might as well be killed for a sheep as for a lamb.

Therefore I followed the fiend's instructions to the letter, which brought me to the Star Inn at Merthyr Tydfil.

I had been to this inn before; it had been one of our watering holes when Jen and I had gone to the Romanies, jumped the broom in marriage (properly sanctified by respected Elders) and begun our wanderings north to Robert Owen's country in Lanarkshire.

It was becoming apparent, by some strange chance, that Jen was now following the exact route which under happier circumstances we had taken before.

A Redcoat troop from Brecon Barracks were drinking within the Public, and I gave a thought now to their bravery during their recent defeat at Majuba Hill by the Boers.

Earlier they had suppressed the power of Cetawayo, the

ferocious Zulu king, and dispersed his army of forty thousand Zulus, winning a succession of Victoria Crosses, there being no more fearful a warrior than a Welshman when he's got his dander up. I, alas, was a very unworthy brother.

Merthyr Tydfil seemed to have got her dander up as well, for the drop-hammers of Cyfarthfa were going like marrow-bones and cleavers, and the Big Wheel was whining like the pit of Hell.

I was directed to the town not by signposts, but by flame-shot clouds mushrooming skywards and I remembered the words of a contemporary writer:

'This was the Crawshay empire where iron bubbles into a thousand moulds: sweat pours here, ale is taken by the gallon, men die in mutilation, children are old at ten: eyes are put out here, sleeves tied with string: the turrets of Cyfarthfa Castle are stark black against the glow, its windows glinting defiance to challenge: hands are cut off here, trouser-legs emptied . . .'

An urchin I came across in Castle Square; a cheeky little face had he, his snub nose cocked up, and it hadn't had a blow for a fortnight.

"Hey up," I called, "can you tell me the way to the Star Inn?"

"Go and ask ye grandpa." Which was as good as one might expect from such a place.

So I entered the Castle hotel where brandy-sniffing toffs were gathered in the hall, and half a dozen chaise and gigs tethered outside.

An Irish serving-maid greeted me with a marvellous curtsey and a first-rate view of the Mountains of Mourne, which is bad for the constitution of a drunk at that time of the morning . . . and up she got bright and rosy-cheeked.

"Ach, for sure, me lud," said she. "T'is down the heart o' the town ye'll be wantin', in Lower High Street opposite the railings o' Saint Tydfil's Church." So out I went again into the weak November sunlight, wondering what I was doing chasing a Romany love when such Irish roses were growing at my feet.

Indeed, and I confess it, this girl composed within me a delight at the charms of womanhood.

"Is there anythin' I can do for ye, me lud?" said she.

I shook my head and left her standing; knowing that had Jen Wildflower been around to take stock of things, I'd have gone out of the place head first.

As usual, Paddy Infernal was hanging about: leaning against a lamp post was he, with his pipe stub in his bearded mouth; and he raised his bowler to me with a grin, shouting, "Did ye turn her down, ye daft nit? Me puttin' the wish in both of ye and her loins throbbing like a festered thumb? What ails you?"

I pushed past him, and he called, "*Jawch*! You're in the big city now: they'll be downin' ye trews and measuring the size of it – you realise. I suppose ye know that while you play the virgin, your Wildflower piece is probably on the batter?"

"Go to hell!"

"That's me intention, but I'm making the best of it before I blister and so should you! See ye on the live coals, son!"

Conscience never gives up. It lurks in dark places; peeps around corners.

"Not if I see you first," I said.

Time was, around 1800, the best hotel in Merthyr was The Crown, but so dilapidated and gloomy was it (the Castle Hotel was then being built) that, when a guest arrived, its landlady had been heard to cry, "Turn the pigs out of the parlour, my duck, for a gent is a'comin'."

The Star Inn was a celebrated attraction then, and to this house one day a star visitor arrived – one named Admiral Horatio Nelson. He arrived with a paramour, Lady Emma

166

Hamilton on his arm, the wife of another; and to the delight of Richard Crawshay of Cyfarthfa Castle, then the Merthyr's ironmaster, paid him a social visit; at which, it is recorded, the latter wept with unrestrained joy.

In celebration of so noble a visitor, they fired a blank shot from an ancient canon. It's breech exploded and killed a small boy. So distressed was Lady Hamilton that she gave eight guineas to his parents to defray the funeral cost.

I was interested to learn that the Star was the meeting-place of intellectuals known as The Philosophical Society, whose members appraised the works of Robert Owen and the great Tom Paine: most of such liberally minded gentlemen being members of the Merthyr Unitarian Chapel.

I was happy to learn also that I was in good company.

Other forces, though, were also at work; not least many reverent gentlemen of the Church of England, who, hating Paine for his books 'The Rights of Man' and 'The Age of Reason', took umbrage at his atheistic stance, and had the soles of their boots studded with nails making the pattern 'T.P.' Thus enabling them to trample his genius underfoot.

There are some who understand the idiosyncrasies of humans.

But where ever you have great men you breed their parasites, and in memory of the hero who saved Britain from the French, the hotel was crowded that night with gentlemen of good birth and luxury who had called in to celebrate, and a chance to drink at the landlord's expense from the cup Nelson himself had used. The tap-room was crowded with aristocratic top hats.

After difficulty I got the attention of my host.

"A room for the night, Landlord – is it a difficulty?"

"An excellent night for a gentleman, sir!" He was large, ebullient, and very Welsh. "What might be your pleasure?"

I said, quietly, "First, can you tell me if you are playing host to a friend of mine?"

"Ay ay! It's a lady, by the sound of it?"

"How did you guess?"

"A yokel barks the question, sir; a gentleman keeps a lady's name under 'is hat, so to speak." He put his chops next to mine. "Who?"

"Travelling under the name of Wildflower," I whispered.

"Room Three, kind sir."

I stared at him, astonished.

"Is it your intention to join her?" he asked.

I drew even closer. "Are you telling me she is already here?"

"As sure as me name's Elias Evans."

"Good God!"

"God don't come into it, beggin' your pardon, sir. You see, being the landlord of such an establishment, famous in circles of 'igh society – national heroes and suchlike – it's me task in life to keep abreast of events. And being of a highly volatile nature, me missus likewise, it's our job in life to ease the drab lives of the gentry. The reunion of lovers and a closing of weather eyes to their shenanigans 'as become the heart and soul of this establishment, innit? And so, if the lady's willing and don't start flingin' bloody chamber-pots about an generally sayin' stop it and playin' Hamlet, it ain't our business what goes on after lights out, me being an ex-army fella – once a corporal in the Ox and Bucks and the syphilitic army of the East. Name?"

"Thomas Mortymer," I said and he wrote it in his register, saying, "And sound in wind and limb, lest I'm mistaken, which is a change these days, for our courtin' aristocracy's largely composed of gouty old gents who can't get it up. So would Number Three on the second floor, adjoining the lady's room suit? Mind, it'll cost ye, for it was the one Nelson and his lovely Emma used."

"Name your price!"

"Ten bob to you, sir." He leaned closer, breathing hops

168

all over me. "You see, Mr Mortymer, me and my missus are of a romantic frame o' mind, and though it's mainly ambition for yours truly these days, we likes to see others at it, beggin' your pardon again. I mean . . ." and here he grimaced at the ceiling, his fat face puckered up. "So, every year regular, on the anniversary o' the night England's hero came, me and my missus go up the stairs hand in hand to Room Three. I calls her Emma and she calls me Horatio, and we lays together in the feathers . . . celebratin' their lovieducks, you could call it." He sighed. "You reckon that's daft?"

"I reckon that's beautiful."

"Mind, it ain't the same as in the old days when we was young coots and fevered, if you get me; but, it's good to stay young and romantic, ain't it?"

"That's what the world has lost, Landlord," I replied, and left him.

Out in the stabling I saw Lark watered and bedded, and looked up from the cobbles to the window of Room Number Three (according to the groom) and here a light was dimly burning.

My heart was thudding.

"Most nights she burns her light, that lady," added the groom. "A week she's been in there now; folks say she's ill."

"The landlord didn't mention that," I answered.

"That pale and thin she is. A decent lady and gent brought her here in their carriage – they found her lying ill down on the Redcoat road." I wondered where I'd heard that earlier . . .

"He didn't mention that, either," I said.

"She's a Romany lady, they do say." He was young, thin, and his elfin face stared up out of his ragged coat. "I takes her travel-bag up to her room and she gives me a penny."

Dusk was falling over the town and I could hear the lamp-man beginning his rounds. Already red light from the Cyfarthfa furnaces was flickering in the shadows and the night-shift drop-hammers threatening on the wind.

"Good-night, sir," said the groom, shutting Lark's stable door. "I'll give 'im a good brushing down first thing in the morning."

"Thanks," and I gave him a tuppence, "and there's sixpence more if you do me this service tomorrow. Yesterday I sent a telegraph to a friend and am expecting his reply. Will you call at the post office at midday tomorrow – I'll give you a note to the postmaster – and collect any reply?"

"O, aye, sir!"

"Tell him *poste-restante* – understand?"

I left him staring at the tuppence; the prospect of a further sixpence had almost paralysed him. Some of these impoverished grooms were actually starving.

Now he bowed to me, knowing me as a gent of wealth and privilege.

The light in the window of the room above the stables had gone out, I noticed.

I tried to anticipate my first meeting with Jen after so long apart, and decided to open what might be a formal conversation by asking if she was all right for money. Then I remembered our joint account in Swansea and that all she had to do was write to Goat Street and ask for a draft and the manager would send it; I grinned, nostalgically remembering her insistence upon pocket-money.

The groom joined me in staring up at Jenny's window. "Like I said, sir, she don't look too good to me."

And at that moment I saw a woman's form move indistinctly behind the window glass.

170

Chapter Twenty-Eight

The night shift at Cyfarthfa was pouring molten iron; the sky over Merthyr glaring with light; rainbow colours were whooping on the clouds as the bungs poured their incandescent fire.

This was the apex of Merthyr's greatness, the peak of its industrial activity, with thousands of tons of finished iron being sent to the ports of the world.

I lay back on the pillows in the Star bedroom and watched the firework display and the granite towering of St Tydfil's Church; its railings, forged even before the time of Bacon the Pig, an earlier ironmaster, withered and shrank in the pulsating glow. The building around me vibrated to the thunder.

Lying there, I thought of the generations that had been charred by the town's cascading fires and elevated into prosperity by its abundant wealth.

I thought, too, of the children whose lungs had been coked by the years of Merthyr's toiling, the wasted limbs, and the human defeats in the face of Crawshay's victory of gold.

Worth millions of pounds at the time of his workers' greatest distress, he had birthed a dynasty of greed that would denigrate his name for generations, and erect an edifice of success that would last in bitterness for a thousand years.

I thought, too, of the one who lay in the bed next door while this maelstrom beat about her; and wondered at my reception were I to turn the key in the adjoining door and present myself before her.

My conscience, refined by parting, was sharpened by immediacy.

Had I the right, I thought, so to present myself without preliminary warning? Indeed, had anything between us changed since the day she had walked out of *Cefn-Ydfa* in the knowledge that our love could never again be consummated?

No, I argued, nothing had changed at all. And yet . . . ?

Were she to know that I was now within touch, might she not share my physical longing?

I lay in a desire greater than anything I had known. It was something other than mere unrequited love, but as if my essence was being torn out of me, leaving behind in the bed a husk . . . No woman of charm and beauty could replace the one I wanted; and she slept on in disregarding tranquillity.

Driven by the need of her, I rose and went to the adjoining door. It opened to the lock, swinging wide to expose a smaller room within.

Jenny's profile was etched against the fire-shot window; I moved to the bed, looking at her colourless face on the pillow.

I saw in flushes of window redness not the girl I knew, but the woman Jen Wildflower had become: the lashes of her eyes spread wide upon her shadowed cheeks; her hair, once shining black, now lay dankly upon the lace pillow; her brow was wet with the fever; so still she lay, as if the essence of her had been sucked out of her body; I clenched my hands and bowed my head.

Unaccountably, for I had made no sound, Jen opened her eyes and regarded me blankly, as one might a stranger. I heard my own voice as in a dream. "It's only Tom, Jen, don't be afraid."

172

Her eyes, opening wider, grew from calm into astonishment, and she raised a hand and pressed it against her face; then, turning away, she began to sob, her fist against her mouth as if to stifle the indignity.

"Jen, don't . . . !" I reached out, but she drew away.

"Oh my God!" she whispered.

"But you knew I was here, didn't you see me come?"

"No, I did not. But why? – *why*?"

"Because I love you. I waited over a month at *Cefn-Ydfa*, but you didn't return. What was I supposed to do?"

"You were supposed to leave me alone! Nothing can come of this!"

I answered quietly, "Jen, I just can't bear us to be apart!"

"But we can't be together. The world . . ."

"To hell with the world! And if you loved me as I love you, you'd say the same!"

She thumped the bed. "Tom, we're *brother* and *sister*!"

"And I don't care. This must have happened before thousands of time, and folks as decent as us have got away with it. For God's sake, who's to know?"

"I will know!"

"Well, I'm prepared to forget it!"

"That is the difference between us."

I sat on the bed; instinctively she drew away.

"Why does it make such a difference? We're only half-related!"

"It is against the law!"

She began to cry; the tears ran down her face and splashed on to her lace nightdress, and I longed to take her into my arms. In a breaking voice, she said, "The . . . the baby, Tom."

I sat silently, watching her.

"I lost it."

I nodded. "Yes, I knew. I followed you to Ossie Primrose's place. Did you have to finish up with that filthy old thing?"

"The tribe was moving north; child-bed women are always left behind till later . . ."

"It's a wonder you're alive!"

"I . . . I didn't know until I got there. A Welsh girl took me to her."

"Yes, Culpepper – she told me. Jen, Jen . . ."

I tried to touch her hand but she pulled it back as if scalded, saying: "It won't work, Tom! I love you, I'll always love you, but my clan says – 'He who lieth with his sister finds no place in Heaven; harken ye to Deuteronomy twenty-seven.' It is the law!"

"And mine, too. The Bible isn't only for you Romanies!" I paused, fighting emotion. "Was it our fault? What about an all-forgiving God? We love one another; that's enough?"

There was a long silence, and then she said with cold finality, "Tom, ours is a love that God forgot, and you have got to realise it."

We sat staring at one another and the gap of disaster widened. I said, getting up from the bed, "So what happens now?"

Jen's voice was calm. "The Elders would say that our son's death was a biblical sign. You go back to your life and leave me to mine."

"My God, it even rhymes!"

"Don't be cruel. Just go – *please*?"

I thought madly, if I take her and hold her against me, this might bridge the chasm between us, but I knew by the sobbing restriction of her breath that there was no hope for us; that generations of public condemnation stood between us. And now my desperation forged the hurt.

"It should never have come to this," I said. "Tell me, would you have treated your beloved David Grey as you are treating me?"

174

She answered brokenly, "It is because I love you that I can let you go. Were you to ask me to die for you, I would do so, but you cannot expect me to deny the law of God." She added as I again drew closer, "No, darling, please don't touch me! I . . . I couldn't bear it. Just go!"

The thundering of Cyfarthfa, until then but a murmur in my consciousness, grew into a sustained roaring, enveloping us both; and a thin wisp of smoke, Merthyr's old 'choke you bastards' began to drift up between us, a talisman of inevitability.

On the other side of the door dividing us now, I listened to her sobbing.

Chapter Twenty-Nine

There's no colder place in the world than Merthyr Tydfil in winter, I reckon. Next morning, with the trees of the valley loaded with hoar frost and the inhabitants blue in the face and coughing tubercular, I came down to breakfast to find the place empty . . . apart from Jenny, who was already at table.

Thin and worn she looked, and I said so.

"That's a dreadful thing to say to a girl!"

The reply was almost light-hearted; an astonishing contrast to her mood of the previous night. I wondered at the sudden change of character, and said, sitting down, "One thing's for sure, you know how to keep a man in his place."

"That has to be, with persistent people like you around. Anyway, am I supposed to be a blushing maiden? Only a week or so ago I had a baby."

"So what's the next move?" I was flippant, but couldn't help it, for to my added astonishment she had picked up a travel brochure for the Continent and begun to read it.

She said, "I don't know about you, but I'm making for one of our old haunts in France – tomorrow I hope to be on the Boat Train from Dover.

"Time was – now so long ago that I can scarcely remember – I fell in love with a chap who took me off in a red caravan; up to Scotland we went and finished up in a little attic in Paris. It had pink curtains at the window and an *estaminet* below."

"Now that," I replied, "is coincidental, for I once took a

176

gypsy girl to Paris; there, at an address in Stinkerque – this was in the *Moulin Rouge* area – I entertained her in a club named the Black Cat; I used to give her sips of cognac, make her tipsy, then take her back to an attic I'd rented, and make love to her red-headed."

My egg and bacon came and I cursed it. Jen asked, "Did she enjoy your love-making?"

I munched at the bacon. "It appeared so, for in the mornings I made love to her again and she never objected."

"How about at lunch time?"

"Only when she asked me to, for we had to eat as well, remember. Since she was the best cook in the Latin quarter it was not possible to think seriously about love then, for her mutton stew set a man up for the day. But best of all was her night attire: she used to put *Paris Matin* perfume behind her ears, which was enough to drive a healthy male demented; this and her pink lace bits and bobs – yes, and black stockings like the dancers wore in the *Moulin Rouge* . . . this girl kept me up half the night."

Jen lowered her face; her eyes were bright. "Do you see anything of her these days?"

"Not a lot. She got some queer bee in her bonnet and made off, just when I thought I'd got her settled."

"That's the way life goes." She added, "Perhaps she's got another chap locked away somewhere."

"I doubt it, she wasn't that kind of a girl."

Jen lowered her teacup and smiled at me. "Was she beautiful?"

I lowered my knife and fork. "Men ignored their wives when she entered a room."

"And you truly loved her?"

I nodded. "I still do."

Jen looked away. "Some gypsies, you know are not very dependable . . . they're a queer lot and have strange customs, like jumping over a broom and calling it a marriage; but that

177

is what a man must expect if he falls for one . . . different customs, different tribes.

"Also, I think your attitude is very exasperating, because you're seeing things purely from a man's point of view. You are a male; how can you expect to know the way a woman thinks? You don't possess a woman's heart."

"They are a perverse lot, I can tell you that!" I drank, watching her.

"There you go again. You men judge women through what you hear; it is wrong of you. Sometimes we're so complex that we don't understand ourselves . . ."

"You can say that again!"

"You talk of making love to her – you tell of that to another person? Do all men talk this way, one to the other?"

"Jen!"

"You make it sound so important – it might have been for you, this rolling around in a bed – but for that girl it was only a small part of the presents she gave you." She made a fist and thumped it against herself. "Also, you talked as if you owned her heart and soul, but Romanies say their souls belong to God."

With which she sat there twisting her fingers in her lap. I thought she was going to cry again, but she did not. For many seconds we sat thus, the air between us finely tuned to a thin note of nothingness, an easily broken magic . . . while the traffic outside rumbled past the window. Suddenly Jen, smiling brilliantly, put back her head, and asked, "You still love this woman – the girl in the Paris attic with the pink curtains . . .?"

I closed my eyes. "I have only just found her; I shall die if I lose her again."

Her eyes softened; fumbling at the neck of her dress she pulled out a little gold crucifix on a chain, and said, "Listen, Tom. Could I forget so easily? As I sit here there is also a need in me for you. I am not a religious person, but I know that we are being watched . . . someone is waiting to see what we will do next. Until then . . . ?"

She held herself.

"How long?" I asked. "Jen, for God's sake, how long?"

She rose, smiling down. "Something will happen: I don't know what, but *something* – you watch. God must be getting pretty old these days, and forgetful – give it a year, Tom. Please? And wait to see if He remembers us."

"I wouldn't bet on it."

I got up and tried to hold her, but she turned her face away to my kiss.

"Goodbye, my darling," she said, and I stood at the table and watched her walk away.

This walking away from me like this was not the first time it had happened, for Jen had been married to my friend, and then he had died: more, she had had a still-born child by him, as I explained before. And right at the time when I thought she might be my wife, she had walked away, as now.

History was repeating itself.

Now, on the platform of Merthyr station I watched the afternoon train steam out for the south, and did not wave goodbye; nor did Jen, as far as I could see, for I had half hidden myself behind piled luggage. Perhaps, like me, she did not trust her emotions.

Lark studied me with mild surprise as I collected him from the Star Inn stable and put my face against his coat.

My weakness when things go wrong is that I turn to whisky, and was well into half a bottle of it when the stable groom appeared with a reply to my telegraph to Jethro. It read:

'To: Mr Tom Mortymer, Star Inn, Merthyr Tydfil, Glam.
Please return early. Old Bid seriously ill.
Also assistance required re new information.
Upper Works House,
Morriston, Glamorgan'

179

I grieved for Old Bid; it was as if another piece of my life had left me; in self-pity I proceeded to finish what was left in the bottle.

New information?

All part of the efficient Pinkerton Detective Agency?

I closed my eyes in a haze of whisky, and thought of Old Bid.

Sod it all, I thought: the Pinkertons, Jethro and the Wildflowers in particular.

Sod everything.

Paddy Infernal was lying on the bed when I got back to my room upstairs. "Ay ay," said he, cradling his head, "as drunk as a coot, eh? I knew you'd find your own level!"

I did my best to ignore him, and he bawled, "Marvellous, ain't it! The first thing to go wrong sends 'im on the piss!"

I said, "It's Old Bid . . ."

"Snuffed it, 'as she? Oh dear me, ain't that terrible? And so bloody hypocritical! Come on, mun, your trouble is that ye rounded up your woman, corralled and branded her, an' now she's bunked the feathers."

"You are disgusting!"

"And you're a boot-faced bloody Pharisee, Mortymer – luxuriating in pastures o' self-pity. Atonement don't come in half pints, ye know, it's all or nothin' when you're flourishin' penitence; and the fact is, me darlin', that ye not askin' forgiveness for puttin' your sister in the club – given half a chance you'd do it again!" He leaped off the bed and went to the door. "See you in Hell, my lovely!"

I lay upon the bed and slipped into an alcoholic drowse, seeing Jen's face rising like a Phoenix in the flickering redness of the room, for Cyfarthfa had begun to ladle her cauldrons again, and there was in Jen's eyes a smile of untroubled innocence. Paddy Infernal yelled, "Ach, to

180

hell, ye hooligan! I'm your conscience, remember, ain't I?"
and left me, slamming the door.

Whisky has a few ways out of a drunk, and one is through
the eyes.

Book Three

Chapter Thirty

Within a vacuum of emptiness I wandered, lost in time and geography.

Leaving the Star Inn, I loaded my few possessions on to Lark and walked him north through Dowlais to Vaynor.

I then struck north again, automatically taking the same route as the one I had taken earlier with Jen when travelling to Scotland. Next day found me through Builth Wells and on the road to Rhayader.

Wrexham shook her spires like lances in the cold winter sunlight a week later, and here I took a week to get going again after Lark cast a shoe, and I couldn't find a blacksmith. To Chester now, then Warrington; feeding at wayside halts; north still, to Wigan and Manchester where I begged a ride on a canal long-boat.

I walked Lark and rode him alternately according to my mood, going carelessly, without thought or planning . . . in a wicked, bare-legged crow of a day and night-time dream. Eating little on the tramp, I drank ale copiously, eyeing peasant wives, weighing up their husbands; there being no randier male than one devoid of a future and trying to forget the past.

I spent a month with a tinker girl outside Bradford, and every time I made love to her she called the name of her husband, who was doing six months for theft in the local gaol. At Kendal I found an inn I was looking for, a little hostelry half-timbered in white and run by a merry-faced landlady who had earlier taken a fancy to Jen and presented her with a tiny crucifix. She had given us the best room in the house, which my girl and I had shared. The bed was of hair and feathers; and I slept that night in the place where Jen had lain. Then, for the first time in weeks my conscience arrived again and sat on the end of the bed.

"Wake up, ye hypocrite," said Paddy Infernal.

I saw his bearded face in cold February moonlight, a beam of blue that painted up his face in cadaverous shadows; the lowering brow I saw, the broken teeth and sunken eyes.

"So ye thought ye could scarper and leave us behind, did ye?" he continued. "But the Master said to me, he said, 'Get after that Mortymer sod and let him know the time o' day, and move, mun, *move*, for if there's a man I canna abide it's one in tears o' contrition all day and doin' everything but eat his dinner wi' it at every opportunity!' What ails ye, don't ye love the woman now?"

I clenched my eyes and turned over in my sleep, for the air in the room had moved and I knew the stink of him. Now he said, "Ye see, my darlin', you canna get rid of me; I'm the air ye breathe and the worm in your brain. I snuggle up in the bed wi' ye like one of your harpies, wi' an ear out for the golden words you say to 'em in dreams.

"I'm your laughter when ye booze out your troubles, and your tears when you remember them, and when you look in the mirror, you see my face. I tell ye this once an' for all, Tom Mortymer – I ain't here for your original sin, which wasn't your fault – I'm with you for the sins that came after; and when the big St Peter blows his bugle I'll be with you then – to testify at the final judgement! I'll open the fiery gates and slam 'em behind you, for the weakling that ye are!"

I flung back the bedclothes, scrambled out and went to the window and the night was cold in patterned stars.

Paddy Infernal was still at my elbow, whispering now, "Mind, you might as well be killed for a sheep as for a lamb, remember, for there's a bunch o' foine women pining to death for a handsome young fella – from here all the way to Lanarkshire – to say nothin' o' the plump wee Scot in the room next door awaitin' your knock; she's got a glint in her eye for ye, so she has! Go on, son, who's Jen Wildflower, anyway?"

I left the bed I had shared with Jen and knocked on the door of the landlady.

"Sure to God, you're the finest bloody pupil I've been handed since a week last Michaelmas," said Paddy Infernal.

March found me outside Carlisle and in early April I bathed, chattering with cold, in exactly the same watering-place where I had bathed with Jen, and although it seemed like a lifetime before, I knew her nearness; for we had shared the same towel, drying one another in laughter, until the bailiff had come out of the bushes and put paid to us.

I saw Jen again as I saw her then, fighting to cover her nakedness as he took our names.

Dreams, all dreams . . .

The river bank was empty; the bailiff was not there, although it was a Sunday.

"Soon the cuckoo will be calling down south," said Jen in my heart, "the nightingale has arrived and the bilberries are flowering, Tom. Please take me home now?" she begged. "Please?"

On that lonely pilgrimage, returning from Lanarkshire, Jen stood before me, as if it were yesterday.

Now, with the coming of spring, Wales had thrown off her winter garments and begun to dress herself up in bright new clothes, Jen told me in my thoughts; so I gave Lark to a friendly farmer with admonishments to treat him well, and caught a country cart back to Carlisle, and at the railway station there booked a ticket through to

Morriston on a track that was now calling itself the Great Western Railway.

The journey was an event in itself, involving unnecessary delays at halts and unknown stations, and was one of the most uncomfortable journeys I have ever undertaken.

In this new phenomenon called the railway era I tried to lose myself . . .

Travel by train was still in its infancy, although engineers, working under the genius of Brunel and Stephenson, had begun to push the network in Britain to astonishing lengths.

Railway mania was at its height; fortunes being won and lost by speculators; even people like Jethro, born to the era of the stage-coach, would have agreed that the locomotive had come to stay.

It was after this journey from Carlisle to Morriston with all its discomforts, that I decided to invest half my capital in railways; an act which inspired local confidence in the coming of the railways . . . I made this new investment the moment I reached Morriston.

Events later proved my wisdom; had I kept my money in tinplate for a little while longer, I could, through the intrigues of then unknown enemies, have ended up a pauper.

A financier being to a financier what a tiger is to a tiger . . .

An equally safe investment was my recently bought Upper Forest House in Morriston, where the new housekeeper (the one following Old Bid) held court. She, Angharad Rees, appeared even more beautiful in pink, as she awaited my arrival. Framed by a portico of Corinthian columns, she looked like a modern Diana awaiting her most eminent guest; though I already had reason to suspect that once 'lights out' was bugled she'd exchange her tea-time attire for her libertine black; having once experienced Angharad's night-time activities.

The greeting was reserved, and I remembered that this was probably because Jethro was now in the vicinity; he having the ability, I suspected, to cool most female ardour.

I could not have been more mistaken; there being no sign of him.

"Some business over in London, I believe," explained Angharad, and poor old Dai Dando, snuffling his tears in grief, confirmed it.

"Thanks for comin' back Maister," he added. "Old Bid would 'ave been the first to appreciate it – handsome is as 'andsome does, she always used to say. Thought a lot o' you, ye know."

"And I of her."

Together we stood in funeral black while Old Bid's many relatives filed past the open coffin, and Dozie Annie had to be supported.

It appeared impossible to me that Old Bid had died; over seventy, true, but in the full bloom an' all, the relatives said. Mind, she did have the pegs, said one, a contemporary name for arthritis, but her heart were golden sound, and what a life of it she 'ad wi' that old Dai, the randy old soak!

"You don't have to tell me," I muttered vacantly.

"But improved a lot recent, ye know; always the same, these fellas, once the pastry's gone flat."

There was Uncle Ben from Coedpoerth and Aunty Nell from Crumlin – next door to the big viaduct; "They do say the rails are haunted wi' ghosts of them that went before. Would you like another, Uncle Albert?"

"There's one thing about the Welsh, they love a good funeral, and I reckon Bid'll be cookin' bakestones and Welsh *cawl* for St Peter the moment she do get up there; lovely old girl, she was . . . and the speeches of that pastor were marvellous when he come to the lovie little bits in the *Song of Solomon*; made me hair stand on end, it did; wonderfully melting, mind – the emotions o' the saints a'flowing in his

189

cadence: glory to the net of God, I always say, he's caught a crocodile this week, an' no mistake . . ."

"Another half o' skull attack for you, Deacon?"

"Make the best of it, I always say, Bron; that's what Old Bid reckoned; 'ere, have another tot o' gin; ye look miserable to death."

Cocooned in their grief, they pestered and whispered.

"Mind, Bid were a morsel below herself since that Angharad come."

"Ay ay, mun – a very tasty piece is that Angie."

"My Joey knew her when she were over Peveril way; said he wouldn't trust 'er with his pet poodle – got Spaniel eyes, he says – never trust a woman wi' sad eyes – she'll be away quicker than Samson's bloody foxes. What time is it?"

"Time we wasn't here, girl. I hate these funerals. When our mam went down, we buried her with ham and green peas, but I anna seen another like it since . . ."

"Dear me – talk o' the Devil – look who's comin'."

"Who?"

"That tarty Angie. Full o' pins and Sunday braveries, she is; but fancy airs and graces do nothin' for my Evan."

Another observed, "My latest is a glutton of a baby, mind. I said to my Alf, 'He's been on the breast two years now; at this rate I'll be putting 'em through the school railings.'"

"What do ye make o' that Jethro fella?"

"Too big an' handsome by far, my duck. Wouldn't trust 'im farther than I could throw 'im."

"And Tom Mortymer?"

"Moral degenerate, take it from me."

"Watch it – 'ere he comes."

On the other side of the open coffin, with Dai Dando looking morose, I said, "Sorry in my heart I am, Dai."

"And me," replied he. "Me soul's ragged and torn, Maister." He sniffed and snuffled in his tears. "I was a sod to our Bid, ye know."

"Don't go overboard, boy; we're all sods to the ones we love."

"She were like a young maiden, really speakin'. Didn't know the time o' day nor which way up she was." He patted her cold cheek with a horny hand. "And proper healthy she looked, right to the end; it did her a world of good that fortnight down in Tenby."

I agreed, adding, "Death is a joke, she always said; St Peter will be pleased to see her."

He nodded, wounded. "By now she'll be giving the sorrows of Baal a goin' over – she 'ad no time for Satan, ye know." Dai bowed his head. "See ye on Resurrection morning, my lovely," and bending, he kissed her marble face.

Auntie Alice attended then; large in the rear was Auntie once removed, as Dai explained, with a bosom for weeping on and wearing a broad-rimmed black-veiled hat, one later buried in error as a floral tribute, and she was weeping to float a battleship.

This is one reason why I love my Welshness; weddings come after funerals . . . in preference; the harmonium sings in a minor key and everything smells of lavender and moth balls.

Rock of Ages it was then, with adenoidal small boys rooting for the top notes and sopranos giving a maternal blessing to their sweet sad octaves – from old crones to mischievous maidens – combining with deep-throated contraltos in the eternal music that is the essence of my country . . .

I actually wept. However many legs an animal has, it does not stop him from being your brother, the red tribes say. Similarly, no supposed division of class and sex had ever stopped Old Bid from being my sister; my mother, even, and my friend.

"Don't take on, sir," whispered Dai in panic, "people are watchin'!"

191

It is in grief that we learn our true values and discover our own unconscious levels.

Later, I asked Dai, "Where the devil has Jethro got to?"

With Old Bid settled comfortably in her counterpane of earth, as the officiating minister put it, we were trying to get back to normal, and Dozie Annie, our long-serving housemaid, answered, "Reckoned he'd be back for the funeral, he said."

Then another came to the fore, and this was Angharad, remarking with pastoral dignity, "Actually, he was due at Maesteg on the midday train from London, but Mr Jethro never could be complimented on punctuality, I fear."

"For heaven's sake, what's he doing in London at such a time?"

"Simple, sir. Ask Jethro."

Jethro, eh? A word about this one. Take note of Angharad.

Her slimness enhanced her height; her long black dress (though I doubt if it grieved for Old Bid) enhanced her new-found authority as the Morriston house-keeper; her hair, blue-black and tied with black ribbon, reached to her waist; she was akin to Jen in her startling beauty, but inches the taller; and she looked as Delilah must have done before Samson brought the house down.

Certainly she was no woman to become jammed across a bachelor's ethics at a time of my greatest need. Meanwhile, wishing her to the devil and back, I couldn't keep my eyes off her, and wondered how Jethro had fared while sharing her company. My own future in Upper House was now unsettled, to say the least; with Paddy Infernal's haunting having a finger in my interests.

I met Dai Dando on the first floor of the house and collared him, asking, "Look, Mr Jethro telegraphed me, saying he was going to London when he told me about Old Bid's illness. Do you know why?"

"Why what, Maister?"

"Why he was going to London?"

"'struth, sir, nowt to do wi' me." He glanced about him as one fearing a listener. "Mind, he did mention as how you had enemies . . ."

"Enemies? Who?"

"Well, like I told 'im – that bugger Bill Bumstead who's butler to the Greys over at Russian house – the fella I booted outta your mam's room while your pa was away – remember? Him for one."

I nodded. "Yes, I've remembered that now."

"Well, he's an enemy, ain't he? – the sod went to transportation for stealin' your ma's jewellery, didn't he?"

"But why didn't Mr Jethro mention to you that he was going to London I wonder?"

The old man jerked his head in the direction of the hall door through which Angharad had just left us. "He don't say a lot with 'er highness around, but he did say, 'Dai Dando, there's some'ut funny goin' on, and I'm gettin' to the bottom of it or I ain't a Pinkerton detective . . .'"

"Go on, don't stop!"

"Well, he be of the opinion that that bloody ole butler's some'ut to do with it, like I said before."

"To do with what – come on, for God's sake!"

"With you and Jen Wildflower." He lowered his voice. "I said to Old Bid, I said you and her are supposed to be brother and sister, like, but she said it weren't nothin' to do with me."

Exasperated, I cried, "Dai, it doesn't matter what Old Bid said, what did Jethro say?" and I shook him for sense.

Dai didn't reply. He stared vacantly past me through the window to the drive, and beyond that to the distant estate gates which were slowly opening. "Lor, love-a-duck, Maister – here he comes, Mr Jethro!" he ejaculated.

"No, it is not, Dai, it's one of the tradesmen – now come on, try to remember; what else did Jethro say?"

193

His old face puckered up and he fought for the facts of it, saying gruffly, "Old Bid understood it, see – she 'ad it all buttoned up."

"But she isn't here now, think, man, *think!*"

"Some'ut about your Romany woman, but dunna tell Angie."

"Yes, you've told me that already. How does MrBumstead come into it? The one you booted out of the house when I was a youngster. Now come on!"

Dai's old pugilistic face was suddenly alight with wonderment, and he raised a gnarled fist in the air and brought it down into his palm. "I got it Maister, I got it! It were some'ut about him goin' up to London to try to find some papers. Ay ay, that's it!"

"What papers?"

"He were goin' to talk to some big nut about it . . ."

"Whom . . . ?" I gripped his hands.

"Don't know, Maister – he didn't say. But he was going to search old Bill Bumstead's place, an' all, and I was to stay outside and keep watch . . ."

"Keep watch for what?"

"Old Bid knew!"

"Forget Old Bid!" I gripped him harder. "Why were you to stay on guard outside Mr Bumstead's house?"

"The Russian Villa, Maesteg."

"Yes, yes, I know where he lives, but why had you to stay on guard?"

"While Mr Jethro were inside it, o' course!"

"But why was he going into Russian Villa – what was he trying to find?"

Old Dai put his face up and howled, "Maister, I anna a full pound these days – you *gotta* ask Old Bid!"

"I am asking you. What was Jethro going to try to find in Russian Villa?"

"Sod me, Maister – I just told ye that!"

He was senile to the point of insanity; I vaguely wondered who was really the mad one, having lately progressed myself in that direction . . . the appearances of Paddy Infernal and my predilection for nightmares having begun to shake my own sanity, for which I had always possessed an unspoken fear . . .

Angharad arrived then with brisk, matter-of-fact authority, and I knew by Old Dai's expression that he feared her; clearly she had overheard us speaking, for she said with languid good humour, "He don't know anything else about what, sir?"

"When the old man can't speak for himself, I'll let you know," I said coldly.

This she ignored, saying, "Clearly Mr Jethro has been delayed in London. I take it you haven't heard from him?"

I walked past her. "He will make contact in his good time."

"He told me he would return in under a week."

"You're privileged; he didn't tell me anything."

Her close proximity was disturbing. Only by aloofness could I hope to keep her at a distance; now, being under the same roof, there was no way of avoiding her.

Having for so long been celibate, my urge for relief was pressing; and though in the last analysis alcohol enhances desire but destroys performance, my need was great. Also, this woman wasn't in Paris, she was here and available at the lift of a finger.

I told myself that Jen would understand, but knew that she would not.

Chapter Thirty-One

Three weeks to the day after Jethro had left for London, a letter arrived for me. Fortunately I saw the postman coming up the drive of Upper House and took the envelope myself; it was stained with rain and had been carelessly handled; its date stamp recording that it has been posted in London a week ago. Opening it, I read:

'Dear Tom

I am sorry I didn't get back for Bid's funeral and hope you received my telegraph in time for you to attend. My investigations upon your behalf have been interrupted by Pinkerton activities, but Dai Dando will appraise you of certain suspicions I now hold, and how best we can come to grips with them. It is now up to you to continue with the investigation I am forced to leave incomplete. I will, of course, continue with my efforts at the first opportunity. Until I write again, therefore my renewed condolences to poor Dai and my affection to the delectable Angharad, whom I hope soon to meet again.

Cool breezes
Jethro'

Clearly, Jethro was playing his cards close to his chest, being distrustful of the open post.

I could ill afford the time for intrigue; for the past

fortnight I had been coming and going to Upper Forest Works trying to sort out the administration, which Jethro had left unattended. Outstanding foreign orders dated back to before I'd gone in search of Jen, and some had already been lost to competitors; but now the tinplate exports were moving out again, and income beginning to increase.

The intensity of losing Jen, sleepless nights and the onset of whisky was beginning to affect my health. Spending one's waking hours in an alcoholic daze is scarcely conducive to coherent thought, and small instances of what was called *delirium tremens* began seriously to affect me, which I've heard can be the harbinger of insanity. This took the form of acute headaches and minor hallucinating; and Jen's continued absence, with no apparent hope of her return instilled within me a hopelessness that led me more to the bottle.

I had been drinking in the study, wondering how I would meet Jethro's request. There being no point in searching Bumstead's rooms in Russian Villa if I didn't know what I was looking for . . . It was also a dangerous venture, especially when aided by Dai, and I began to wonder if any of us were completely sane; Jethro's contribution to date being vague to the point of idiocy.

I do not know what put me harder on the bottle on this particular night, other than my overwhelming need of Jen and the complexity of the web in which I had become entangled.

I recall finishing one bottle of brandy and opening another; sitting in the dusk of the study contemplating its amber slant in the glass; then, bottle in hand, stumbling up the stairs to my bedroom. Here, outspread on the counterpane, enduring the swimming senses of the saturated drunk, I was awakened by the clucking of hens and was astonished to see an enormous cockerel sitting on my bed-rail. For many seconds it sat there, easing its clawed feet, and while I stared at it in astonishment the cockerel said, "Well well, the fella's back home at last, sure to God!"

I had known drunken visions before, but never an animal that spoke, and I peered at the thing through my fingers, wondering where I had heard its voice before; then I knew, for the bird spoke again, saying, "At weekends I get out to see me special customers, ye see, by which I mean murderers, thieves, adulterers and fornicators, plus a few incestuous bastards who insist on coverin' their relatives." Raising its beak it crowed at the ceiling, shook its fine red coxcomb and added, "Remember me?"

Paddy Infernal.

Clucking, red-eyed, the cockerel peered at me.

Morriston was making iron and the night-shift was thundering in bell-clashes and whining rollers; the window was a sea of fire. Pinned by terror, I stared at the vision on the bed-rail, then guzzled at the brandy, seeking escape.

"Go back to Hell!" I whispered.

The thing flapped its wings, shrieking, "Ye silly bugger, I've just come from there! And don't you blame folks for the milk ye spill yourself, Mortymer. I'm your conscience, remember? – and I'm only doin' me job. What's more, it's no good tryin' to lay the blame on that poor sod, Bill Bumstead, for like the rest of you he's got bad feet chasin' around after the hens!" He crowed again at the ceiling. "Don't yet realise the fella's beaten ye to it? – Oh dear me, where's our beautiful Angie?"

I shrank back, sweating in the hot flush of the brandy.

The cockerel continued, "You've been back here nigh a month and ye can't see what's happenin' under your nose, can ye! While you're mooning around for a love that God forgot, old Butler Bumstead's out o' the pantry and into your housekeeper, and her pining to death for you!"

I found my voice, shouting, "He's welcome to her!"

"Ach, the fella's got a tongue at last! But can't ye see what

198

you're missing, me darlin'? She's a foine set-up strumpet, broad in the haunch, firm in the calf and a bosom for weepin' on, with more tricks in her than a harem, and I'd rather be in Angie than in the Army." It fluffed up its feathers and hopped along the bed-rail, clucking to raise the neighbourhood.

Upper Forest Works opened with drop-hammers then; flakes of plaster drifted down from the ceiling and the night was filled with whip-cracking and the screams of horses. Furnace light was baying on the walls and the cacophony was riven by the cockerel's shriek, "Sure to God, man, isn't one in the bed worth two in Paris, or where ever your silly Romany bitch has gone? Angie's waiting on the landing, and who's to know? Into her mun! You'll be dazzled by the lustre of her eyes for her beauty would ravish the heart of Solomon's bloody eunuchs. Do ye even know where your Romany is at this moment?"

I thought: Jen, *Jen* . . . !

"Hell's bells! Jen, Jen, is it! Will ye stop bloody romancin' and get down to facts? She's finished with ye, Mortymer – she's done a runner, son! You can bet your sweet life that by now she's on the batter wi' some beardy old frog and lovin' every moment!"

It bounced up and down on the bed-rail, clucking, "But take the lovely Angie for a trip in the dark, me love, and I'll clad ye in silk and finery, so I will; for a live cat is better'n a dead tiger when it comes to the honeyed middle. Your couch shall be of spun gold, your cushions of silk and the woman beneath ye lovelier than the Whore of Babylon. Are you listenin'? Between love-making you'll feast and dance hilariously, so in the name of Satan, what more do ye want?" Red-eyed it peered. "How's that bottle doin' for a start?"

I held it up half empty. The room swam about me.

"Then open another and get it down ye, boyo, for it's doin' no good under the stopper and ye've got to be at your best for the beautiful female . . . and unless me eyes deceive me, here she comes now, the marvellous creature!" It hopped on to the floor, went to the door and bowed low as Angharad entered like a Diana. Consummately graceful, she came into the room in a black see-through gown; opening her arms to me in greeting as it dropped to the floor, and she stood there as bare as an egg.

"Don't hang around, woman," said the cockerel, "you'll catch your death. The fella's awaitin' ye, me darlin', come in, come in!"

"I dreamed of you, Jen," I said, seeing six of her, and was aware that the air was perfumed, the pleasurable scent that was the embodiment of Angharad. This was unexpected since Jen smelled of the wild places of the Romany and the thyme she pinned to her petticoats . . . while this one brought the perfume of the exotic, a craving of the senses.

I hesitated, and the cockerel shrieked in my indecision, "Why, ye pitiful hobbledehoy, ye've got it made! What more do ye want? Invite her in!" and for answer I held up the bedclothes and the woman slipped in and her body was cool against mine.

"Dear me, said the cockerel, I began to think I was back among the virgins, me darlin' – go on – enjoy the girl!"

In the reek of the brandy I sought the mouth of the woman beneath me, saying in gasps, "Jen, *Jen* . . . !"

"Ach, you're a marvellous pupil, Mortymer – get going!" said Paddy Infernal. "Get going!"

Chapter Thirty-Two

I decided to continue with the investigation into William Bumstead, which Jethro had left unfinished.

"Mind you, sir, if we get caught in the 'ouse," said Dai, "it'll be Mr David Grey who'll be seein' to us, not the butler!"

"What of it?"

"Shoot us, more'n likely. Since he's retired they do say he's a terror."

I was perplexed by Jethro's need to investigate the butler. True, if there was just cause for a vendetta against my family, William Bumstead had one ready made.

I had always thought his imprisonment for his escapade in my mother's bedroom unjust; knowing her, what she was when it came to affairs during my father's absences, the butler was probably more to be pitied than blamed. More importantly, I had always believed the accusation of theft against him to be a trumped up charge designed by the police to protect my mother's name; a five year transportation to Botany Bay for something a man didn't do was a punishment practically guaranteeing a vendetta.

Nevertheless, I was aware that against this particular individual, I possessed not the slightest proof.

Therefore, it was with some reluctance that I began the journey from Morriston to Maesteg on what could prove a fruitless operation, especially since I didn't even know what I was looking for.

"Mind you, Maister," said Dai, beside me in the trap, "he

anna all sweet-juice an' honey, this ol' Bumstead; I knowed him since a lad, and he were either diggin' holes in the road or bustin' folks' windows. His mam used to spread honey on his mouth to sweeten up his lies, for he'd *cleck* on ye in school as soon as look at ye."

I began to wonder, as the pony trotted along, which of the two of us – Dai or me – was the more infantile, but comforted myself with the thought that at least on that day I was sober.

The night was cold for April, with a right old palaver going on in the hedgerows, for stoats were hunting and tiny things dying and torn birds complaining to the crescent moon: nothing else sounded but the crunching of the trap's wheels and the rat-a-tat of the pony's hooves, until we came to three old drunks serenading outside the Farmers' Arms a mile or so short of *Cefn-Ydfa*; and I thought of the day I had left the old mansion; now a lifetime ago, it seemed, with Jen as my bride.

"Best leave the trap clear of Russian Villa", suggested Dai.

"That's what I thought. And let's hope you're right about Bumstead being away."

"Ay ay – regular as clockwork he takes his holidays every year in April. Mind, the maids'll be in – they're up in the attics, and their housekeeper's in the main wing with the Greys. I used to clean out the stabling when Angharad worked for 'em, so I knows it backwards."

We were within sight of Grey's villa now; the place was in darkness save for a porch light.

Now sheltering in a thicket, I saw Dai's face silhouetted against the crescent moon, and said, "I'd forgotten that Angharad once worked with William Bumstead."

"O aye, sir – for a couple o' years, before she come to us." He added, "More than one thing ye forgot lately, Maister – like ol' Bumstead owing us one for you Mortymers sending him to transportation . . . and messin' up his life."

Dai's face was corpse-white in a sudden brightening of the moon, and hostile. I replied coldly, "He was our butler and we trusted him. Officially he went to the Colonies for stealing my mother's jewellery. Anyway, that's what came out at his trial."

"Not true, Maister. He never touched her jewellery, I say. I ain't on ol' Bumstead's side, mind, but we got to be fair. You knows like I does what he were up to in 'er bedroom."

There was a silence; he had never talked like this before, and added, "He got flogged on the ship goin' over, and was on the triangles twice after, trying to escape; beaten up some'ut cruel for somethin' he hadn't done. No wonder he hates ye all."

A strange time to raise such an issue, I thought, and made to move, but Dai gripped my arm.

"Folks say I ain't a full pound, being addled between the ears with fightin' fellas three stone larger, but sometimes I'm as sane as you, Maister, and this be now. I got no time for Bumstead, but he's a servant, and servants got to stick together or maisters swarm all over us, says my Bid." He tightened his grip on my arm. "So before you go into that house and do that fella more damage, remember that the old Book says, 'An eye for an eye' – 'ave you ever stopped to think that if your mam invited him?"

"All right, Dai – that's enough! It was you who booted him out of *Cefn-Ydfa* for it, remember!"

"Ay ay, I did it for your feyther. But whether you likes it or not, Tom Mortymer, your mither were at the bottom of it!"

"Right. You've had your say. Are you in this with me, or not?"

The old man straightened. "Straight orf, Maister, for I'm on your side and allus have been. But my Old Bid, she says to me, 'Dai Dando, one day you gotta tell those Mortymers that it ain't all good maisters and bad servants.' Bill Bumstead never touched the Mistress's jewellery – all he did was bounce her on the bed, which is what she asked him!"

I took a breath for a smart reply, but decided against it. I was hearing now the servants gossip so rarely heard in the rarefied atmosphere of the Upstairs Rooms; and there was an unusual justice about it. Poor old Dai with his limited intelligence was only repeating the scandalising of others, and suddenly he said, grinning up at me, "Mind, if you be a'feared o' goin' in there alone, Maister, I'll come wiv' ye, for I loves ye splendid!"

"No. I'll go in alone, but don't talk about my mother like that again!"

Befuddled, Dai stared blankly; his momentary intelligence departed, then said sadly, "Mind you, she were a lovely little skirt was your mam, Tom; but, like Old Bid said, she'd got her brains mainly in her drawers, so I can understand ol' Bumstead wantin' to get 'em orf her."

I left him then to save me the sin of murder.

The butler's rooms were at the rear of Russian Villa; this I knew because once, when visiting Jen soon after she had married David Grey, I had entered them by mistake, and Bumstead himself had redirected me to the Gray's magnificent drawing-room.

But those days now seemed a lifetime away, and all the windows of Bumstead's quarters were in darkness.

Owls were hooting their heads off in the big walled garden, and at the back door I found myself walking on a carpet of stitchwort, their five-petal flowers stark white in the moonlight: a pair of blue-tits nesting nearby began squabbling at my intrusion, and I momentarily stood listening, sensing a threat; it was as if unknown eyes were following my movements.

Beside the back door was a window; to my amazement its sash opened to a touch as if expecting me . . . Swinging a leg over its sill, I crossed the floor of a little bedroom and went into a narrow hall. Pausing, I listened: silence, utter silence rang in my ears.

Faintly from above I heard the distant voice of a woman;

probably a maid in the attic, I reasoned.

Certainly on this floor there was no activity, yet my entry had been made with such ease that I was suspicious.

The thought struck me that Jethro might have earlier accused the butler he suspected, and that this had put the man on his guard . . . ?

A board creaked in my proximity and I pressed myself flat against a wall; it creaked again, louder, and I realised that I myself had caused it by transferring my weight. Taking a chance I lit a match: the hall about me sprang to life, exposing a narrow door that swung open to my shoulder; the match spluttered, burning my fingers. I lit another.

I was in a small, book-lined study: leather volumes, books in line, flashed their gilt in the light; and then I saw a desk and a hand-lamp upon it. The match went out. In the dark I fumbled with the lamp glass; raising it, lighting its wick, I stood taking in the detail of the room: a small table, a chair and a little writing desk.

It was then that I smelled the perfume; and heard again from above stairs the soprano voice of a woman, and this time a man's bass reply. The air moved; the perfume came more strongly.

Perfume is a woman's signature, this was Angharad's . . .

I recall thinking with faint humour that but a few days before she was miles away in my bed in Upper Forest House; so if she was entertaining Bumstead upstairs now, she certainly got around . . .

I began seriously to search; first the drawers of the writing desk, then files on the book-shelves behind me. Nothing of importance came to hand – some household bills for coal and lamp-oil, replacement of silverware from a Maesteg jeweller, and the usual nondescript items of cost-accounting entered in a ledger; the items meticulously entered in a copper-plate hand, that of Gaffer Adams.

Then my eyes caught something more important – a file of

cuttings from *The Cambrian* newspaper reporting my father's and Clare Wildflower's death in Lake Geneva. This caused me no surprise. The man who had collected these had once been a servant in my father's house; naturally he would be affected by the tragedy, although . . . and I stared into the lamp . . . Surely Bumstead would by then have been serving his prison term in Australia? Somebody else, therefore, must have collected these. Still, it was of small importance and I shrugged the thought away.

Through the study window then I caught a glimpse of Dai Dando hunched up in the moonlight near the thicket. Seeing him waiting, moved me into action, and I searched the room quickly but carefully.

Finding nothing significant, I inwardly cursed Jethro's suspicions in sending me on such an inconspicuous errand, and was about to leave in the manner I had entered when renewed voices from above quickened my interest. The female voice I could now identify – Angharad's . . . but not the man's. Was it Bumstead with her, or another? True, this was the butler's official quarters, but I had no proof that it was he.

In moonlight I was on my way up the stairs to the landing above when I saw the half-open door of the bedroom from which the voices were coming, so paused, level with the landing; and saw in a sudden blaze of the moon a naked man standing in the bedroom with his back to me. He was middle-aged, of athletic build; with his hands upon his hips he stood facing a woman in the bed and I recognised her in the light of the moon.

Then the man laughed softly, a chuckle I had somewhere heard before, and as he suddenly moved in the light, he turned, and I saw his face clearly.

Jethro.

I watched with disbelief as he went to the bed and gathered Angharad into his arms.

Jethro and Angharad!

Chapter Thirty-Three

My search unsuccessful, I was about to leave Russian Villa by the way I had entered. With a leg over the window sill I reached out to turn off the lamp, then heard a soft command, "Oh no, you don't; stay – stay where you are!" and turned to find myself confronted by a man with a pistol.

William Bumstead, the butler.

I recognised him after momentary hesitation, for the years had changed him; no longer was this the man of the good looks and presence that I remembered, but one strangely dwarfed by the years between. The big horse pistol he held gave him command of the situation.

"Come back into the room," he said, and I obeyed.

"Tom Mortymer, eh?" He peered at me in the glow of the lamp. "Now tell me what you're doing here."

In such a situation the captive is sheepish, and so was I, saying, "I'm in trouble, and believe you to be the cause of it."

His eyes strangely bright, moved furtively from one object to another in the room. "And now you are going away disappointed! You and I have a long history of deceit, Mortymer, but I'd not have believed you'd stoop to this."

"I had my reasons."

"Enlighten me."

This was an intelligent man; rumour had it that he was of the usual cast of gentry illegitimates; a son of high breeding who had fallen from grace through a hapless marriage and gaming. The theft of my mother's jewellery, for which he had been sent to the Colonies, was the pettier crime he had confessed to at his trial; this being a lesser offence than sexual harassment, said Dai. Yet it had been his unfair conviction for theft that had led to his demise.

The fact that Mr Grey, a respected Maesteg industrialist, had employed him immediately upon his to return to Wales, was proof enough of public sympathy for the man.

On the face of it I could understand Jethro's suspicion that Bumstead was waging a vendetta against my family, but in terms of absolute proof, there was nothing yet to be laid at Bumstead's door.

Now he said with careless grace, "Incidentally, I came across old Dando outside the house – on watch, he said, the old fool – his brains are scrambled – I sent him about his business . . ."

I did not reply.

"A different situation to so many years ago, Mortymer, when as a thriving pugilist he tossed me out of the house – remember?" Gesturing with the pistol, he waved me to a chair. "We have much to discuss, so why not sit down?"

I obeyed, watching the gun, which, strangely, Bumstead had placed conveniently within my reach; abstractedly reflecting upon the ludicrous situation now presented: the captor and his burglar about to discuss his motive for the break-in. Bumstead frowned at me in the yellow light, saying, "You appreciate, I suppose, that I could have shot you out of hand? No court in the land would have convicted me for such action." He emptied his hands at me.

"Here I am, a respectable citizen returning from a holiday to find a burglar rifling my possessions; my age alone would give me the benefit of jurisprudence!"

"Clearly you know the law," I replied.

"Better still, Mortymer, I know the way the law works; it may be an ass, but is corrected by the jury system – crooked judges, policy corruption, and false allegations – all come to grief in the face of twelve good men and true – with the proviso, of course, that they are untainted, which was not so in my particular case."

"Really? From what I heard, you got a pretty fair trial."

"From what you gathered as an adolescent, no doubt. One has to be the victim, not a callow onlooker, when one is being tried for theft from one's superior in this accursed country."

I said, "You surprise me. Though I tend to the *avant-garde*. I believe our judiciary to be reasonably honest, but perhaps I'm misinformed."

My cynicism didn't anger him, and a small sense of pity touched me; the lamp brightened in a flare of the wick; and his face – once he was a truly handsome man – was that of one aged by sickness and privation; something I had not noticed before.

Quietly, he said, "Perhaps for the first time you should be informed of the situation in which I found myself, Mortymer . . . if you could for a few moments devoid yourself of the clap-trap that has been fed to you by relatives and the Press . . . ?"

His voice was harsh and strained, its inherent beauty that I remembered, gone.

"If I stand accused of betraying your father by an adulterous affair with your mother, then I plead guilty; but no man, least of all one of young years could have resisted her wiles . . . no, don't interrupt me, I'm entitled to this hearing.

"I was unsuspecting when I entered service as a butler in your father's house – and Mission trained – that in itself is a laugh, is it not? For me it was acceptance into the priesthood or, if I failed this, domestic service. Within a week I was under your mother's spell."

He leaned forward, his eyes narrowed and glittering in his haggard face.

209

"Had such a beauty thrown herself at your feet, how would you have fared? Believe it or not, until then I'd never had a woman.

"She planned every move, organised my every activity – to await her signal the moment your father was clear of the house; and I blame him as much as myself, for he blundered on, letting her play the role of a virtuous wife even when she was the talk of the county!"

His anger was rising now and he was speaking with difficulty.

"The night you and Dando caught me in her room was not the first, Mortymer, but one of many such occasions. I was the toy with which she played – no doubt you find this difficult, but by God, you will learn the truth of your mother."

I interjected, "You were sentenced to five years transportation, not for your affair with her, but for theft of her jewellery."

He was trembling now; it spread from his hands to the sagging folds of his face, and he replied, "Wrong again! I swear it to you, as I swore on the Bible all those years ago, that I never touched her jewellery. It was a charge alleged by your mother and trumped up by the police to smother the scandal which would have resulted. She was no good, Mortymer, do you hear me? Your mother, perhaps, but I've known harlots with better ideals."

The lamp, burning lower, spluttered on the wick; shadows loomed deeper about us. In a moment's quiet the voices upstairs sounded again in whispered consultation. Bumstead asked, "You hear that?"

I nodded.

Unexpectedly, he said, "No business of yours, of course, but the reason I returned here sooner than expected, and in view of your own unhappy situation I will not bore you with more tales of infidelity. The woman you hear upstairs is mine; the man one of many she entertains during my absences; it is a common enough complaint from betrayed lovers."

It was the way he looked at me. Then he said, "I know of the situation that brought you here to search my rooms, but understand this: I hold no sympathy for you damned Mortymers, and you'll find no evidence anywhere to link me with your personal troubles, what ever you've been told. My hostility to your family died with your father's death." He added bitterly, "I have enough troubles of my own through that one upstairs, without other complications."

There was about him a directness; his honesty shone through with unremitting persistence, and his sadness lent this substance.

I was tempted to ask him how Angharad came into the equation, it being news to me that, although she had worked with him at the Greys, I'd heard no talk of other mutual interests . . . True, few of those privileged to live 'above' knew what was happening to those 'downstairs', though not a lot missed people like Old Bid.

Further, I wondered if Bumstead even knew the identity of the man on the floor above us now, or if, indeed, they had even met; but decided against it on the grounds that I was a big enough fool as it was.

The lamp flickered again and Bumstead leaned forward to turn up the wick; tears shone in his eyes.

"Best be on your way, Mortymer," he said. "Neither of us have done too well tonight . . ." He hesitated. "I . . . I will take no action against you, if you, in turn, promise that nobody will know of anything you've heard or seen here tonight."

"Of course."

He went on, "It may be insignificant, but when it comes to your own complicated existence – the departure of your wife – I suggest you need look no further for evidence than

211

that sitting under your nose. There's no point in being a fool so consistently . . ."

I did not reply; he added, turning away, "As for young Jenny, remember that in the difficult days after her first husband's death, we shared the same roof. Ask her, and she will give you proof that in our short time together I did my best to make her lot reasonable in a house curiously opposed to Romanies . . . of which I remind you, I am one."

Picking up the pistol from the table, he left me, and I heard his footsteps echoing on the stairs.

Outside Russian Villa, I took the stopper out of the flask I carried and guzzled Satan's Brew to clear my head.

"Are you there, Dai Dando?" I called.

"He is not," came a reply, "for I made a face at him through the thicket; he was away. I couldn't see the sod for dust."

Paddy Infernal again, sitting in a crook of a tree above me, and he said, his face up at the moon, "Gawd, *what* a cock-up! You insist on goin' into everything head first, don't ye! If a fella can get hold of the dirty end of the stick, mate, it's you."

"Aw, shut your gob!" I said, talking in his language.

"Shut me gob, is it? Can't you see that the man who's just put a boot behind ye is one of Nature's gentlemen? That he's had no truck with the filthy accusations you've made against him?"

"I accused him of nothing!"

"Without a shred of evidence you break into his rooms! Hasn't he enough hassle wi' your Uncle Jethro rogerin' his missus wi'out you bustin' in to search his private papers?"

"How did I know Jethro would be there?"

"Because he's your uncle, ye daft nit – he's a Mortymer, isn't he – and if there's spare skirt lolligatin' around, your all faster on the job than Samson's bloody foxes," and here he

212

crossed himself, – "and him seducin' that harlot Angharad for the past six months?"

"Don't be ridiculous!"

"Ridiculous, is it? That only goes to show that you're up the wrong street again; now listen to me, listen and learn, Mortymer. You're luxuriatin' in the wrong pastures, for you're too small a man to handle the likes of Jethro. Why do you always insist on ignoring what's goin' on under your nose?"

It stilled me, for that is what Bumstead had said; I took another swig at the flask; the voice from the tree continued, "Have you stopped to think, me darlin', that all your troubles began from a certain date? Right from the moment that lovely Jethro came into your life? Check it back. Who killed the animals on Flatholm? Where was Jethro when Gaffer was knocked off – I'm tellin' ye this – he didn't do it himself, for all his supposed suicide note . . . Who tipped off the Scots about you lyin' with your sister, and who forged the Works cheques and blamed it on to Gaffer?"

"Wrong!" I said. "Gaffer confessed!"

"O aye? And you believed it? What did his wife say about it? And while we're on the subject of Upper Works, have you had a look at the books there lately, for ye were fool enough to put your Uncle in charge there while ye scarpered north after your missus, remember? God, man, there's one born every minute!"

I clenched my eyes and tipped up the flask; the raw whisky seared my lips; my head swam.

"That's right – go on – a few home truths and he's back on the whampo! You're no good, Mortymer. Like poor old Bumstead, you're both innocents in a world of tigers; neither of you could organise a piss-up in a brewery, and the way you're goin', ye'll finish up wi' nothing – no business, no money, no mansion and worst of all, no missus! Like I said

213

before – at this precise moment, she's probably hittin' it up in Paris wi' some ol' fat Frenchie!"

"You're disgusting!"

"And I'll be saying I told ye so when you learn the truth of it, for this is the last time I'm warning ye. Forget Bumstead and weak buggers like him, and get after your precious bloody Jethro – he's the cancer in this particular growth! The Pinkerton Detective Agency did ye say – *my arse!*" and he shouted laughter.

I leaned against the bole of the tree and stared up through its branches. The bearded face of the thing above me grinned down.

"Do you expect me to believe a single thing you say?" I asked.

"Gawd help ye if ye don't, me darlin'," said Paddy Infernal.

Chapter Thirty-Four

I could scarcely believe it when, within a day of my igno-
minious attempt to search Russian Villa, I received a letter
from Jethro which bore a London postmark. Unbelievable this, because he would not have had time to travel
from Maesteg to London in order to catch that particular
postmark . . . but try as I may I couldn't work out the
conflicting times involved, being too far gone on a bottle
of vodka to make sense of anything.

The letter read:

> 'Andover Hotel
> Pudding Lane
> London

My dear Tom

I have not been idle in my attempts to clear your good
name and bring you peace of mind.

The more I examine it, the more I consider the letter
written by your father to Jenny's mother to be both
extraordinary and worthless. To this end I have sought
proof of Jenny's true parentage. I am delighted to be
able to tell you that I have unearthed the true facts
of her birth, and that your worries as to your blood
relationship are now at an end.

Truly, it astonishes me that this proof, so readily
available to me and in the public domain, has not
surfaced before.

Such is the value of documentation I hold, Tom, that I will not enclose it herein, but suggest that you, Jenny and myself should meet at an appropriately secure place, where I can hand it to you and explain it in detail; and can think of no better rendezvous than Drift Cottage on Flatholm, a place so dear to you both. I do not have her address in France, so please write and ask her to come. Shall we make it June 10th next? I enlist you to keep secret both the time and the place of this meeting.

Meanwhile, as the bearer of such delightful news, I send you my most sincere congratulations. With affectionate greetings

Jethro   May 16th 1885'

The effect of the letter upon me was one of unrestrained joy, and I cursed myself for doubting the integrity of one who, at the expense of his own work, had laboured to produce such a happy result. I wanted to shout from the roof-tops that the nightmare of our existence was now over; that I could live with Jenny for the rest of my life in peace and happiness.

Having in mind Jethro's counsel against spreading such news abroad (and I must say that this surprised me) I sent a letter to Jen's Paris address instead of by open telegraph.

'My darling,

I have just received the most important information from Jethro, and enclose a copy of his letter to me, for you to read for yourself. It is surely an act of God that my own relative should have arrived to solve our dilemma, and I bless the day he came into our lives.

Jethro has bound me to secrecy, so it appears that guilty people may be involved. Therefore I beg you to

216

reconsider your decision to stay away from me, and come posthaste to Drift Cottage on Flatholm Island (yes, I still have the key!) meeting me there on June 10th, when I am sure that Jethro, with the Pinkerton Agency at his disposal, will once and for all put an end to the nightmare that has for so long kept us apart.

Your devoted husband

Tom   May 20th 1885'

After posting this, I was going up the drive of Upper Forest House when I met Angharad on her way to shopping in Maesteg. With the sun upon her face under her pretty lace bonnet, she looked more like a young girl off to Sunday school, than a scheming adulteress. Pitying Bumstead, her aggrieved lover, I wondered at the weakness of Jethro, for women were plentiful in the Maesteg area, with beauty and quality at no premium. Also, I now wondered at the outcome of his confrontation with a heart-broken Bumstead in the bedroom of Russian Villa . . .

We passed one another, Angharad and I, with happy Good-Mornings and little sincerity, and I told myself with some satisfaction that within a week of her homecoming, Jen would give this one what for. There being no better example of zeal when it came to a woman on her own patch removing the competition.

Dozie Annie, our parlourmaid, accosted me upon my return home. Accosted is the word, because Annie remembered me from my childhood, and far from retaining her inherent shyness, her emancipated attitude was now that of Mother taking me over.

"How do, sir!" said Dozie, her usual greeting.

Time was, when we were young and suffering pangs of adolescence, I used to pinch her under the bustle; but encouragement came in small doses from a then highly

217

virtuous Dozie. Later, however, she had begun to issue favours to the Maesteg males; in which, being the Young Master, I luckily could not participate. This culminated in poor Dozie getting in the family way, an appalling situation in those days, and she was groomed for the Workhouse, the home of such domestic strays.

But on the basis that only good girls got into trouble, my father intervened: Dozie was given a downstairs bedroom and produced a son called George, who was the doyen of the house; and raised him there with official family blessing.

That was so long ago now that I can scarcely remember . . .

"Mind, you'd not recognise my George now, sir," said Dozie, and held up a feather duster like a protective weapon. Time was she would have used something heavier, for I was a randy young sod in my early teens. An early experience of the difference in the genders being through a hole in the floor of my attic bedroom, when I had observed Dozie in the bath.

This history, a remembrance of earlier yearnings, moved between us like a faint erotic dream.

"No, ye wouldn't recognise my boy these days if ye saw him in the street, sir," said Dozie proudly, referring to George – his father having long since joined the 32nd Ox and Bucks to escape my father's affiliation order. She added now, "That grown, he has. When he was little, Old Bid cooked him a hegg for 'is breakfast every mornin', and it's made him very muscellous."

We were now in the study of Upper House; I had come in there to do some Tinplate correspondence and Dozie had stayed, being privileged by our affinity; now she was swiping the dust from one place to another.

No beauty, this one, her face peaked and pale under her mop-cap. People said she was a pound short in the upper storey; but they didn't know Dozie; she knew her way around, all right.

"How old is he now?" I asked, knowing it full well, and shuffled papers at my desk.

Blackbirds were shouting at the morning, and the room was shot with sun-shafts; fantail doves were coo-cooing.

Dozie made a face at the ceiling, "My George? Twenty-two come Sunday."

"He is still in the army?"

Actually, I was wishing her a penn'orth, because I wanted to get things cleared up, having a mountain of unanswered letters needing replies.

One was from Opand, my Swansea bankers practically demanding my presence at their premises again; they were in the middle of an audit of the firm's accounts and certain irregularities had come to their attention, they said. What with one thing and another – Jethro's brief but peremptory bookkeeping and my own disinterest in the business – things at Upper Forest Works had gone from bad to worse.

"Oh no, sir – didn't I tell ye?" Dozie interjected into my thoughts. "George left the Army after four years wi' Colours, and is now a journalist in Fleet Street – I told ye, didn't I!"

"Yes, yes, of course! What newspaper?"

"*The London Mercury*. Three sovereigns a week they pays him, ye know!"

"That's excellent!"

She preened at the sun. "Gawd, he's got on an' no mistake, sir. When I started in Service, I got that much in a year. Mind, it don't impress Miss Angharad much . . ."

I gave her a happy smile. "I shouldn't let that worry you!"

"Now that's just what I said to Dai Dando. 'Dai,' I said, 'she's a frosty old piece when I talks about my George, as if he ain't of no importance.' Do ye know what Dai said, 'Annie, me love,' said he, 'she's a maiden lady, see. She'd be different if someone put a bun in her oven.'"

I forced a grin. "Trust Dai!"

"Would . . . would ye mind if I said some'ut personal, sir?"

"I have no doubt you will, Annie," I answered brightly, now wishing her to the devil.

"Since your wife went . . . went away, ye've kept a bit to yourself, so to speak . . .'aven't you!"

It was out. Sweat had formed on Annie's forehead and she wiped it into her hair, adding, "Not my place, like, but wi' Old Bid gone to Jerusalem and old Dai a bit spare up top, there's no one left but me, and . . ." She faltered. "Well, I'm a bit older'n you, see, and . . ."

"Spit it out, Annie!"

"I mean, while I ain't a great one for Church, and all that, but . . . it's best to try to keep oneself decent, ain't it?"

"Of course."

She raised her small wry face; to my astonishment her eyes had filled with tears. She said huskily, "I . . . It was terrible sad to see your Jenny go, sir, and it ain't my business why she went, save what I pick up downstairs, but . . ."

"But what?"

Clearly she was in a dilemma.

She waved a hand at the wine decanters on the sideboard, saying, "It be terrible to see you drinkin', sir. I mean, old Dai's an old boozer, ain't he? But you're different, like, and . . ."

"Is that all you are trying to say?"

For answer she was silent, standing before me like a chastised child; then, "Well, no, Mr Tom . . ."

"What, then?" My tone was peremptory.

"Well . . ." and she faltered.

I said, "My drinking is my business, Annie!"

"I ain't talking' about the drinkin', sir. 'Mind ye own business, Annie,' said old Dai, 'if Mr Tom wants to drink 'imself to death, it's up to him, ain't it?' and I agree. Oh no, sir, I'm talking' about old Danny Wildflower."

220

"Who?"

"Danny Wildflower – you know, your Jenny's father."

"What of him?"

"The chap Jenny's mother used to pull around on a trolley . . ."

"What about him?"

She took a deep breath. "Well, all this gossip about 'im not being her pa an' all that . . . it's codswallop, sir. Mind, I was only four or five when your Jen was born, but I remember old Danny – tossin' me up and catchin' me, and him and Clare callin' at our house to take me out wi' Jen only just born . . ."

I rose at the desk. She continued, "An' . . . and he had no broken back then, Mr Tom."

I said, "Are you telling me that you remember Jenny's father before he had his accident?"

"Clear as a bell, sir . . ."

"What else do you remember – come on!"

"I remember they brought 'im home on a stretcher, and Jen's mam cryin' and the colliers making her a wheeled trolley thing so she could pull him around on it. And it were only after he died that your pa and Clare Wildflower got together, when Jen were about two years old . . ."

Truth dawning upon me. "And that was after Jen's father, Danny Wildflower, had died?"

"O aye, sir – over a year after."

We stood in silence. My world stopped dead on the clock of joy. I said, "Annie, in God's name, why didn't you tell me all this before?"

She emptied her hands at me. "Not my business, were it? What the toffs get up to upstairs ain't none of your business, young Annie, they said, and don't you make it so, or ye'll land in hot water . . ." She added faintly, "Besides, you never asked me, did ye?"

It was a bitter and recriminating thought, that all the

anguish and heart-searching Jen and I had suffered had been totally and conclusively unnecessary. That while I had been casting around for diverse and complex reasons for the misery of our situation, the reasons for it were non-existent.

The answer to the tragic conundrum lay not only within my own house, but actually within reach. All I need have done was to call the parlourmaid and ask her one simple question, "Are you telling me that Danny Wildflower, Jen's father, was alive at the time of her conception?"

And the answer would have been "Yes".

"Are you feelin' all right, Mr Tom?" asked Annie, peering at me. "Ye've gone very pale . . ."

Strangely, Dozie Annie's statement, couched in everyday conversation and abstract innocence, had more effect upon me than Jethro's claim to our innocence through professional investigation; and surely, if he could spare time to conduct an affair with Angharad in my vicinity, surely he could have called into Morriston Works or Upper Forest House, and informed me of his findings face to face.

Annie was basic and substantial; Jethro – whom I had not met for months now – appeared shadowy, almost mythical.

The fulcrum of his investigation, and its outcome, was apparently the finding of Jenny's birth certificate, which he claimed to hold.

Such a discovery was surely worth more than a passing mention in a belated letter, when our future, since we were a heartbeat away from a nightmare, was so dependent upon his actions.

What was needed now was not vacuity, but firm statement; not tenuous promises, but tangible facts; nothing less than this, I was sure, would entice Jen back to me.

I railed against Jethro's delay; that the three of us should meet on a date as far away as June the 10th, a whole month, appeared an eternity of nervous expectation, and I wondered at the reason for it.

Chapter Thirty-Five

A beautiful summer was now into us; Wales washed out her green and gold garments under each fresh rush of the run, and I was high and alive with me that evening as I climbed down at Sully into the boat of the ferryman (new to me) and watched him tack his little craft in a welter of foam; skylarks sang their eternal love songs. There was not a cloud in the sky on that brilliant June day.

June the 10th!

I braced myself in the prow of the little clinker-built cutter and watched the southern shore of my beloved Flatholm come up in brilliant sun-spray, and there was in me a great joy at the prospect of seeing my girl again; yet somewhat sullied by the prospect of having to share her with Jethro, who would be there, too, of course.

The boatman's voice interjected into the thumping waves and battering wind. With his hands cupped to his mouth, he shouted, "Are you anything to do wi' the woman I brought over this afternoon?"

"A woman you brought over? What woman? Did she say her name?"

"Was she likely to? She 'ad a ticket."

"Did she say why she was coming over?"

"No chance. A hoity-toity piece, if you ask me. I reckon somebody took her tongue."

The cutter rocked and dived to the swell, and we hung on.

"What did she look like?" I asked.

"Black hair. Small. Got bangle earrings." He bent to the tiller, swung the cutter to a new tack, and the south beach foreshore came up out of the spindrift. "I likes me women gossipy, I do; when they're gossipy ye know what the buggers are up to. Close women 'ave close thoughts – I got one at 'ome."

"Dear me," I said, "I'm very sorry for you."

"You're welcome, mate! She had her nose up, this one, if she's your'n, you're welcome."

"Thanks very much."

"Think nothin' of it, boyo, the philosophy's free."

"I'll make a note of it," I bawled back. "You don't like women?"

"Not particularly, nor you neither; the last old tart I took over 'ad three chins and were grandma o' one of the Gunners!

The cutter ground on the sloping shingle beach and I jumped out at the prow.

"See ye again!" he bawled.

"Not if I see you first, you bastard!"

A voice in the wind followed me up the beach, saying in a whisper, "Dear me, just hark at that! He can't even get on with the boatman."

"You sod off," I said, sick of people.

Paddy Infernal again, even on Flatholm; I was never going to be rid of him.

Once clear of the beach I ran all the way to Drift Cottage.

It was only a year or so since I had lived here with Jen, and it seemed like ten; but the wearying frustration, disappointments and tears were banished at a stroke now. I felt reborn, vitally alive, then dispirited, because if she wasn't here already (and it was now past eight o'clock, with daylight fading) the boatman might be mistaken and she might not be coming at all . . .

224

Remembering where we had hidden the cottage key, I felt along the eaves until discovering it. The door swung open and the beloved little room stood before me like the opening to another life.

The same faded oil painting of the ram dying in snow (Jen had picked it up for sixpence at a jumble sale) was there; the same tatty sampler above the bed (now piled with blankets) saying 'God is Love', and I stood there wondering if He really was . . .

Apart from the usual musty smell of unused habitation, all was exactly as we had left it, a tribute to the honesty of the people of the island.

All the familiar sounds of the cottage came back to me in those moments of entry: Jen's laughter, Shelduck's hovering cries, Goat's raucous bleating, Donk's hee-haws and the eternal wind, blustering in the chimney.

Now, sitting in my old armchair, I wondered why Jethro was leaving it so late, for shadows were deepening in the room. Indeed, if he or Jen left it any later, they would miss the last ferry from Sully.

It was then that I became aware that I was no longer alone . . . for a smell of decay had come to my nostrils; and I saw in the glow of the searchlight's beam, a hunched figure standing in a corner and knew it instantly. I saw him more clearly as I lit the ceiling lantern.

"Well, well," said Paddy Infernal. "You do get around, don't ye! Now I'll tell ye somethin' free, me charmer; if you're waitin' for your beloved uncle, you're wasting your time, so treat yourself to a snifter while you're waiting."

And I saw shining on a shelf by the oil-stove a bottle growing out of the gloom: whisky . . . a bottle that wasn't there before. I didn't drink now, and told him so.

"Ach, to hell wi' it, son – who's to know? Ye see, Mortymer, while I used to be your conscience and personal

225

confidant, I've played out that role. I'm here now as your clairvoyant . . ."

The shadows further deepened, and I heard only his voice, "But when it comes to demonology, bewitchery and sorcery, you'll never find a better practitioner, take it from me. For I can give ye, hook, line and sinker, advance notification of what's goin' to happen to ye tomorrow or a week next Sunday.

"For instance, you're there sittin' on your arse, waitin' for your Uncle Jethro to arrive, yet at this precise moment he's on his way to an audience wi' St Peter."

I scarcely heard him, such was my sudden thirst; it was as if salt had been suddenly injected into my veins, and my mouth was parched. Therefore, while his chattering continued unabated, I was wiping my mouth in the approved antics of the alcoholic, staring fixedly at the bottle.

"Ye see," said he, "if you're here for a cosy relationship wi' darlin' Jen and a copy of her birth certificate, then you're up that creek without a paddle again, son, for that's the very last thing you're gettin', so ye are! In fact, me lovely, you're more likely to get a kick in the arse from Bumstead, the butler, and a lot o' tongue pie from Jen, and shall I tell ye why?"

I didn't reply, being busy getting the cork out of the bottle; and drank, eyes clenched, gasping to the sting of the whisky.

"Ach, for sure," said the voice, "t'is the elixir of life, so it is! I wouldn't mind a sovereign for every drunk I've sent to hell in the name o' me old friend, Johnny Walker, and soon I'm away to supervise the next fella on me list. Meanwhile, I'll now be singin' the love-song of the bottle to ye, for I've hooked ye again, so I have, as sure as me name's Paddy Infernal." He came out of the corner, sat on a chair and turning up his bearded face, sang tunelessly in a cracked tenor:

"When dull care do attack you,

drinking will those clouds dispel.
Four good bottles will make you happy,
they rarely fail. If a fifth should be
wanted, ask the gods, t'will be granted,
Then you'll easily obtain a remedy for
your pain . . ."

Then he stopped singing, pointed at the door in panic, and whispered, "Away to go, I am! Someone's comin'!" and vanished.

"Are you there, Tom Mortymer?" asked a cultured voice outside the door. "And will you light the lamp, sir, for I cannot see my hand before my face."

I turned in my chair, recognising the voice. The lamp glowed under my hands, the shadows were banished, and the man who stepped into the light was William Bumstead; he was wearing a cloak and carrying a brief case.

"Good God!" I whispered. "What are you doing here?"

"That, my friend," said the butler, "is a very long story."

Reaching out, he took the bottle from my hand. "It is of paramount importance that you stay sober for a change." Throwing his cloak before him, he sat down in a chair at the kitchen table. "No doubt you're surprised to see me?"

"I'm astonished! I was expecting Jethro." I added, "He wrote asking me to arrange for my wife and I to meet him here."

"No, Mortymer, it was I who wrote to you . . ."

"You sent a letter to me in Jethro's name? Why?"

Bumstead smiled. "All will become clear in due course."

His tone was calm. "Last time we met, your Uncle Jethro was being entertained in my quarters by your maid, Angharad, do you recall?" He peered at me in the light of the lamp, adding, "Are you sober enough to understand what I am saying, Mortymer?

"This damned uncle of yours began to be a nuisance – the amateur detective rooting around for evidence, so Angharad and I decided to be rid of him." Saying this, he drew from his cloak a big horse pistol and laid it on the table between us. The whisky was now getting at me and I stared fixedly at the bottle inwardly cursing my stupidity in getting myself under the influence at the time when I needed my wits about me.

The man's voice droned on and I heard it, not in my consciousness, but as within an evaporating dream. Certainly, the drink I had just taken was of overpowering strength; never have I felt so befuddled; I concentrated hard, trying to focus his face, and heard him say, "You'll realise by now that you've been taken for a fool; more, you'll also understand that should you show the smallest violence towards me, I would have no hesitation in blowing your head off your shoulders; do we understand one another?"

Vacuously, I nodded, fighting for intelligence; Bumstead continued, "Even to you, Mortymer, something should now be totally apparent – that this is the end of the road for you – in other words – pay-day."

Suddenly, within the daze of my mind, I remembered Jenny, and said, staggering up, "Where . . . where's my wife?"

Reaching out, Bumstead pushed me back on to the chair. "Good God, man, don't you know? If, as you say, your wife is to join you here on Flatholm, it's probably time she arrived. Indeed," and here he smiled, "she might even be already here, my friend! Meanwhile . . ." and here he opened the brief case and brought out papers.

"But I am more concerned with you, than her." He tossed the papers on to the table, saying, "These documents, legally drawn up, are the basis of a transfer – the assets of Upper Forest Works from your name into mine. Do you understand what I am saying?"

I asked flatly, "Where . . . where is Jethro?"

"I am not the least concerned. These papers . . ."

"Where's Jethro? I am not going any further with this until you tell me what you've done with him!"

Picking up the pistol he examined it with meaningful intent, and said, "Ah well, I suppose you'll have to know some time. Suffice to say that he is not now competing in this particular game."

"You've killed him, haven't you!"

"Oh come, we're not savages! Seeing the game was up, he committed suicide."

"You're playing the fool with me, Bumstead . . ."

"And isn't that a bloody change! You and your line have been playing the fool with my life for as long as I can remember!"

With an effort I shouted, "My line, as you call it, is nothing to do with me! I had nothing at all to do with you going to prison."

"Perhaps not, but to repay me for the past you are now going to reimburse me for pain and suffering. The sins of the fathers, it is called . . ."

"Where's my wife, and what have you done to Jethro?" Awkwardly, I leaped to my feet, caught my foot in the chair and went headlong. Bumstead stood over me, the pistol in his hand.

"Back on your feet and sit down again," he said, and for many moments we sat, staring at one another, then, "Your family sent me to the Colonies, Mortymer, and these papers reimburse me for what they did to me there.

"Can you, for one moment, understand the misery of a man falsely imprisoned – the sadism of transportation, the brutality aboard ship and the blood-stained triangles of the convict settlements?"

Unbuttoning his cloak, he pulled up his shirt, momentarily turning his back to me, and I closed my eyes to the white scars where the whips had cut; weals as thick as a man's fingers criss-crossed his flesh.

"And for what, Mortymer, shall I tell you? For protesting my innocence – three floggings – three lots of fifty on my back, eighty strokes of the bush-cane on the backs of my legs and five lots of fifty on the breech for refusing to state my guilt for a crime I never committed – sent in an annual report from Van Dieman's Lane to Parliament. All this for a man who has never stolen a penny in his life!"

I sat in silence, numbed by the vehemence of his allegations.

"But more, Mortymer, much more! I was young then. Can you imagine, in your respectable little world, the depravity of that convict colony, when the nearest women are on the other side of the world? Unspeakable offences are committed against innocence, and when we are returned to our own country, you expect us to act as normal people!"

"I did not do this to you!" I shouted.

"Perhaps not, but since it is too late to get satisfaction from your father, I intend to get it from the remaining Mortymers."

I closed my eyes. "What do you want from me?"

"Upper Forest Works, for a start. *Sign!*"

I stared up at him. "I have sunk every penny in that project!"

He nodded. "Yes, I'm aware of it. In today's money about eighty thousand pounds," He pushed the documents towards me. "Two signatures where I have marked with a cross in pencil."

"And if I refuse?"

"Then I will sign them for you, but for me that will not be quite the same; part of this retribution is the pleasure I get out of watching you do it."

"You're mad!"

"So I've been told before."

I did not move; motionless on either side of the table, we sat, and hatred was upon his face; then he directed the pistol at me again, saying, "You know something? I've dreamed of this. In the lice-ridden bunks of the settlement it was with me in my waking hours; but I knew that one day this would come about, for you are the product of a debased system, the son of a fool and an amateur whore. Your father let your mother flaunt her immorality and kept her under his roof long after he should have divorced her!"

He saw my knuckles tighten on the chair and chuckled softly. "That's right, enjoy the role of the outraged son – do better – take a chance and come for the gun – it would delight me to blow your stomach into your backbone. A fair exchange? I lose Upper Works and you die." He tossed a Waterman pen on to the table.

"Sign."

I took a deep breath. "Not legal. You've nobody to witness it." I tossed the pen back to him.

He said, "If you take the trouble to look, you'll see that it has been witnessed already."

I glanced at the last page of the document. Jethro's signature was entered as a witness; realisation of the truth of what had happened over the years now began slowly to permeate my mind.

"A forgery. Like all the letters?"

Bumstead nodded. "And an excellent example, although I say so. God, Mortymer, for a man making a fortune in tinplate, you're not very bright, are you! You send me to the Colonies for five years for unrestricted leisure, surround me by revolutionaries, sadists, thieves and murderers, and expect me to keep out of mischief? This, you know, is the disadvantage of the British legal system – it deals collectively; it lumps together the dregs of its communities and expects the individual to end his term as lily-white, ready to take his appointed place as a member of decent society. Well, you can't have it both ways. I went in as an innocent – mission-trained out of my Romany clan, remember – and

231

came out as a forger trained to perfection by the best professionals in the business. But note something carefully – I did not use my new craft on any but the guilty. I possess excellent testimonials from David Grey, the industrialist and might have continued so into my pension, had I not been pledged to repay you Mortymers for the misery you brought into my life."

I took up the pen, saying, "Upper Works is of little importance to me. Revenge yourself on me if you wish, but let that be an end to it."

"You refer to your wife?"

"Yes."

He replied carefully, "When her first husband died she lived in Russian Villa, as you know. Ask her if she has any complaint of the way I treated her then. As butler there I behaved to her as a friend. I have nothing against Jenny Wildflower."

"You had nothing against Gaffer Adams," I replied, "but I have no doubt that you killed him."

He did not answer this.

I continued, "And no doubt at all as to who informed the Scottish authorities that my wife and I were in their vicinity?"

"Yes, but not until you yourself alerted them by a childish offence against Scottish law. Be reasonable, you asked for it!"

"And the letter my father was supposed to have sent to Clare Wildflower warning against my association with her daughter? You were responsible for that?"

He nodded. "A forgery of which I am inordinately proud, Mortymer. Your father wrote with a dangerously unusual hand; it needed all my skills, some forgeries being easier than others. Old Gaffer, for instance, who was classically educated, enunciated like a peasant, but wrote copper-plate!"

"You transferred funds from his Works accounts into your name?"

"No, Mortymer, no – from your Works accounts to Gaffer's name, when I then appropriated it."

"After which you shot him."

"Good God, no! Little people like Gaffer, astonished at their own success, can never bear the thought of public disgrace. It was suicide."

I said, "You really are the most cold-blooded bastard!"

"But a realist – men like you, the dreamers, are food and drink to men like us." He raised the pistol again. "There's too much talking – give me the pleasure of watching you sign. If you don't, I'll kill the pair of you, your woman as well!" He glanced at his watch. "In the next five minutes."

I said with a lightness I didn't feel. "You'll have a job – she hasn't arrived!"

The reply came instantly. "Oh, yes she has, as you'll discover."

I watched the gun; it was rigid in his hand, and thought, for my head was clearing, it would be dangerous to have a go at him, and said, "You won't get away with this; lawyers will come into it; such signatures will be subject to meticulous scrutiny . . ." and heard my voice as an echo in the room.

Jenny was here? On the Island, he had said. I didn't believe him, but dared not take the chance. To make a mistake now could mean the end of us both. Bumstead's features, I noticed, had changed from his pose of languid indifference to an inner ferocity; the penal hardships were suddenly implanted upon his face and I saw his finger tighten on the trigger.

Picking up the pen, I signed the documents.

"Excellent," he said, and tossed a pair of handcuffs onto the table, saying, "Right. Now put these on. You're too big to be walking around with your hands free."

233

I pushed them away. "Why should I? Now that I've signed, you'll kill me."

"Only after conducting further business."

"I beg you to leave my wife alone!"

"Ah, now, that is what I like to hear!"

His expression now convinced me of his madness; his features were contorted as he took down the lantern.

With one hand he gathered up the papers and thrust them into his brief-case. Now manacled, I watched him. Opening the door of the cottage, he prodded me out into the night.

In the beam of the lighthouse I saw that we were not alone; grouped outside were old friends out of the past, and never were they more welcome: Shelduck Two was there, still dragging his injured wing; two brown rabbits were either side of him (probably relatives of Bun); patient old Donk, now adopted by the soldiers, had She-cat sitting on his back.

"Who's this bloody lot?" asked Bumstead, for the moment he moved, they followed.

In single file now, with She-cat in front (clearly she thought she was going to sea again on *Aquila*) we went, followed by Bumstead and the clients of the old Casualty Station: a ridiculous retinue making its way to the Coaling Wharf on East Beach; and as we went I prayed that my captor was bluffing; that Jen had ignored my request for her to come to meet Jethro . . . he who was no doubt already in his grave.

As Jen and I would soon be, I thought.

Book Four

Chapter Thirty-Six

I did not need the lighthouse's alternating beam to see the tall mast rising out of the shallows of the coaling wharf; such was the fierce moonlight, as our sad little trail of humans and animals trudged over to East Beach; and strangely, I was not surprised to recognise the mast standing in reflected silver, having seen it so many times before.

"Your *Aquila*," said Bumstead. "Did you know that I had acquired her? Your loss, my gain!"

I was tiring of him. On the hundred yards or so from the cottage I had been assessing my chances; a quick swing and a leap upon him, then club him into unconsciousness . . .

With my fists free, it might have been possible; but even with the most successful timing, with the gun in my back, all Bumstead had to do was to squeeze the trigger.

My lovely old boat, once as white as a snow queen, he had repainted black. She was now butting the wharf to the incoming tide.

She-cat, as always in the past, was first aboard; leaping on the thwarts, then down into the tiller-deck. The other clients, now joined by a flock of starlings and black-backed gulls, stood in disconsolate groups on the wharf, or wheeled above us with unearthly cries like outraged witnesses to the drama unfolding below them.

Standing in the well-deck beside the companionway door

was another I recognised, for the moon, temporarily obscured by cloud, had suddenly pulled up her skirts and again flooded the night with silver.

Angharad!

The truth was now coming out, enemies exposed; the riddle unravelling.

Bumstead and Angharad!

I might have known it, for they were worth one another: the latter said with forced cynicism, "Well, well! Tom Mortymer! Are you sober?"

I glared at her for reply.

"Just fancy seeing you here!" she added.

I found my voice. "You'll be seeing a lot more of me, be sure of it!"

"Where is Wildflower?" asked Bumstead, looking about him.

"Locked in the fore-cabin."

"Did you search her?"

"Of course, do you think I'm pixilated?"

"Didn't she have a bag, or something?"

Angharad nodded.

"Where is it?"

"I've got it here." She indicated Jen's little travelling bag.

"Then bring her out; I want her in here."

"If she can stand," said Angharad bitterly. "Did you have to hit her that hard? I think you've broken her cheekbone."

"She can take it; she's a Romany."

Realisation began to arrest me. Bumstead raised the lantern higher as the fore-cabin door came open. Jen was standing there, supporting herself against the frame; blood was coursing freely from a cut over an eye and her right cheek was puffed and bruised. As I started forward, I felt the gun against my stomach. Bumstead said quietly,

"She isn't as bad as she looks. I had to hit her; she's a wild-cat."

I said between clenched teeth, "Right, but every bruise you get back double!"

I heard Jen say faintly, "Tom . . . They met me at Cardiff . . . from the train. They told me you were coming . . ."

Nausea contained me. I heard myself say, "Don't worry, Jen – it will be all right, do you hear me . . . ?"

"There's too much bloody talk here," said Bumstead; seizing Jen's arm he pulled her into Aquila's stateroom. "Sit down, the two of you!"

Now, side by side at the stateroom table, Jen and I faced the other two, and Bumstead, while Angharad covered us both with the gun, opened his brief case. Tossing more papers before us, he said gruffly, "I can't make your parents suffer for my lost years, but thank God I can take it out on their son!"

"All right, you've had a bad time! Take all I've got, but does my wife have to pay as well?"

Strangely, it appeared to placate him, for he answered more coolly, "It's a point . . . but doesn't merit consideration. Sacrificial courage is all very well, especially when a man doesn't fear death." He smiled. "The best revenge of course is to hear you beg!

"Do you really think I'd let Wildflower live to tell the nation that you met your death in a vendetta at the hands of a mad convict?"

Bumstead laughed falsely, his head back, and it was then that I recognised the derangement in his eyes.

He said, more quietly, "I am not an ogre; indeed, it could be said that some of my instincts are guided by gentility – certainly as a family we go back a very long way. Protection of women has always been the concern of my forbears . . ."

"Oh God, spare us that!" I interjected.

239

The tide had turned now: *Aquila* was alternately floating and rasping on the seabed as she swung by the prow. Within a minute or so the draught would be deep enough to take her to sea. As if reading my thoughts, Bumstead said, "In your wife's case I feel I must give her a sporting chance, for I know she's a wonderful swimmer.

"We once shared the same roof, as you know, and were friends. Nevertheless, I doubt if she will make land, not in this current . . ." and he took a deep breath in contemplation and pushed a document over the table towards me. "All of which is a tremendous pity, but there you are . . ." He added, "I already have control of your Morriston Works; this document covers both your interests in Upper Forest House, its grounds and appurtenances – in your joint names – tax purposes – very commendable . . . Further . . ." and he smiled into Jen's face, "it includes the railway shares recently purchased by your husband in your name."

"And if she refuses to sign?" I asked.

"Than I will shoot her first."

Sick of him, I shouted, "This is a pantomime! You're going to kill us, anyway – get it over with."

"Oh come," said Angharad smoothly. "What's the hurry? I'm thoroughly enjoying it!"

"And you go to hell!"

"Go to hell, did you say? What's a little going to hell matter between friends like us?"

Jen raised her face at this, saying above the wind, "What have I done to make you hate me so much?" Then to Bumstead directly she said to my astonishment, "You are a Romany, like me. Your quarrel surely isn't with me, but with the Mortymers. I often remember your kindness to me after my first husband died in Russian Villa . . . no, don't interrupt me, Mr Bumstead – please hear me out . . .

"You and I, being gypsy blood, were treated as strangers in the Grey household: you the butler, I the daughter-in-law

240

– both beyond the pale as far as fine people like the Greys were concerned, do you remember?"

He replied: "I will always know you as Jenny Wildflower; for you are of my tribe . . ."

Momentarily, they looked at one another with what appeared to be almost affection. The boat was now moving gently to the tide, the wind plaintively moaning in the rigging. Jen continued, "A tribe to which one could return when in trouble – remember that, too? I went to my people recently when my second baby was coming, and they took me in . . ." She took a deep breath.

"Mr Bumstead, you now have control of my husband's Works." Saying this she swiftly signed the new document before her. "Now I give you my share of the house, but allow me to keep the little money that goes with it, please, so that I have something left with which to make a new start . . .?"

I whispered, "Jen, for God's sake . . ." but she continued, ignoring me.

"Wales is not my true country. While in France I spent a wonderful time among my own people – your people too, Mr Bumstead, the true gypsies. Do you know the poverty of the French Romanies? If you leave me a little money, it will help to get our clan upon its feet . . . with a little left over for my future . . ."

Angharad said with a bright smile, "Watch her! There's a man at the bottom of this!"

"Of course!" said Jen. "Jacques Pierre is his name! Oh, if only you could meet him! Why do you think I ran away to France? Because I was ashamed of my so-called marriage? And now I am in child again by my Jacques! Also it is against Romany law to kill a woman carrying a baby – remember?"

Reaching out to Angharad, she then said, while I sat in astonished silence, "Please, my bag . . . ? My face is bleeding again . . . and I need another handkerchief." Angharad,

241

without a second thought, took the bag off her shoulder and slid it across the table. For a moment or two Jen rummaged within it, whispering inaudibly to herself as a woman does when in search of something; and at that moment, She-cat, who had earlier been investigating kittenishly on a rack behind Bumstead, slipped . . . and fell in a lurch of the boat. This attracted the man's attention, and he turned to the noise.

Light flared in a small explosion.

Shot in the head, Bumstead dropped face down on to the table, and as I stared at the speed of things, Jen levelled a little two-barrelled pistol at Angharad's face, saying, "Right. Now it's our turn. You took everything from me – the baby I wanted more than anything in this world – by God, Angharad, you made a mistake by getting mixed up with a gypsy mother!" and she fired again.

Angharad screamed as the bullet struck her. Gasping, she slipped easily into death.

All in seconds: it was so quick that I could only stare at Jen's expressionless face, and her eyes were as cold as an official executioner's.

"Bloody hell!" said a hoarse whisper into my ear. "Did ye see that? She had the pair of 'em! Take that minx to bed, and ye'll wake up late in the marnin'. Domesticated, did ye say? You'd be skating to Porth on 'er dish-cloth."

Chapter Thirty-Seven

With a five knot and fourteen feet tide running east to west in the Channel, we cast off into its spate with me, still manacled, on the tiller and Jen on the sails; we tacked into the teeth of it, and took *Aquila* out to a hundred yards off East Beach, fighting for every inch of water; and while the bright moonlight helped us, it was also an enemy, since I didn't know if the East Beach gun-battery was manned, or not.

"Do you think they might have heard the shots?" Jen beside me now, wiping spindrift from her face, and she hung on to me as the sloop buried her prow and came up streaming, for she never liked a windward tack.

"Just pray they didn't!" I shouted back, and my words were drowned in a roar as green water came tub-washing over the starboard rail. Then to make things difficult, just as I had set us on a course for Jackdaw Point, the clouds shut off the moon and left us tossing in total blackness.

"What are you going to do, Tom?"

Jen clung to me as the boat bucked and heaved; momentarily directionless, I lost bearing and the wind took us into irons. Becalmed now, the mast swung madly across the pale stars; then the moon blazed again and I saw Jackdaw Point loom up in a threat of foam and hissing surf.

"Prepare to go about!" I shouted and Jen leaped to the old command, caught the for'ard sheet and flung herself across the thwarts as sea and tide simultaneously struck us. *Aquila* jumped like a live thing, flattening herself on the breast of the sea. Free of immediate danger, I held her on an easterly tack, then swung her again into the teeth of the wind; the rock-strewn Point receded. In the few seconds before the moon died again, I had her on a southerly run nearly opposite Dripping Cove.

"What happens now?" Jen, beside me again in the calmer water, cupping her hands to her mouth.

"Down to the lighthouse," I yelled back, and as I said it the lighthouse beamed, flooding the night with brilliance.

"Into Deep Fathoms?"

"Of course!"

"Oh God, no, Tom!"

"It's over a hundred feet deep – they'll never be found."

I glanced at Jen. The light was sparkling on her, brightening her clothes; her hair was soaked and strangely tufted; she looked like some ancient sea-sprite flung up from the depths of the ocean. At that moment she clasped me, shouting, "Tom, you can't! They're entitled to a Christian burial!"

The light died, and we were in blackness again: I said, "It's them or us!"

"I can't bear this!"

"You should have thought of that before!"

"Can't we take them ashore and bury them?"

"Christ, woman, they're dead! Does it matter where they lie?"

"Oh please!" her hands begged. "You can't just throw them over the side!"

"That's what they were going to do to us! Anyway, I'm not doing that. I'm scuppering the boat, and they'll go down with her."

I did not bother to explain, because Jen knew that offshore from Lighthouse Point was the deepest water of Flatholm: a hollow in the sea bed dug by aeons of tidal scour. old sailors, tainted by ancient lore and sea-tales, actually claimed that the hole was bottomless, which it was not; but at over a hundred feet deep at low tide it would serve my purpose.

By modern standards nothing, as far as I knew, had been brought up after sinking in Deep Fathoms. For, while no deep-sea divers had ever investigated its murky depths off Lighthouse Point, nose-peg amateurs had reported rotten driftwood rising to the surface from ancient wrecks. And while the thought of Bumstead and Angharad sharing such a fate evoked no particular response in me, it was anathema to the highly sensitive Jen; the alternative was a Coroner's inquest followed by a trial of suspicious characters like us.

There were other potent dangers: for instance, ownership of *Aquila* could be easily proved; doubtless its absence from Cardiff would already be logged by the harbourmaster; her recent direction seaward reported by coastguards.

Even more importantly, although I had seen no habitation lights in the quarters of the East Beach gunners, anyone could have recorded *Aquila* on her arrival and departure from the coaling wharf.

It was a calculated risk I was prepared to take. The option was to sail to Newport, our nearest port and make a clean breast of everything, and I couldn't see any mileage in that. I might get away with a charge of murder, but I couldn't see how Jen could escape a hanging, or at best, life imprisonment. In seconds, from the moment of the murders, the risks had to be assessed and the decision made.

Therefore, I had decided on sinking the evidence into the sluggish depths of Deep Fathoms.

The nearer we came to Lighthouse Point, the brisker was the tide, and now we were running goose-winged and free straight into the light's beam; it was dazzling in its intensity.

Jen, now huddled in *Aquila's* prow, was sobbing; I could hear her in quick surges of the wind.

I had dropped the mainsa'l, leaving the foresa'l up for

directioning while the tide took us as straight as an arrow. About two hundred yards offshore I dropped anchor, and *Aquila* swung to the eastern tide. Expecting this, Jen came aft, her face streaming with tears. I shouted, "Pull yourself together, there's no alternative! But get these handcuffs off. The key . . ."

"Here, it was in Bumstead's pocket. Oh Jesus, Tom, the way his poor eyes watched me while I searched him for it . . ."

"Imagination, Jen – the man's dead. As we will be if we don't handle this properly."

I had to be rough; she was breaking down.

Now she stood before me, braced to the pitching of the boat. "Wouldn't it be best to give myself up?"

"No, it would not – I'm in this, too, remember."

"But I fired the gun . . ."

"Doesn't matter, I'm equally guilty in law."

Leaving Jen on the tiller, I went down the companion-way steps.

The scene below appalled me.

Astonishingly, the initial position of the bodies had changed; the dying movements of the boat, through some ironic juxtaposition, had thrown the two of them together, so that they were now facing one another; the effect was horrible, because Angharad's arms were now around her lover, a final paroxysm of death; before her soul fled, she had crawled over and embraced him.

Momentarily, I stood above them, and even as I watched, in a sudden lurch of the boat, they actually touched face to face . . . as if performing some mystic rites; a communion of dead lovers, kissing.

Sickness rose in my throat and I swallowed it down.

Going for'ard, now free of the handcuffs, I pulled up loose planks of cabin flooring and reached the cabin drain-plug; sea-water fountained up to the pressure. Coming back,

246

leaping over the bodies, I did the same with the aft bib-cock, then commanded Jen, "Right. Now we swim for it! Take your clothes off and tie them around your neck."

As I said this the lighthouse beamed again, turning night into day. Tearing off my own clothes (for *Aquila* was already settling for'ard and the sea was swilling around our ankles) I knelt, naked, and tied my clothes into a bundle. Side by side we worked with gasping haste, crouching to avoid exposing our white bodies to the beam. We waited. The light died into the dim, watery moon. "*Now!*" I shouted.

Jen went overboard first and I followed, swiftly overtaking her; for she trod water at my bidding: I wanted to be the first into the danger of the rocks. I had calculated it badly; at full tide, the surface should have been quieter but approaching the shore, I saw rocks of monumental size, lashed with foam like white bears feasting.

Jen was swimming behind me; indeed, her hands once touched my feet. In brilliance and black blindness we swam, according to the whims of the light; and then, as I reached an opening in the rocks the light died again, and a pursuing wave, driven fiercely, caught me up, enveloped me, and flung me unerringly through a gap in the rocks on to sand. In a moment Jen followed, sprawling on top of me.

Spreadeagled, we lay gasping, face down in the sand, exhausted by cold; breathless, but alive!

When, a few minutes later, we sat up looking for *Aquila*, the sea was empty.

"Oh, God!" exclaimed Jen, wiping water from her face. "I've left my bag behind!"

"And the gun – it's still in the cabin!"

"Well may ye take the name o' the Deity in vain!" said a voice in my ear, "for ye've made a right botch of everything over the past ten minutes! Do you realise you've put paid to the best two propositions I've had in me bag since the French

247

Revolution? Couldn't ye see that it was the destruction of innocence?"

I saw Jen stare at me, as she wiped water from her eyes, for I had put my hands over my ears. The whispering continued, "Cursed be your house, Mortymer, from the cradle to the grave. In return for the deaths of these beloved people, I'll see to it that no child of your body graces a woman's loins . . .! So that's the end of you accursed Mortymers!"

Trembling, I rose to my feet.

"Are you all right, Tom?" asked Jenny. Her arm went about me as the voice said, "And so, you congenital idiot, you left the bloody gun behind" and it bellowed ironic laughter. "Now how did that happen to such an intelligent fella, or could it be that somebody else had a hand in it . . . ? For one thing's certain, son, it's the best piece of evidence ag'in you both in the jigsaw. In the name of His Satanic Majesty, can't ye see ye've come to the end of the line?"

With Jen's arm about me, both as naked as babies, we went up Lighthouse Beach, cowering at times to avoid the beam . . . and across the fields. Unseen, we reached Drift Cottage. Shivering, I slammed the door.

God, I needed a drink. For all my love of Jen and all my promises, I needed a drink so badly that I could have screamed, and as I stood, gasping, with my back against the cottage door a voice whispered into my ear, "Ach, ye've got yourself into a rare old state, me darlin' And though I've no wish to add to your sadness, son, it's me duty to keep the pair of you informed. Have ye stopped to think, for instance, that this terrible fella Bumstead might 'ave topped your parents in Lake Geneva long before he began his shenanigans against you and your missus?"

Red eyed; now shaking uncontrollably, I listened to the voice, "For sure, it's a heavy load on your conscience, lad – don't ye realise that if you hadn't booted him out o' the house, your folks might be alive today?" and he thrust a whisky flask against me.

"Tom, Tom, for God's sake!" cried Jen, fighting to get at it.

Paddy Infernal yelled, "Och, to hell! A tot or two o' the hard stuff'll make a new man of ye, so it will, and there's another full bottle for ye next door on the floor of the bedroom, remember. Now tell this bitch where she gets off," and the last thing I remembered was pushing Jen away.

It was the final act to my approaching degradation.

I remember lying in the bed within convoluted shapes of coiling snakes and laughing demons, the extremity of alcoholism, when time and space cease to exist within the trauma of brain delirium. I knew a retching sickness and an onslaught of devils I had never seen before: great coloured animals vied with each other for my attention, their cries obscene, their horns raking the sheets. Above me the slanting ceiling was a mass of coloured murals, the last analysis of the infected drunk. And my companion was the little tramp now shrunk to the size of a dwarf; sitting astride me he shouted, his small face puckered up, "Are ye awake, Tom Mortymer, for I want a word with ye before you descend into the pit of hell."

Vaguely I was aware of Jen's cajoling voice, her arms tightening about me; the voice went on, "The Man in the Big Pew may be a fisher o' men, me lovely, but I'm a fisher of souls, and tonight I've landed yours in me net, hook, line and sinker. I've taken your sobriety and given you drunkenness; I've exchanged your morality for lust and bought your decency for pints. So now come quietly, and I'll meet ye in an Elysium field of decay and blazing coals. Sure to God, I've never had such a success in me life, for I'm watching your spirit rush hell for leather into the arms of me personal Inquisition. Are he with me, Tom Mortymer, you poor broken sod, or are your ears gone loose?"

Jen Wildflower was calling my name . . . "Tom, *Tom* . . .!"

"Now take a last swig o' the brandy to help you on your way, son," added Paddy Infernal.

That was the last I saw of him.

Epilogue

1905

It is said that God, because He couldn't be everywhere at once, invented mothers. Of one thing I am sure; He never intended them to be treated by the world as badly as has been the case. From the sun-black mammy suckling in Africa to the stringy matriarch telling everybody where to get off in Bond Street, they need all the pity He can give them; mothers usually being behind the door when consideration is handed out. My own mother, known locally as Dozie Annie, certainly had little to boast about in having me.

Indeed, she is a case in point. Perhaps I never adequately forgave her for having me out of wedlock. The truth of one's origins invariably slips out in close-knit communities like Maesteg, and being called a bastard in the playground at the age of ten, is scarcely productive of good family relationships, particularly when it is true.

Because of this, the affinity between myself and Mother (Dozie Annie, the butt of local jokes) began seriously to fade after I left Upper Forest House (the home of the Mortymer family) in Morriston, and set up home with one beauty after another in London.

Here, rising to the editorial chair of *The London Mercury*, I retired early at the age of fifty (when most of my lovers had left me for more virile competitors) and settled down to a pipe and advanced middle age in respectability

251

and little compensation: young men manufacture fanta-
sies and leave old men to their visions, so my friends
were few.

Looking back across the editorial room with its rush and
bustle about nothing in particular, I now had time, before
collecting up my papers for a dog and stick quiet . . . to
puff at my pipe in bachelorhood and wonder what the
hell it was all about. In retrospect, while a woman in
a bed was acknowledged as the essence of enjoyment,
these days I would throw stones at it. Take it from me,
you young ones: viewed from the wiser perspective of
approaching senility, it is worth nothing more than a good
winter sneeze.

Biology always plays the last card in the game of life, so
Dozie, my mother (remembered more kindly in her doze
of lavender and lace) now became more clearly observed;
and probably because I had nothing better to do (for
I must be truthful) decided in my own loneliness that
she wasn't such a bad old crow as relatives go . . . and
paused betimes to remember the guts of it . . . the sweating labour and joyful eyes of a mother delivered out of
pain.

She had started her labour they tell me, on the floor of
the stables of the mansion of *Cefn-Ydfa* with Old Bid, the
cook, in attendance; and Dai Dando (now long dead) said,
for it was he who had discovered her, "Oh, my poor little
duck, what you doin' out here?"

"'aving a baby, Dai, please don't tell nobody!"

At which point Iestyn Mortymer, the master of *Cefn-Ydfa*
came in from riding, and said at the stable door, "What's
happening here?"

"It's our Annie 'aving a baby, sir," said Old Bid.

"But that can't be . . . only yesterday . . ."

"It's a seven monther, sir; she strapped 'erself up."

"Bring Annie into the house, and you come with her," Mr

252

Mortymer commanded. Thus was I born, not in a stable, but in one of the best bedrooms of *Cefn-Ydfa*.

"Mind you, George," said Dai to me later, "you was a big sod, especially in the 'ead – you bloody nearly killed 'er."

And now, this same mother was the sole occupant of Upper Forest House in Morriston; all the blood Mortymers including Tom having taken the rocky road to the grave.

Was it my own loneliness, I wonder, that reminded me on that hot June day of my duty to my mother? Or was it one of those inexplicable occurrences that are part of psychoanalysis? More likely just plain guilt, I reasoned later, because, as they say in Eton, when a boy's face shines, look behind his ears.

Coincidental with this sense of guilt was a much more potent happening; one that caused me to send a headline article – the last of my editorship of *The London Mercury* – down to the printer in the basement with accompanying photographs of the lighthouse area of Flatholm.

The headline read:

'TWO BODIES ASHORE ON WELSH ISLAND
(from a special correspondent)

The skeletons of a man and a woman were this morning taken from the remains of a small yacht presumably wrecked many years ago on the rocks below Lighthouse Point on the island of Flatholm, which lies in the Bristol Channel off the coast of South Wales . . . '

My intention being made urgent by a report of an earlier skeleton which was found in roughly the same area, called *The Unsolved Mystery of the Hanging Man of Maesteg*: a headline I myself had coined for an article I had written five years before when a reporter on the *Mercury*.

History, it appeared, was about to repeat itself, but

253

this time, given luck, I might help the police to find a murderer?

Unsolved murders, especially where skeletons are concerned, are usually thin on the ground through time-span – motives and reasons being long disseminated.

Skeletons editorially may be acceptable in single numbers; but when people start making a habit of it, there must exist a story; and when one is journalistically wounded by the pen, it never completely heals.

Therefore, on the morning after my official retirement, instead of clearing the editorial desk and taking a taxi to the penthouse flat I had rented, I found myself again in a First Class compartment on the Express from Paddington to Swansea, and Dozie Annie, my mother.

God knows what reception awaited me, for I hadn't been home for years.

It was not only a nagging conscience that took me to Morriston: news that Mother had now taken to her bed, coincided with the tragic discovery.

The last report I received before leaving London was the Coroner's. Both skeletons showed evidence of bone damage, it said; the man having been shot in the head while one of the woman's ribs had been fractured near the heart; a wound also thought to have been caused by gunshot. I was unaccountably convinced that the skeleton of *The Hanging Man* found some years earlier in an underground coal gallery at Maesteg, was linked with those now discovered in the debris of the wrecked yacht.

Parents get even with reprehensible relatives by falling ill just at the time when you hope to find them hale and hearty; thus adding remorse to the sense of guilt, and so it was with Mother.

My taxi from Maesteg put me down at the drive entrance to Upper Forest House and the place was as lifeless and shuttered as a monastery in Lent; three times I jangled the entrance bell without reply; then footsteps sounded within, and the door slowly opened.

A woman about my age stood in the doorway, evincing an air, like most Romanies, of aristocratic independence. Her bangle earrings matched the dark sheen of her skin; her hair, plaited either side of her face, was black and I knew her for one of those who towed their caravans around these parts.

"Yes?" Her dark eyes questioned.

I said, "I'm Annie Evans's son – George. May I come in?"

The eyes swept over me. Once, clearly, she had been beautiful, but the years, as for me, had more closely stamped their authority now, and I saw that she was a little older than I'd thought. (You can tell a horse's age by its teeth, a man by the back of his neck, and a woman by her throat.)

Inside the house, although mid-summer, it was as cold as a Spanish prison, and our feet echoed on the decorative mosaic of the great hall.

"My name is Jen Mortymer," said the woman. "Since your mother moved in from *Corn Hwtch* about a year ago, I come over from Flatholm from time to time to keep an eye on her."

"Thanks very much," I said, and followed her into the spacious drawing-room.

"Thanks very much isn't good enough, Mr Evans." The reply was instant. "Your mother is lonely and you should be more responsible: a woman her age shouldn't live by herself in this great barn of a place. Do you realise she's ill?"

"I didn't know, Mrs Mortymer."

She looked me up and down as if judging a porker contest.

"She tells me you're leaving Fleet Street. I had hoped you were moving in here."

"It . . . it wasn't my intention."

"Nor mine to continue coming over from Flatholm once

255

a week. I've been doing it because she's the last of the old retainers. My husband, Tom, was very fond of her."

"Ah yes, Tom Mortymer."

She nodded. "He died two years ago, about the time Annie moved in here when dear old Dai Dando passed away. I still say she'd have done better staying on at *Corn Hwtch*." She looked around her vacantly, as a woman does when there is little more left to say, adding, "Your mother's incontinent now, Mr Evans. A district nurse comes in daily, but you ought to do better than that – she really needs constant nursing, and from what I hear there's no shortage of money." She added tersely, "Or perhaps you'd prefer to put her into a home?"

The antagonism was growing, possibly because of my unresponsive silence. Being better able to express myself upon paper; oral interviews, especially if lacking empathy, have a disastrous effect upon my psyche. Yet, a strange and unusual affinity bound me to this woman, even allowing for her intolerance.

I found myself saying, "I am sorry about your husband, Mrs Mortymer."

We stood uncertainly, and I added, "My . . . my mother told me of his death in a letter, but the newspaper was in difficulty at the time – projected take-overs and God knows what – and I fear it slipped my mind . . ."

"Don't let the same thing happen with your mother, Mr Evans. Now's a good opportunity to give her the attention she needs – remorse is a useless commodity: it's no fun in the cemetery, give me my flowers now." She fussed and fidgeted with her gloves. "Ah well, back to my other patients!" and she went to the door.

The sun was a ray of gold upon her face as she opened it, and I thought she looked beautiful.

"Patients?" I wasn't interested in her reply, but wanted to delay her.

"Surely you've heard of my Rescue Centre on Flatholm?"

"Mother mentioned it, but not in detail."

"She knows more about it now, for I've just been telling her; it has grown enormously since Tom and I started it all those years ago. We now have an official vet – he comes over from Sully once a week, and with public donations coming in, it's my intention to build a little Rescue Hospital; lots of shearwaters and other seabirds get injured in migratory flight, and the morning clinic is crowded out these days with buns and . . ." She paused, gulped and said with an effort, "Tom would have loved to have seen the hospital built, but . . . well, there you are . . . it's the way life goes!"

Her eyes were bright and I thought she was going to cry; then she patted herself to see if she was still there, as women do when fighting tears, and added, "Ah well, if I'm going to catch the Flatholm boat, I . . . I'll have to get going," and raising her face, smiled brilliantly. "I'm sorry I've done all the talking. How long are you going to stay?"

"I'll stay until Mother is better."

She nodded, saying, "Good. There's a full-time nurse starting in the morning, so you'll receive her bills in due course – kindly leave your home address when you go."

"Certainly."

"Goodbye, Mr Evans!"

"Goodbye, Mrs Wildflower."

"No – Mrs Mortymer – I'm a widow now, remember!" She offered her hand.

"I do hope you will come again . . . ?" I said.

"Not all the time there is somebody here with Annie – I simply can't afford the time with so many other invalids . . ." She hesitated, one eyebrow slightly raised as if fearing a reaction. "But surely there is nothing to stop you visiting my brood on Flatholm?"

"I will come!" and wondered if I sounded too enthusiastic.

I was still standing at the door as she went down the drive, and continued to stand there, as if she had taken my legs with her; she having made upon me a greater impression than any woman to date . . . one reason why so far I had managed to side-step the altar.

Mother was sitting up in bed, awaiting me. A glance told me that in another few days I might have been too late. Life appeared to have taken her by the throat and thumped her into skin and bone since I had last seen her.

Holding her, unseen, I wept without tears.

Nobody could have envisaged that the carroty-haired misfit with the turned up nose, known in Maesteg as Dozie Annie, would one day end up as the mistress of Upper Forest House; and even more unbelievable was it that what was left of the Mortymers should look upon her as a beloved friend: such affinities do not exist much between master and servant today. To be fair, my mother, the embittered husk of a woman betrayed, possessed little in terms of personal attraction. Yet, not only had she acquired Upper Forest House with its land and appurtenances, but had also become rich through the will of Tom Mortymer, deceased. Worth consideration, when as Mother's surviving relative, all such assets would one day come to me!

However, financially comfortable in my own right, I was much more interested in the story rocking Wales at the moment . . . the identity of the skeletons recently discovered in the wreck of the yacht.

"You met Jen Wildflower, George?" (Mother meant Mrs Mortymer.)

"She opened the door to me."

"Beautiful, ain't she!"

I did not reply; for as long as I could remember, Mother had never flagged in her efforts to see me ringed by the nose; she was still at it.

"Who you living with now, George?"

"Nobody."

"Then who's going to shake a leg for ye when you retire from Fleet Street?"

"I'll manage quite well on my own."

This set her up for the usual confrontation.

"Oh no, ye won't; you'm hopeless in a house, and ye know it. Time was I used to come and dig out your places – one flat after another, but I'm past it now. You was never like your pa, ye know: everything 'ad to be Bristol ship-shape wi' him – ye could tell he'd been a sailor. And he were no philanderer, neither, like the vicar called him once – never liked that vicar, I didn't, talking about my Bert like that. He were the only fella I knew who was white all over inside an' out. It were the Boer War that took 'im, or he'd 'ave been here to see me buried." She dabbed at her eyes with a little lace handkerchief. "I want you to think well o' your feyther, George."

"He was one of the best, Annie," I said.

"Ay, ay! He were a good 'un!"

He was, in fact, one of life's natural bastards born legitimately. He had courted her; disdainful of her generosity, he had seduced and left her without a penny, and I'd pledged myself to the day that I might catch up with him. Nature has her own ways of relieving grief, or few of us would be alive, and false compassion had built an image within Annie's longing heart; caricaturing her lover into what she prayed was a good husband and not the village waster who put one serving-maid after another into child and Swansea Workhouse.

One of these unfortunates (not too bright) was Annie Evans, my mother.

"You'd 'ave loved 'im, mind!" she added.

"He was my father, I love him now," I said, for if a lie is worth telling, it's worth repeating.

"God bless you both," said she then, and slept.

The new nurse didn't come for a week. Bright with summer's disposition she arrived to live in; with a breast for weeping on, she was a big woman who took us over with ebullient confidence; and Annie glowed with new energy. We had a bath chair delivered; got her into it and out into the conservatory's sun.

Sitting there planning, Mother surveyed Upper Forest's shining acres.

"What about that Jen Wildflower, then?" she asked optimistically.

"Mrs Mortymer? What about her?"

"You promised her you was going over to Flatholm. You interested in her, son?"

"Not particularly, but there's a good story knocking around on her island."

"You mean the wreck of the yacht, and the bodies?"

I nodded, lighting my pipe. "If there's anything in it I'll cable it back to the office."

The nurse came in with morning coffee, put down the tray and went out again, saying over her shoulder, "I say there's more in that than meets the eye, sir."

I nodded. "Have they identified them yet?"

"Not that I've heard," she answered, "But yesterday they found a gun in the wreck of the boat, I heard say."

I thought: if I don't get over there soon, this story will be ancient history, and the nurse added, "Lovely place, mind, that Flatholm! My hubby hopes to buy a boat and get around there and Steepholm, when he can afford it."

My mother added, "Jen Wildflower and Tom used to 'ave a boat when they lived on Flatholm, ye know."

"What kind of a boat?" I asked.

"Search me, son – just a boat. They used it for fishing and more than one dish o' cod and flounder they dropped into Upper Forest for poor old Annie." She put a finger under

260

her chin and made no eyes to mention, adding, "That was before they left Flatholm the first time, mind."

The nurse returned with Mother's morning medicine. Recalling that the doctor was due at midday, I was keen to get going to catch the 2 o'clock ferry from Sully. Idly, I asked, "What made them leave?"

"Flatholm?" Mother shrugged. "They 'ad a bit o' bother with some of the locals, I heard – old Dai Dando knew more'n me about it."

"Bother?"

"Well, it seems they kept animals even then – patching up injured gulls and suchlike, and somebody on the island kept knockin' 'em off."

I waited while she took her medicine.

"Did they find out why?" I asked.

"'cause they was strangers, I suppose. Boiled one o' their animals, too, I heard."

"They did what!"

"Like I said – they 'ad a pet cat, a big tom, and then they came back one day and found 'im in the saucepan on their stove, skewered, knotted up and boiled hot for eating – and he still 'ad his fur coat on, poor sod."

"How terrible," said the nurse, and fluttered me a smile.

Mother made a wry face. "Aye, well folks is queer, ain't they, everybody knows that. One way of getting rid o' them off Flatholm, I suppose. But accordin' to old Dai, who ever done it killed off their chickens, too and cut the throat of a goat they were milkin!"

"Good Good!" I said. "Why?"

"Didn't like 'aving them around, I suppose."

"So they left the Island?"

"That's it. They was living in a cottage, Dai said, so they locked it up, took the ferry to Sully, harnessed up their 'orse to their gypsy caravan in Thomas's field, and went off."

"To where?" I asked.

"Up to Scotland, of all places, said Dai, and after a while they took a boat to France."

"Why France?"

Mother emptied her hands at me. "Lots of Romanies in France, mind."

This was getting interesting. "And then?"

"Then they come back to Maesteg and *Cefn-Ydfa* – Master Tom didn't have this place till later, though he lived 'ere after Jen Wildflower left 'im, poor lad."

I had turned away to the window in contemplation, looking out on to the bright summer-lit fields: curlews were calling, I remember.

"Why did Jen leave him?"

She did not reply, and I knew she had something under her apron that would soon come out.

"Come on, Mam!" I prompted.

"I reckon that's their business." Lips pursed, she sat.

"How long was she away from Tom?"

"About a year – no, more, if I remember!" And she looked huffed and impatient. "Anyway, it's all past now, so why don't you go over to Flatholm and see Jen Wildflower – she's an attractive piece, and I'd like to see you settled before I pops me clogs."

I said, carefully changing the subject, "You remember – it must be five years or more ago now – how you tipped me off about the first Maesteg skeleton, 'The Hanging Man', I mean. I came down and did a piece for it in the *Mercury*?"

Mother nodded.

"Do you think the finding of these latest bodies has any link with that?"

"'course not!"

"I think there is; don't you recall that you suggested I should write a book about the Mortymers – old Dai Dando called it 'the love that God forgot' – remember?"

She remembered all right; I could see it in her face. I

262

added, "Then you suggested that the Mortymers ought to write it themselves? Come on, surely you remember that! Did they produce anything?"

There was a long silence: then, "They produced a book," said Mother, disinterestedly.

"What!"

"Like you said, we suggested that they wrote a book about their times together on Flatholm, and they did!"

"*No!* Did they publish it?"

"Not likely. I got the manuscript in the safe here."

I was astonished. "What's it doing in there?"

"They had no safe place to keep it on Flatholm."

"You say you've got the whole book? Last time I heard about it they'd only finished one chapter!"

"The whole book – nigh forty chapters."

"Have you read it?"

"Can't read, can I? Why do ye think they trusted me with it?" She shielded her eyes from the sun, adding, "Jen Wildflower's writing a final chapter now, she says."

"A final chapter?" I was stupidly repeating her.

"One she's calling 'Expiation'. Now that her Tom's dead," she said.

"Because her husband's dead?"

"Gawd, you're like a ruddy old parrot, mun!"

"Did she say why?"

"Why what?"

"Why she's writing a final chapter called 'Expiation'?"

"Search me, I don't even know what it means."

I replied, "Expiation means 'to make amends'."

"O aye? There's new words croppin' up every minute . . . Ah well, now that I'm poorly, I'll have to hand it back to them, in case I kick off first, won't I?" She made big eyes at me, patting her chest.

"Don't you believe it, you're good for years!"

We stood unspeaking, then she said, "That book is

between the Mortymers and me, George – understand? Not even you can lay eyes on it, cause this Annie promised them so."

"I'm your son."

She ignored this, saying, "When my time comes, it goes back to the Mortymers for tearing up if needs be – the solicitor's put that in me will. Everythin' else is yours, but not that book . . ." and she sighed, slipping into another dream, and whispered, "Aye, you're my son right enough, but like Jen Wildflower said, you're still a journalist . . ."

Later, when the house was quiet and coo-doves had stopped calling from the woods, I got out of bed, lit a lamp and went downstairs.

In the study the old safe faced me. It was my 'Grandfather' Iestyn's, and had been brought over from *Cefn-Ydfa* mansion; its iron and brass was cold to my touch, and I stood there in the flickering candlelight, fighting temptation.

Mother had forgotten that I knew the safe's combination – in fact, I had known it before she did – since the days of my adopted Grandpa . . .

But, and to my credit, I could not bring myself to open it and run an eye over the Mortymer manuscript.

Later events, however, diluted my ethics.

Next midday found me going ashore on Flatholm from the Sully Island ferry, and I noted that the little island appeared substantially served by visitors; there being nothing like a morbid curiosity about death to enliven a tourist, and people were so crowded around the Lighthouse area where the skeletons had been found, that I gave up and inquired the way to Drift Cottage and its occupant.

The cottage, leaning with age, was almost a tumbledown. Upon the door was a hasty note telling that Jen Wildflower

264

was shopping in Swansea, and would be returning on the evening ferry. Above the note was an inscription:

'To The Memory Of A Beloved'

and above this were the words:

'ANIMAL RESCUE CENTRE'

Surmounting all was a twelve inch high brass cross dovetailed into the stonework and in the foreground, as if awaiting the return of the cottage occupant, sat a little man in a high-backed chair with his knees cocked up. Looking into the sun was he, his scrubby bearded face alight with smiles, and the moment he opened his mouth I knew his race.

"Well, well, good-day to ye, sir!" cried he, and getting off his chair, took off his battered bowler hat and bowed low, sweeping the grass with it. "Are ye visitin', or am I mistaken?"

I answered. "Certainly I'm not expected!"

"Nor I, if it comes to that," said he with a flourish. "But they tell me the foine woman livin' here opens her sanctuary to all and sundry, if they come wi' the statement that they're fond o' God's creatures!"

I thought he was delightful.

"What's more, since she's a Romany lady, she'll tell ye fortune if ye cross her palm wi' a threepenny piece; and all contributions gratefully received by the Kingdom of Animals!"

"I've heard she's kind to them," I said, sitting on a rock beside him.

At which he leaned confidentially towards me, saying, "At one time there was a fella here as well, don't ye see, but the Man in the Big Pew called him, so now she's alone. Have ye business wi'd her?"

265

The wind blew from Weston-super-Mare, and it was perfumed.

"No," I answered. "Just a visiting tourist."

"Not a relative, then?"

I shook my head.

"Ye see, sir, the reason why I'm asking, is because I'm wantin' to find out more about this business o' the skeletons, and it struck me that this Jen Wildflower could enlighten me a wee bit. Do ye know anythin' ye'self, at all at all?"

"Only what I read in the newspapers."

"Do ye reckon she 'ad anything to do wi'd it?"

"With what?" I asked.

"The skeletons."

"I shouldn't think so for a moment."

With that the little man took a flask from his hip pocket, and turning it up to the sun, guzzled at it, then offered it to me. "Have a sup on it, me lovely, for talking about folks dyin' makes me miserable to death."

"I don't drink," I said.

"*What*?" He was aghast.

"Teetotal," I explained.

"Ye can't be! There's no teetotallers in Wales; it's a wee bit o' the old nose-varnish that makes the nation what it is!"

"It's a fact," said I. "Never a drop has ever passed my lips."

"And you a journalist! God bless the Pope – sure, a swig o' the nectar of the gods would have ye luxuriatin' in Elysium dreams – go on, take a sup wi'd a mate!"

I pushed the flask away again, at which he took a fighting stance, shouting hoarseiy, "So, you're a parsimonious pew-hopper are ye – a Bible in one hand and a nun in the other, I expect! Come on, be a man, for I'm a gatherer of souls, don't ye see, and today I'm after the big literary fishes."

I was walking away now, having had enough of him, and he bellowed after me, "Well, you've had ye opportunity, ye boot-faced bloody puritan, so if you fancy your chances wi'd the widow o' Tom Mortymer, ye've another think comin', for her chap were a man! I taught him the beer-belly arts from a dram o' the hard stuff to ten quarts o' home brew, and he were none the worse for it. Thrice cursed are fools who turn their backs on Paddy Infernal's friendship, so black be ye house!"

Some pretty unstable people must be living on Flatholm Island, I remember thinking. Vaguely, I wondered how he knew I was a journalist.

Much more important things were happening down at Lighthouse Point where divers had again come in from Trinity House to search for clues about the skeletons. More, it appeared that I had arrived at an opportune time, being the first national journalist to be on the scene when a gun was produced for inspection by the policeman in charge of the investigation.

"A Duval, by the look of it," said he, turning it over to the sun.

It was an insignificant-looking little thing, pearl-handled and decoratively engraved, most of which had rusted away.

"Like the registration number," he added, peering. "Not a hope in hell of getting it now."

"Since you know the make, the continental police . . ." I began.

"Not a chance," said he. "Hundreds have been turned out in the past ten years. Half the Paris ladies of the night would have to empty their handbags – and I'm not even sure that it's a Duval, but I'll send it over to the laboratory.

"And this, too, sir," shouted a diver, wading ashore through the rocks. "A bag of some kind, I think." But it was dropping to pieces in his hand.

"Do you think that's the murder weapon?" I asked, indicating the pistol.

"I'm not sure of that, either," came the reply. "Foreigners

have been smuggling up and down this coast for centuries; the place has been a half-way house between South Wales and the Channel ports since Jesus was a baby . . . gun runners, wine, tobacco – everybody is at it."

"The pistol was found in the wreck?"

"No, it wasn't – deeper down, says the diver. Everything breaks up off Lighthouse Point."

"Will you give me a statement for the *Mercury*?" I asked.

"Not even for you, George Evans . . . except . . ."

The inspector was sweating in the sun; and added, "One thing you can report – we've found the name of the yacht.

"It was a sloop called *Aquila*, registered at Cardiff. Originally belonging to a couple living here called Mortymer, she had a few owners and was then bought by a man named Bumstead – butler to Mr David Grey the industrialist. The Greys reported him missing from their house in Maesteg some years ago."

"So he's on the register of missing persons?" I was taking notes now. "What about the dead woman?"

The inspector shook his head. "We've no idea. Could have been anyone."

"And Bumstead?" Having remembered who he was, I was even more interested.

"Aha! Now here's a thing! Our Mr Bumstead had a record a foot long!"

"Enlighten me."

"Transportation to the Colonies for theft and forgery. In fact, you might know more about him than me, because years ago he also worked for the Mortymers." The inspector paused thoughtfully. "That would be in your mother's time."

I shook my head; there are limits to one's involvement in police investigations.

"You haven't had the Coroner's verdict yet?" I asked, to change the tack of things.

268

"Any time now. Hold things on the back page, George, 'til I've got something official.

"You've got no opinion of your own?"

The inspector nodded. "But not for publication. Personally, I think it was a lovers' quarrel . . . The identity of the woman is the clue to it all, I think, and we haven't yet any idea who she might be; and Bumstead himself is an enigma. We know he was a forger with a police record, but as far as we know, was not a womaniser."

"Who shot who, then?"

"Your guess is as good as anyone's. The finding of the gun helps, of course, though no crook would be seen dead with a weapon like that. I think Bumstead probably tried it on and got shot for his pains."

"Then the woman turned the gun on herself?"

"That's my belief: we'll have to see what the Coroner makes of it . . ." and then the inspector narrowed his eyes to the fierce sunlight. "How old is your mother, George?"

"Too old for you!" I tried to humour the situation.

"She would have known Bumstead. Do you think she'd know anything about his courting antics? She was with the Mortymers for most of her life, wasn't she . . . ?"

"She's too far gone, Inspector – she doesn't know what day it is."

Pigeons were coming home to roost. The last thing I wanted was embarrassing questions about the Mortymers, to whom Mother owed so much.

Clearly, the answers to most of the questions might lie in the book she was keeping in the safe . . . and, as if reading my thoughts, the inspector said casually, "I've questioned Tom Mortymer's widow, of course, but she has no information – apart from the fact that they once owned the *Aquila*. When they left Flatholm years ago they sold it to a Cardiff chandler."

"From whom Bumstead bought it, presumably," I said.

269

I hoped that was the end of the conversation, but wondered what would happen if the inspector knew about the book . . . Without a doubt, this might prove one of the most important stories Wales had read in a decade. I also realised that by the way things had gone to date I was already withholding vital police evidence.

I was leaving Lighthouse Point when the inspector said, "They must have had a cat aboard the boat – a little more useless information; this morning, one of my chaps brought up its skeleton."

"Surely that is not important?"

"No, except that one of the old people here remembers that when the Mortymers owned *Aquila*, they had a pet that always insisted on being aboard . . ."

"What are you inferring?"

He made a face. "Nothing, but I'm short of facts, and one snatches at straws. I take it you've told me everything you know?"

"Good gracious, I don't know anything!"

"I'm not saying you do, but your mother . . . ?"

"I'm not having her bothered, Inspector."

"I could get a doctor's certificate, you know."

"I doubt it, she's practically on her deathbed."

It was unethical and unworthy of me, but the phrase kept echoing in my head . . . 'If Mother died and the solicitor came into things officially, I'd lose every chance of seeing the Mortymer manuscript . . .'

Professionalism overcame my inherent sense of decency.

That same night found me down in the old Mortymer study in Upper Forest House, staring in the moonlight at the Mortymer safe.

A clock in the hall was chiming midnight, I remember, when curiosity overcame a lifetime of hard-earned principles. Raking my memory for the safe's combination, I opened it.

270

THE LOVE THAT GOD FORGOT

I read the manuscript from beginning to end, starting at midnight and finishing it at ten o'clock in the morning, when the nurse took up Mother's breakfast.

"Mister Evans, Mister Evans!" I heard her shout from the landing above, and went up the stairs three at a time, with the last pages of Book Four – 'In Expiation' – still in my hand.

My mother's eyes were open, even in death, and I will remember them for the rest of my life, for the expressionless eyes of the dead can carry an indictment and the only way I could erase their condemnation lay in confession.

A fortnight later, hearing that Jenny Wildflower had returned to Flatholm Island, I caught the ferry from Sully and walked from the landing point to Drift Cottage.

The morning was bright and fair; the wind caressing the island was sweet with scents of pastoral Wales; the smoke-choke of Swansea and Morriston being unusually absent; and seemed in tune with my mood of gentle understanding of another's troubles.

Life, it appeared, had treated Tom Mortymer and Jenny-Wildflower with a poignant share of tragedy.

This time, Jenny Wildflower, one of the guilty, was at home; proof of this being the line of patients awaiting medical attention outside her door . . . a motley array, including shelducks, black-backed gulls, a cat from the lighthouse with a bandaged paw, a hen crow, a lame dog and brood of half-tamed rabbits watching from a safe distance.

"Good-morning," I said brightly outside her door, and she raised her face like a nun at prayer . . . her eyes dancing with recognition.

"If you have come for treatment, sir," said she, "please give your name to the cat and take your place in the queue."

I thought she was delightful.

Now I could see more clearly that she was no longer young; I judged her age at over fifty, but such was her careless grace that it defied the years; indeed there was about her a Pan-like quality . . . a 'Jenny of the Light Brown hair' now that once had been Romany dark, my mother had told me; hair that still reached to her waist, but now was streaked with grey.

"Please come in, Mr Evans."

I did so, watching while she splinted and tied a seagull's wing.

"Boys will persist in throwing stones," she observed, and bit the twine with her teeth. "If I had my way I would outlaw stone-throwing and guns. Do sit down.

"I would like to say how grieved I am at the death of your mother, Mr Evans."

"She died in her sleep; I would have had it no other way." I paused. "The life she had was happy, largely determined by you Mortymers – as I said before, I will always be grateful." We were silent within the loss. "You'll come to her funeral?"

"Of course. I am making a posy of wild flowers from Flatholm, which she can hold in her hands."

I said, "It is my first loss by death; I find it difficult to come to terms with it."

She smiled sadly, holding the next patient, a rabbit, against her face.

"After a few years of it, one becomes an expert," she said.

"You live here alone now?" I asked, although I knew full well that she did.

"Yes, my husband died some two years ago."

I knew this, too. Now she was humming softly to herself as she worked on the gull, and whispering to it words of comfort. She asked, "Surely you must have known my husband, Tom?"

I nodded. "I met him twice – once when I was very

272

young, before his father sent me off to the Redcoat School in Camberley; and once, in nineteen hundred, when I tried to persuade you to write a book about your work here on Flatholm with the animals – remember?"

"Good gracious! Truly, I'd forgotten that!" and she laughed and clapped her hands together like a happy child.

She had not forgotten of course. One does not so easily forget the writing of a book.

"And since the death of your husband you've carried on here alone?" I asked.

She sighed. "It seemed the logical thing to do – what Tom would have wanted."

"And the Upper Forest Works at Morriston?"

She shrugged. "There's been a manager there since Tom died." She smiled. "You'd know about all that?"

"Mother kept me pretty well informed. The Mortymers were her life; you did her pretty well, all things considered. Respect for old retainers these days comes under the heading of old codgers."

"Retainers? Annie was part of the family." Her hands paused on the bird. "Is that why you're here, Mr Evans – only to thank the Mortymers?" Suspicion touched her eyes.

"Not quite," I answered.

"I thought not!"

To the gull she said, setting it down on the door threshold, "And that's you, Sook! Come again in a week, and I'll have another look at you." She added, "Now then, what about a cup of coffee?"

There was about her movements an elfin charm. Remembering when I first saw her at Upper Forest House, she now appeared daintier.

While she was boiling the milk, I wandered outside in the sun and wondered at the diplomacy of raising long-dead issues, for little could be gained by resurrecting the past, other than an extension of present misery.

After all, I pondered, Iestyn Mortymer, her father-in-law now dead and forgotten, was the fulcrum of Bumstead's vendetta against the Mortymers, not Jen Wildflower.

Yet it was she who had actually shot to death Bumstead and Angharad, and try as I may I could not release myself from the professionalism I had served all my life. That justice must be seen to have been done; and that nothing must circumvent its natural course.

More, and I knew this also to be true – here was a story that would set the country by the heels. The book itself, being a full confession of the facts of two murders, was now not the property of the few, but in the public domain. Indeed, now that I had read it I would be withholding police evidence if I failed to expose the truth . . . that Jenny Wildflower, of Upper Forest House, had killed William Bumstead and Angharad Rees assisted by her husband, now deceased, and had caused their bodies to be lost at sea.

It was a culpable indictment, and, if proved, would attract the death penalty through the book's confession.

We drank our coffee in the sun, sitting side by side in the open doorway, Jen and I, and she said, while the patients, disturbed at the delay, gathered about us in an inquiring circle, "I will be leaving here soon, Mr Evans."

It turned me.

"Leave such a lovely place, and such a satisfying job?" I put down my cup. "You surprise me!"

"Yes . . . I have no alternative," she said at nothing. Clearly, she had something more to say and I did not interrupt her. She continued, "It is a long story, but rapidly coming to its denouement, like all good stories. Soon the police will come and take me away. Surely you know of the book Tom and I wrote?"

"What book?"

"The one you and Annie suggested we should write about

the Animal Rescue Centre we had opened here . . ." She faltered.

"I don't know what you are talking about," I answered.

"On come, Mr Evans, this is why you are here, isn't it? It was you and Annie who suggested that we should write about our experiences with the Animal Rescue Centre, and . . ."

"And . . . ?"

"And . . . well, one thing led to another and we became totally involved in the thing. Surely you remember?"

"Truly, I do not," I lied.

Her eyes searched my face. "Well, if you don't know about it, you very soon will, for it will be in the hands of your mother's solicitors. And . . . and perhaps that is all to the good, for it will bring things to a head and be the end of everything."

"Can you enlarge on that?"

She replied, "At your mother's suggestion – yours, too – my husband and I wrote a book, as I said. When it was finished, we didn't know what to do with it, so asked Annie to keep it in her safe, away from prying eyes.

"Its last chapter we called 'In Expiation' – because it was in the nature of a confession I felt we had to write. As I said, under your mother's will it will soon be in the hands of her solicitors, like the rest of her papers. The initial idea was that she would will it back to us in the event of her death."

"And you haven't had the book back, is that it?"

She nodded, disturbed, and said, "When Annie died it came as a shock to me, for she appeared indestructible. Nevertheless, a week or so earlier I had intended to visit her and ask to have the manuscript returned to me."

"With no thought of publishing it?"

"No, no! Publication was out of the question, all the time either my husband or myself were alive. Nor did I want to see it in the hands of solicitors."

"Of course not."

275

She faltered again. "Death has protected my husband, you see, but . . . I am still vulnerable."

I smiled at her and a new understanding brought by her confiding moved suddenly between us.

"This would appear to be some book!" I said.

"It . . . it is more than that; it is an indictment." She moved uneasily. "God knows why I'm telling you all this, a perfect stranger . . ."

"All right. But having written it, what did you intend to do with it?"

"Destroy it, once I got my hands on it."

"That's pretty dramatic!"

"Not if you knew the contents. At the time it seemed all right to set down the truth on paper, but now it could destroy me."

I said easily, "Would your present worry be connected, in any way, with the two bodies recently washed up on Lighthouse Point?"

For reply she stared at me.

I added, "Might it tell, for instance, of how William Bumstead and Angharad Rees met their deaths?"

"How could you possibly know this?"

"Because I have read the book, Jen Wildflower," and opening my brief case, took out the manuscript and put it on the table behind us.

"You are right to be worried; as you say, the last chapter, 'In Expiation', could be a death sentence . . . that is, if one didn't know the entire facts of the tale from beginning to end."

She did not immediately reply, but rose, and ignoring the manuscript on the table, wandered around in front of me, her hands clasped: tears were upon her face.

I said, "Curiosity overcame me when Mother said she was keeping it in the safe: I opened the safe and read it. But what will you do with it if I let you have it now?" I added, "By law

276

it belongs to me – all possessions and effects, according to my mother's will . . ."

"I would burn it, as I said."

I chuckled. "At least you're honest. But I'm a journalist, JenWildflower, and professionals like me simply don't go around burning social documents, to say nothing of suppressing evidence of value to the police . . ."

"And so?"

"So I suggest that I now keep it under lock and key, with the promise that it will stay that way until my heirs and assigns, such as they are, can let the world know the real truth of how a pair of villains can destroy decent people without giving them a second's thought." I got up, taking her hand. "In my opinion, you see, the bright pair they've just unearthed from under Lighthouse Point deserved to die."

We sat in silence, and there was nothing of embarrassment in it; with heads inclined, we listened to the chattering of the gulls. It appeared enough just to be there in each other's presence; there was peace in it. Eventually, I said, "I do not know what to call you. Sometimes Mrs Mortymer comes to my mind, but my mother always referred to you as Wildflower . . ."

"Jen Wildflower will do."

"Then tell me, Jen Wildflower, where your husband comes into this story now?"

"He doesn't; my poor Tom is dead." She looked at me. "No doubt Annie mentioned that he was an alcoholic . . . ?"

I shook my head. "She was one who never encroached upon private grief. You have him here, on the Island?"

"In a way, for I buried him out there," and she waved a hand at the sea. "He never told me so, but that was where he always wanted to be." She smiled. "Every time the tide comes in, it brings him back to me."

"You're still in love with him!"

"Of course. The purest and best love lasts for Eternity, and that is what we shared, Tom and me. But, surely I am preaching to the converted!"

"A doubtful convert, Jen Wildflower. Such a crusty old bachelor as I has had many lovers, but few loves; in truth, I suppose I was married to a newspaper: I put it to bed every night, but never went with it!"

"This," said she with finality, "is something we will have to resolve, for I know a spinster with a matronly interest in gentlemen of advanced middle age," and she lent me a wink. "One of laughing eyes, they say, and a marvellous sense of humour has she – the sister of the lighthouse-keeper – and amazingly of a literary bent . . ." She leaned towards me with mischief in her face. "In my old age, you see – I match-make! Come to tea next Sunday and you'll never go to bed with a newspaper again!"

"I am overwhelmed!" I said, entering the farce.

"You will be when you meet this spinster!"

I said, "Remind her that she'll be tangling with a libertine. In younger years I have pursued debauchees and courtesans. Only the unchaste spring to mind, for although teetotal, I am a most romantic bachelor."

For reply she wagged an impish finger at me, saying, "Do not underrate the Flatholm islanders, Mr Evans, for while we entertained the disciples of St Cadoc with decorum, we also feasted and drank with our lustful invaders, the Danes – to say nothing of the Lords of Glamorgan, who liked their Welsh females appreciative – no doubt you've heard about Iberians when it comes to love!"

"Tell your spinster that I'll expect a little more than talk of love-spoons," I said. "But more, please, about this available woman?"

Jen smiled. "Now, let me see – she is no longer young, of course . . ."

"You've already made that point."

278

"And, being matronly, is today on the plump side – her sylph-like figure having disappeared with her youth."

"As did mine," I said. "Proceed."

She put her finger in her mouth like a thoughtful child. "Indeed, the last time I saw her she was on the busty side, if you get me . . ."

"All to the good. I prefer the artists of the French Renaissance – a man in advanced years likes something to get hold of, without being too indelicate . . ."

"And she is inclined, when excitable, to revert to the patter of the Romany – a sort of vulgar gibberish – however, my late husband, with whom she was most friendly, thought it quite attractive . . ."

"As would I, without a doubt," I answered. "But what makes you think, Mrs Wildflower, that she would be the slightest bit interested in me? Look at me – turned fifty, balding, a little paunchy, and being a discarded journalist, not even wealth to boast about!"

"Ah, now! Of money this spinster cares little; believe me, she has enough of it for you both!"

I said, "When you see her again, is there a single redeeming feature about me of which you can boast, for surely that's essential?"

Before replying, she came closer and looked into my face. "I shall tell her that you have the most beautiful eyes, Mr Evans. They are sky-blue, an almost exact copy of the eyes of Tom Mortymer . . ."

"Will it suffice her?"

"And you are masterful, like him," and she stepped away as if remembering who she was, and again patted her chest to see if she was still there, adding, "Come to tea next Sunday, sir, and I will parade my patients in your honour. More, I will have that spinster waiting in her best dress to meet you, and together we will take afternoon tea. But now, before you leave for the ferry –

279

and you'll have to hurry now – what about this manuscript?" She picked it up.

"Put it under the bed until next Sunday," said I, and made my most elegant schoolboy bow, "I just can't wait to meet that spinster." I then made my way across the fields to the ferry landing-stage with my heart thudding against my shirt and my boots so lop-codded, as Romanies might say, that they scarcely touched Flatholm.